Praise for *Pushing Upward*

"Pushing Upward *is brave writing, a young woman's journey toward her dreams, avoiding traps and falling into them, slipping back and finding the grace and will to go on—and so it reflects on our own journey and makes us braver, too."*

— **Gerald DiPego**, screenwriter for *Phenomenon, Message in a Bottle, Instinct, The Forgotten, Angel Eyes*, and *Sharky's Machine*

"Pushing Upward *brought up shocked and poignant recognition, as it rocked both my forty-three-year-old self and my five-year-old self. I found that when I took breaks from reading it, I treated my children differently. The best words of advice I ever read about parenting were: 'Children may not always remember what you told them, but they will never forget how you made them feel.'"*

— **Julie Novak**, mother

"Andrea Adler gives readers a wonderful coming-of-age story set in the retro-70's, when payphones were necessary, a call was 10 cents, and Batik clothing was all the rage. . . . Pushing Upward *explains how the I Ching is used as an oracle for daily living. The story has a surprise ending, pulling all the drama together and allowing the reader to witness Sandra's 'overnight' transformation. . . . This is a story all generations . . . can appreciate."*

— *Retailing Insight*

"We may all be searching for an oracle, a teacher, the way to free ourselves from our addictions or our past traumas. We do so through self-inquiry, dedication, and practice. We love to walk the path of transformation and read stories of those who have stumbled over the rocks and followed the breadcrumbs to find their way home. Pushing Upward *is an uplifting novel and well worth the time spent perusing its entertaining pages."*

— *LA YOGA*

"Andrea Adler deftly interweaves themes of love and betrayal, friendship and higher guidance, ego and surrender to create a compelling and thought-provoking read."

— **Miriam Knight**, *New Consciousness Review*

"Sandra Billings is really all of us—at one time or another— in our lives: searching for meaning, for the next step, for the right person and the right part to play. And like all of us, she's got demons to work through and angels, in strange and surprising shapes, to guide her. It's a thoroughly enjoyable journey, filled with surprises and the ineffable wisdom of the I Ching. I highly recommend it."

— **Barbara Marks**, editor of New Thought books

pushing upward

ALSO BY ANDREA ADLER

Books

The Science of Spiritual Marketing: Initiation into Magnetism

Creating an Abundant Practice: A Spiritual and Practical Guide for Holistic Practitioners and Healing Centers

Audios

Moving Through Fear Gracefully

To Advertise or Not to Advertise, That Is the Question

Aligning with Our Soul's Calling

All available at: **www.HolisticPR.com**

pushing upward

a novel

andrea adler

HAY HOUSE, INC.

HAY HOUSE, INC.
Carlsbad, California • New York City
London • Sydney • New Delhi

Published in the United States by: Hay House, Inc.: www.hayhouse.com®
Published in Australia by: Hay House Australia Pty. Ltd.: www.hayhouse.com.au
Published in the United Kingdom by: Hay House UK, Ltd.: www.hayhouse.co.uk
Published in India by: Hay House Publishers India: www.hayhouse.co.in

Cover design: Amy Rose Grigoriou • *Interior design:* Riann Bender

Grateful acknowledgment is made for permission to reprint excerpts from the
I Ching.

North American Rights:
WILHELM, RICHARD: THE I CHING, OR BOOK OF CHANGES (THIRD EDITION).
Copyright © 1950 by Bollingen Foundation Inc. New material copyright © 1967
by Bollingen Foundation. Copyright © renewed 1977 by Princeton University
Press. Reprinted by permission of Princeton University Press.

International Rights:
German copyright law public domain.

Library of Congress Cataloging-in-Publication Data

Adler, Andrea.
  Pushing upward : a novel / Andrea Adler. -- 1st ed.
      p. cm.
  ISBN 978-1-4019-4125-3 (tradepaper : alk. paper)
  I. Title.
  PS3601.D57P87 2012
  813'.6--dc23
                            2012019241

Tradepaper ISBN: 978-1-4019-4125-3
Digital ISBN: 978-1-4019-4126-0

1st edition, September 2012

Printed in the United States of America

To Brian, for his patience
To Cynthia and Gene, for their ceaseless support

Sometimes the journey takes us to India,
to travel barefoot along the Himalayas,
or to Australia, to live among the **Aborigines**.

Sometimes the journey takes us to
Los Angeles . . .

The year is 1974.

CHAPTER 1

The beginning of all things lies still in the beyond
in the form of ideas that have yet to become real.

— *I CHING*

Panic had settled into the crevices of my bones. I'd become a powerless victim of circumstance. I was confused, totally stuck in this moment of complete fear and helplessness. Not knowing what to do, I closed my eyes and lay there, trying to be comfortable on the bumpy mattress whose springs had worn out long before I'd rented this apartment. *Sandra, you are not allowed to swallow, exhale, or blink until you have a precise plan of action. Not a move.* Holding my breath while my body remained rigid on the concave bed, I waited for the top of my head to open up so I could receive some kind of guidance—praying that insight into this dark tunnel of existence would reveal itself. Really soon.

My life had become a tragic myth. Not yet suicidal, I was in a state of severe uncertainty and knew that some kind of action had to be taken, really soon. I just wasn't sure what. My creative soul burned to express itself in ways that my present job at Martha's Boutique could never provide. My artistic skills yearned to be challenged in ways that no longer included the exclusive talent of selling women's clothes. My heart burned to be reciting the words of great playwrights, keeping an audience on the edge of their seats as I delivered soliloquies from Ibsen, Chekhov, Shakespeare, Williams. But I was stuck in a nine-to-five grind, and didn't know how to get out.

I gave myself permission to breathe, but I still couldn't blink. So I continued to lie there, counting the brown watermarks on the ceiling, tracing the water leakage to its origin, which diverted my attention just long enough to allow a thought of genius to slip through a narrow passageway into my brain. *What would I do if I were a struggling artist living in Paris? What would I do there to support myself?* It took less than two minutes to come up with the perfect scenario: if I lived in Paris, I would check out the Parisian newspapers for housekeeping or governess jobs. I could have a roof over my head, a small income, and free time to paint.

I tore off the blue polyester bedcover—knowing this was at least a beginning to an action I could pursue—and tripped over my shoes on the way to the front door. I grabbed the *Los Angeles Times* from the doorstep . . . and saw the eviction notice taped to my door.

Shit! I decided to ignore it. I waited for the screen door to slam on my butt, and plopped the paper down on the old oak table. I tore through the sheets, in hot pursuit of the classifieds section. *Where is it? Where is the goddamned classifieds section? Here it is.* I looked eagerly up and down at each ad: *HOUSEKEEPER/live out. Daytime DRIVER needed for six children. COOK for gay couple. BABY-SITTER for triplets. GARDENER/COOK/DRIVER wanted for elderly couple.* Give me a break! Not one job for a live-in.

I headed to the kitchen and yanked open the refrigerator door, looking around for the jars of peanut butter and jelly. Smearing these ingredients onto a cracker would totally satisfy this craving I had to chew. But I was out of both. I slammed the door and returned to the paper. Again, I looked through the ads—up, down, side to side.

Nothing. I went back to the fridge, flung open the freezer door this time, frantic to put something—anything—in my mouth. I began to paw around for one of those chocolate-covered ice cream bars. Just thinking of the soft ice cream and hard chocolate crust made saliva well up in anticipation. But all I could see behind the freezer-burned loaves of bread were orange-flavored bars. Whatever had possessed me to buy those? I *hated* orange. I tore off the wrapper of one anyway, threw it in the sink, and sucked the hell out of the orange coating. I began to pace around the tiny living room.

All of a sudden, as if a large chip from a meteor had fallen from the sky and hit my brain, I thought: *Why don't I place an ad of my own?*

I stood there in complete awe of my own genius.

The orange coating had melted off its stick and was halfway down my knuckles, so I licked the remaining nasty liquid into my mouth, and probed the classifieds columns to see how the other ads were written. Then I saw it—a sign, clear as day: DISCOUNT COUPON FOR ONE PERSONAL AD. The deadline was today!

Knowing that the next set of letters about to be formed would be *the* most important selection I'd make in life, I closed my eyes, prayed for inspiration, and spent the rest of the morning trying to edit a torrent of words down to twelve—which I finally did. And then I, Sandra Billings, placed an ad of my own:

Drama student in need of RM and BRD
in exchange for housekeeping.

CHAPTER 2

The superior man
refines the outward aspect of his nature.

Male responses came pouring in like a school of salmon swimming upstream. Within a week, I'd heard from a firefighter, a stockbroker, a wrestler, and a radio announcer—as well as a "carpenter by day" who dressed up as a woman at night and wanted me to go with him to cross-dressing bars. Can you imagine? I also heard from Maria, who, I think, was a lesbian. I wasn't sure, but she said she lived on a boat in Marina del Rey. I have nothing against lesbians. It's just that living on a boat wasn't the kind of stability I was looking for . . . at this time.

After a week of returning calls, sneaking into the back room of Martha's Boutique, where I worked as a salesgirl, and speaking to Maria and fifteen men with all kinds of arrangements and proposals, there were three I seriously considered: Mr. McKeilly, Mr. Kapoli, and Mr. Wilson. None of them sounded great. But they were the best of the calls. I would meet them all on Thursday. Martha was renovating, so I had a few days off.

Thursday morning I jumped out of bed, put on my clothes, grabbed the bran muffin that had been sitting on the kitchen counter for I don't know how many days, and ran out of the apartment. I climbed into my cobalt-blue, on-its-last-legs Fiat, checked the rearview mirror to make sure my mascara hadn't smeared—and sat there for a moment, knowing I must be out of my mind to even think about living with a stranger, let alone a male stranger. On the other hand, there was a certain relief. I was leaving a stale existence and entering unknown territory. If I didn't take these chances now—step outside of my comfort zone—what kind of an actress could I expect to become? I had to take the leap—for myself *and* for my career.

The winding streets of Benedict Canyon were elegant and sensual. Gunning the Fiat up curving streets between wooden ultra-mods and stucco Spanish colonials, I was greeted by yards burgeoning with shrubs and tall, spiny flowers, hugging close to the sides of pink mansions. As the tires of my car caressed the smooth, banked roads, richly colored leaves swayed to and fro. I inhaled the scents and took in the sights, not wanting to miss a chimney, a tree house, a flowerpot. There were octagonal windows and lawns that seemed to go on and on, trees and bushes bearing early spring blooms of all kinds. I kept driving until I found Kurt McKeilly's street. I eagle-eyed the house numbers looking for #24. Kurt said I'd have no problem seeing the numbers from my car. "They're gold-plated," he'd pronounced distinctly. "Just look to the right of the door," he'd added in his seductive English accent.

Twenty-four. There was the house number, in gold, just like he said. I pulled the old Fiat into the massive circular driveway, turned off the engine, and sat there. *Holy shit!* My eyes scanned the sprawling white ranch that was really more like a mansion. A long wooden fence circled the back of the house, where two beautifully groomed saddlebreds grazed on high grass. *I hope he doesn't think I'm going to take care of these horses. I know nothing about animal care.*

I was tempted to slam the oversize gold-plated knocker down on the elaborate carved door. But I had an aversion to loud noises, particularly self-inflicted ones. They always felt like sharp pins penetrating my skin. I rang the doorbell instead.

I could hear dogs barking on the other side of the door, and then footsteps. A tall, wiry man with a pointy gray mustache opened the door, one hand cradling the bowl of a pipe. The pipe was long and oddly shaped, definitely from another country. He opened the door wider. Now in full view, Kurt was tanned, good-looking, and wore khaki safari clothes. His gray hair and mustache glistened in the sun.

"You must be Sandra." He stepped outside and closed the door behind him. "Kurt McKeilly. No problem finding the house?"

"No, the directions were fine, thanks."

"Well, then. It's a beautiful spring day, isn't it?" he said, standing there on the paved entryway, his hands on his hips, inhaling deeply. He could have easily passed for a successful English actor, and sounded like one. I remembered his silky voice from the phone, and the way he took long pauses after each sentence.

"Yes, it *is* a beautiful day," I agreed, trying to keep the conversation moving, wondering why he was just standing there. *I have no time for pauses, Mr. McKeilly. I have two more interviews after this one.*

"Why don't you come in and have a look." He gestured me in with his pipe, which appeared not to be lit. "By the way, I did mention to you my family of animals, did I not?"

"Ah, no."

Kurt swung open the oversize door to the flagstone entry, where two black Labrador retrievers, a Great Dane, three Samoyeds, two white cats, and six ducks greeted my feet, calves, and thighs. Taken aback by the unexpected sniffs of welcome, I proceeded through the door with tiny, mincing steps, making sure not to tread on a paw or anyone's webbed feet.

"Down, Greta. Jennifer, you, too! Don't squash Sammy. Sammy's the duck with the spotted beak," Kurt explained. "Be good, girls. This is Sandra. She's our guest."

Now, I've always been a stickler for maintaining eye contact during a conversation, but there was no way I could look this guy in the eye. I was too engaged in the sights and sounds of the panorama unfolding before me. Snuggled between lush green foliage and S-shaped ponds was a virtual village of cages containing two- and four-legged animals. Circular rock slabs became pathways leading creatures of all kinds from one habitat to another. And this was just the front hallway. I followed Kurt into the sunken living room from which his richly decorated jungle motif radiated outward, craning my neck to see how tall the treetops were. Between overgrown leaves I could make out majestic beams where two ropes hung down and formed knotted loops.

All of a sudden, two russet monkeys jumped from one rope to the other and then raced each other to the top. As I watched them run up and down the rope trying to catch each other's tails, Kurt McKeilly's Labradors were sniffing away. One had his nose jammed into my crotch; the other had his nose between my buttocks. I tried to push them aside, but they persisted in finding each other's nostrils somewhere in the middle. Kurt finally noticed their innocent game.

"Shadow! Janelle! Stop this immediately!" Reprimanding the dogs, he escorted them out by their collars to another wing of the house.

I was now left alone in this African jungle.

Wait till Rachel hears where the ad led me this morning.

From the other side of the room, I heard: "Pretty girl, pretty girl, what's it gonna be? What's it gonna be?"

I jumped, spun around, and saw two multicolored parrots sitting tall and straight in their silver cages.

"Pretty girl, pretty girl, what's it gonna be?"

"I don't know," I snapped back, and then wondered why I'd even replied.

"Are you ready for your tour?" Kurt asked with great enthusiasm, suddenly reappearing at my side.

"Ah-h-h-choo! I'm not sure."

"Handkerchief?" Kurt pulled out a white cloth from his shirt pocket.

"No, thanks. I have Kleenex somewhere." I searched my purse and pulled out a wad of tissue. "What do you do for a living?" I'd been dying to ask.

"I sell insurance to third-world countries and collect rare artifacts." He dipped into a humidor sitting on the bookcase and began to pack tobacco into his pipe. "During my travels, I started falling in love with these magnificent creatures and began, well . . . collecting them."

"How long are you away when you go?"

"Up to three months."

"*Ah-h-h-choo!* Look, Mister, *ahhh*, Kurt. I should tell you from the get-go, I am highly allergic to animal hair." I blew my nose again, stuffed the tissue inside my purse, and headed toward the door. "I could easily get an asthma attack here. Have you ever seen anyone experience an asthma attack? It's not pretty. Your lungs flare up. You can't breathe." I reached for the door handle, and turned the knob. "What if you're out of town and I need to go to the hospital—who'd look after the animals?" I reached out my hand to shake his. "I know you'll find the right person." *It's just not me,* I said under my breath.

I didn't wait for a response. I opened the door, walked quickly to my car, jumped in, and left skid marks on my way out of Kurt's driveway. Then I proceeded to West L.A. at no less than thirty miles over the speed limit. It wasn't a total lie. I did have asthma . . . when I was younger. It just never escalated like I'd described it.

One down, two to go! As I looked at my watch, my stomach felt queasy. I didn't know if I was sick because of the last interview or worried about the next one. Whichever it was, I had to ignore these feelings and keep moving. I didn't want to be late to meet Saul.

I'd only spent a few minutes with Saul on the phone. His voice was cryptic, distant, as if he were disguising his true identity. Maybe he had a cold. Maybe he was a spy, or worked for the CIA. In either case, I felt uneasy. Sure, I wanted to spend weeks exploring my alternatives, process each candidate, make an intelligent decision. But there was no time. I needed to be living with one of these callers within the next two weeks.

No matter how desperate my situation was, my first glance upon walking into Saul's place told me *this* was not an option. The apartment was stacked to the ceiling with magazines. Small

Saul, with long white hair and a long white beard, looked like he'd stepped out of a Saturday-morning cartoon. He looked totally wild, Einstein wild. Only this animated character was no crazy genius. He was just crazy. It appeared as if he'd saved every magazine he'd ever read, categorized them all by number, and color-coded them by year on ten-foot-tall, built-in library shelves. I had to suppress my laughter as he rolled along on a wheeled ladder, sliding from shelf to shelf.

Saul came down from his ladder and showed me the rest of the place. Every room was stacked with more magazines, more newspapers. Not as high as the ones in the living room. Still, newsprint, in all shapes and sizes, was the prominent feature of decor throughout his abode. The coup de grâce was when he showed me "my" room, the room where I would sleep if I were to accept his offer. It was a five-by-ten-foot walk-in closet with an old dusty mattress on the floor. Picky or not, I needed a tad more creature comforts than Saul's apartment would provide.

On my way out the door, I tried to be diplomatic. "You have a fascinating lifestyle here. I just don't think I'd fit in."

I closed the door gently behind me and ran down the three flights of stairs instead of waiting for the elevator. I walked around the block twice before I decompressed enough to get into my car. And then I collapsed into the bucket seat, rested my hands on the steering wheel, and whispered to myself and to whoever happened to be listening, "I'll brush my teeth three times a day. I won't swear. I'll volunteer at the children's hospital down the block. Just make this next guy normal. Let him be the one."

Fortunately, traffic wasn't too bad. Most people were at work. I just wished the smog would disappear so the sun could peer through.

Frank Wilson's condo looked impressive from the outside. It was nicely landscaped. The wood-paneled exterior was newly stained, shutters freshly painted. I was feeling hopeful. But when Mr. Wilson opened the door, the interior was not as well maintained. His condo looked more like a Dumpster with windows. Dirty clothes were piled on chairs, on the floor, on the couch. Dried Italian takeout was stuck on dishes spread over coffee tables, and Frank himself was seedy-looking. He was gangly, had atrocious posture, and slumped before me, chewing on a half-smoked cigar.

I should have turned around and walked out right then. But Frank ushered me into the kitchen and asked me to sit for a minute. Since I was dripping sweat and the air-conditioning cooled my face and lymphatic orifices, I sat and listened to Mr. Wilson confess that he'd just gotten divorced and lament how lost he was without a woman. How he wanted someone to talk to when he returned home from work. While Frank talked, I glanced at his gray hairs, noticing how unevenly they had mixed with the few remaining black strands of youth; then I spotted thirty or so transplanted dark strands poorly placed at the center of his scalp.

The tall man with no spine unfolded from his seat and asked me if I'd like to see his new rare amethyst. The fact that I loved rare gems, coupled with my desire to demonstrate compassion (a virtue I'd been working on the last few weeks), convinced me to accept his offer.

As I followed him down the corridor, I thought, *How much compassion should I be displaying here?*

The hall smelled of mold, the linoleum floor gave under our weight, and the walls were conspicuously bare. There were no pictures, no wall hangings, no tokens of any present or memories of a past. He opened the last door on the right. It was his bedroom. *What have I done?* I tried to stay calm as he reached for the stone sitting on his dusty dresser top. *Deep breath, Sandra.* He brought it close to me and put it in my hand. *Look interested.* I raised the amethyst to the light, and was surprised to see how magnificently deep and rich the color was. *What's this guy doing with expensive crystals? He should be spending his money on housekeepers.*

As I stood searching for my voice, hunting for a cautious phrase to express my appreciation, Mr. Wilson grabbed my shoulders and pushed me onto his bed. Within seconds, he was on top of me, like a dog in heat, undoing his pants. I could hardly breathe. All I could see were his nostrils, flaring wide; his nose hairs lodged instantly in my memory. My body locked with fear. Terrified that he might pull out a knife or tie me up with some itchy rope, I flailed around mentally for a way out. How the next set of words stumbled out of my mouth, I'll never know.

"Mr. Wilson, I could really get to like it here," I whispered in his ear as I tried to squirm my way out from under his rancid flesh. "I'm just going to the bathroom for a minute . . . you know." Like I was going to insert a diaphragm or a take a pill or something. "I'll be right back," I breathed into his ear. "I *really* like you."

One more squirm and I was off the bed. I smiled, coyly, with a wink.

"Hurry back!" he shouted.

I left him fondling himself in anticipation, closed the bedroom door behind me, and then ran like hell down the hall to the front door. I tried to open it, but it had some weird lock I'd never seen before. *How am I supposed to unbolt it?* I kicked it quietly, then loudly. I looked around the cluttered living room for something, anything, that would help me force the door open. Could I grab one of the wooden chairs, swing it back with all my strength, smash the picture window, and jump out? *I sure as hell can!*

I must have jiggled something loose on my last kick. The lock came undone, and I bounded like a cheetah to my car. The keys in my hand were shaking so hard I could hardly unlock the Fiat. My legs were trembling. I couldn't feel my feet, which kept slipping off the pedals. Somehow the car coughed to life. I jammed my foot on the accelerator, refusing to look in the rearview mirror in case he was running after me or standing at the front door, and drove straight home.

This was enough torture for anyone to go through on a Thursday afternoon. Disappointed, disillusioned, I desperately needed a soft lounge chair on a thick carpet of green grass overlooking a blue ocean, a tall glass of Tab with a slice of lemon, the sun beaming its rays on my face, and fresh air moving through my lungs to help me forget this entire day. I needed a crystal ball to see the future so there'd be no more surprises. And I needed to talk to Rachel immediately.

CHAPTER  3

The tree itself affords no foothold for the wild goose,
whose feet are not made for clutching . . .

Rachel's line was busy.

And she thinks she's so psychic! If she's so telepathic, why doesn't she feel my intense desire for her to get off the goddamned phone? I slammed the receiver down and collapsed on the bed to review my day. Depression set in quickly. What a waste. The ad was a stupid attempt to change my life. What was I thinking? *Sandra, when are you going to learn? Just because you want something, doesn't mean it's gonna happen . . .*

I got up from the bed, went to the fridge, and quickly devoured the leftover Chinese food, along with some cheese sticks, crackers, and a granola bar. I wasn't hungry, but I couldn't help myself. Then I went into the bathroom, and threw up everything I had just eaten. No need to feel or look bloated . . . and disappointed.

A bubble bath was next. I turned on the hot and cold faucets full blast, poured in some lavender bubbles, and slid into the tub. When it was almost full, I let out a humongous sigh of relief. *Ahh-hhh!* Water, particularly bubble-bath water, always brought a sense of calm to my fragile nerves. *If only life would slow down, like it does in this lavender pool, I might be able to move through the ups and downs more gracefully.* But this was not my destiny, not yet anyway. As soon as I dunked my head under the faucet to wash my hair, the phone rang. The decision to get out of the tub or not was no decision at all. I had placed an ad. I couldn't miss a call. I grabbed the towel and dashed to the hallway to pick up the phone.

"Hello?"

"Hi. My name is Peggy. I'm an actress, too. Isn't that bitchin'? We could do scenes together—that'd be so far-out! Do you get high? I can get some pretty groovy stuff . . ."

"It *would* be groovy, Peggy. But I don't do drugs. Sorry." That wasn't entirely true. I did smoke a little grass with friends. "Thanks for calling."

I hung up, brought the phone into the bathroom, and returned to the scented water. I was just sinking back into the thick, welcoming lather, when the phone rang again.

"Hello?"

"Hi there, little lady."

Oh no! The guy sounded like a sixty-year-old cowboy.

"An actress, eh? Well, this could be your lucky day. How would you like to live in the lap of the luxurious Hollywood Hills? For no extra charge, you get a hot tub, a sauna, and me. I give massages to all my tenants, and . . ."

"So kind of you to offer all your services. But I've decided to stay where I am."

Back to my interrupted indulgence. Peace at last. I slid back in, rested my head on the plastic pillow that never really supported my neck, and had just drawn a very deep breath . . . when the phone rang again. I jumped up, got out of the tub, sat on the edge shivering, and picked up the receiver.

"Hello." I must have sounded gruff.

"Hello, my name is Emma. I read your ad in the *Los Angeles Times.*"

"Yes," I said. Not wanting to extend any unnecessary effort.

Still, I listened intently. The woman told me that she owned a spacious two-bedroom apartment she would like to share. "Spacious," she said. I noted the word. "You will love my beautiful home," she went on. "The neighbors are friendly, and the neighborhood is quiet and safe." She also mentioned that her husband had died the previous year. I couldn't tell her age. It was hard to decipher. So was her accent; I couldn't quite place it. But I liked how she enunciated her words, the way she pronounced each syllable. I always admired people with proper diction. There were also sparks of energy and enthusiasm in her voice, as though she were a small child wanting, almost needing, to make new friends.

"Think about it overnight," she said. "If you're still interested in the morning, give me a call and we can set up a time to meet."

She gave me her number, and I wrote it down on the mirror using my Coral #4 lipstick. Then I drained the tub, knowing the moment for any kind of reprieve was over. As I dried my hair and got dressed, I thought about how lovely and refined the woman's voice was. How she chose her words so precisely, and how she paused and listened. But she sounded like she might be fifty or even sixty. How could I possibly live with a woman my mother's age? My neck started to cramp, the muscles along my shoulders started to tighten. I began to perspire, everywhere. I went to the sink, splashed cold water on my face, and scrutinized myself critically in the mirror. *Sandra, I know you don't want to live with an old lady, but what are your choices? You're being evicted, and you'll soon have no job. Martha had made that pretty clear yesterday.*

I tried Rachel again; her line was still busy. Returning to the living room, I sat down on the rocking chair the previous renters had left and decided to keep dialing until she got off the phone.

Rachel was an actress, too. She was twenty-three, two years older than I was. We'd met about a year before at an audition in which neither one of us was chosen. It was our *destiny* to meet. We both walked out from a casting call that day complaining about everything we'd hated in the industry: the phoniness, the pretentiousness, the lack of compassion, the nepotism. No sooner than that and we were on our way to becoming best friends.

Rachel supported herself by delivering singing, dancing, and otherwise dramatic messages to strangers. She tried to convince me how fabulous this job was, and that I too should become a "star messenger" at Frederick Clark's Specialty Agency. She'd constantly try to sell me on how flexible the hours were, how she was never bored, and how there were always interesting people to meet. I suppose these perks made the job bearable, but it was not for me. I wanted no part of a business that made a mockery out of the acting profession. I wanted to be taken seriously.

Depending on the client and the occasion, Rachel was asked to do some pretty lame things, ranging from dressing up as a one-eyed ogre for a children's birthday party to masquerading as a nun. Her most unusual assignment, bar none, was when a wealthy lady executive hired her to play the part of a saucy stewardess for a flight on a private plane. Rachel had to get all dressed up in a Playboy bunny costume and flirt with the executive's boyfriend, who was taking a chartered flight to San Francisco for a business meeting. The plan was that if the boyfriend came on to Rachel, she was supposed to turn a cold shoulder and ignore him for the rest of the flight. If he didn't come on to her, she was supposed to hand him a note from the lady executive proposing marriage.

It turned into a mess. Rachel ended up having a huge crush on the guy, even though he didn't come on to her, and she didn't want to give him the note. Toward the end of the flight, she realized her job could be in jeopardy, so she placed the note on the tray she served his drink on. She watched his passionless expression as he read the proposal, and then slipped him her own phone number on a napkin. Rachel waited for weeks for him to call, but he never did.

Rachel had as much success with guys as I had. Zilch! I think she intimidated men, because she was smart *and* funny. Slipping that guy her phone number was uncharacteristically subtle for my friend. She was more often loud and crass, and never one to hold back her words or her emotions. The stories she'd tell me of her one-night stands would have been heartbreaking if they hadn't been so hilarious. I'll spare you the details.

Rachel was an only child. Her mother had died when she was eighteen, and her father had remarried, so she claimed, the reincarnation of Medusa. She hadn't spoken to her father since he'd moved to Las Vegas with his new bride, years ago. Every time Rachel tried to invite them to L.A. or offer to drive to visit them in Vegas, Medusa would find some excuse and prevent the reunion from taking place. I could tell that Rachel was upset by her father's lack of interest; he'd never once reached out to see her. Though Rachel never confessed this to me, I knew she yearned for close family relations as much as I did.

My own family portrait wasn't much prettier. Daddy had had an ongoing affair with alcohol since I could remember, and Mom . . . well, she was way too paralyzed with fear to take any kind of action. Like get a divorce. The fact that her denial of my father's disease might be breaking down the nucleus of the Billings family was inconceivable to her. So we all ended up pretending that the problem didn't exist. We'd pretend that the reason Daddy slurred his words and walked like a drunk was because of a new medication he was on for his ulcers. We'd pretend the reason he threw martini glasses was because work wasn't going well.

Work *wasn't* going well. Daddy's construction company was going broke, which created a lot of tension in our household. On any given night between my eighth and my fifteenth birthdays, dining at the Billings family home was not exactly about gathering around for a fun-filled evening. It was a dismal, debilitating sport. Steven, my older brother, and I had to guard our every word. *No teasing allowed* at the table. Daddy wouldn't tolerate it. If Steven or I cracked a joke or laughed or squealed on each other during dinner, we'd have to dodge silverware and glasses, watch the black belt slip out from the loops of our father's pants, and be humiliated right there in the kitchen as we stood there bare-assed. He'd whack us until we bled and promised that we wouldn't squeal on each other again. I never could digest a meal.

I thought this was just a phase Daddy was going through, that as soon as his houses were fixed up, he'd stop drinking and we'd all get along. But things never changed. They only got worse.

Daddy took his frustrations out on Steven; Steven took his frustrations out on me. In fact, Steven's mission in life was to make *my* life hell. It wasn't the kind of hell normal siblings go through. His acts of sabotage were downright cruel, mean-spirited. He'd do things like hide my ice skates the day of the big skating competition, embarrass me in front of my friends by taking my bra to school and showing everyone my small cup size, or lock me in the backyard shed for hours—and then throw in a live mouse for added fun. He made a big mistake that time! The day he pulled that stunt, Daddy came into Steven's bedroom, just next to mine—at two in the morning, in his inebriated state—slipped off his belt, and whipped Steven big-time. Was I sorry for him? Hell no! Steven never should have locked me in that shed. I thought I was going to die in there. I screamed for hours. It took weeks before my voice came back.

Daddy whipped me on occasion. But nothing compared to the times he beat Steven. Now, this might have seemed like a blessing, but it wasn't. Throughout the years, Steven's revenge was much worse.

I untwisted the black-coiled telephone cord from around my finger and dialed Rachel's number again. Her line was still busy. *God, that girl can talk!*

I loved being around Rachel, for several reasons. The first reason was because we both came from dysfunctional families. The second was because I always felt thin standing next to her. She was tall, about five-foot-eight, a hundred and fifty pounds. I was five-foot-six, a hundred and forty pounds. Give or take a pound—depending. Rachel's bones were bigger, giving people the impression she was heavier than she was. She had an enviable size-C rack compared to my measly Bs, which my push-up bra helped me to achieve. My wavy hair was consistently dark brown; Rachel's hair was straight one day, frizzy the next, and changed colors with her outfits. She hated her freckles. She'd wear way too many moonstone rings, six or seven gold chains around her neck, gobs of makeup, and bold batik bell-bottoms that totally embarrassed me—I mean, she was partial to God-awful hand-screened footprints of obscure animals! But Rachel loved them. She said her cousin Cannoli (yes, like the Sicilian dessert) gifted her these outfits from his trips overseas as a photographer, and since she adored *him,* she adored the outfits.

We'd take long walks down Sunset Boulevard window-shopping, people-watching, but inevitably, people would be looking at *her.* She always stood out! If it weren't for Rachel's latest attempt at auburn hair, and her oily complexion, she could have been a real stunner. Regardless of what that girl looked like or what she was wearing, though, just being in her presence would make my day. Her dry, sardonic sense of humor always made me laugh.

Another reason I liked Rachel was because she didn't take her acting as seriously as I did. For me, acting had become my salvation. It allowed me to be anybody but me. It also gave me an outlet for my creativity, which was bursting at the seams, and an art form I'd begun to respect and had become good at. For Rachel, it was simply a diversion, something to have fun with. This was good for our relationship. It prevented competition.

She was also the only person with whom I could share my deepest spiritual pursuits. This was very important to me.

We knew there had to be more to this mundane existence than getting up, going to work, coming home, eating, and going to sleep day after day. We knew there had to be a bigger purpose, a perspective on life that was deeper and more profound than what we had been taught. We just didn't know where to look, let alone where to find it. We thought about going to church or to a synagogue, but we didn't want "religion." We wanted something more. Something beyond the doctrine and lectures on guilt and our sins. Beyond the preachers' and rabbis' interpretation of who *they* thought God was. We wanted our own truth, our own understanding. And we wanted it—yesterday!

Then, one day, in God's benevolent way, destiny revealed itself . . . once again. I discovered an awesome book—and its uncanny ability to unravel the mystery of our lives.

I was strolling down Melrose Avenue one day and smelled an intriguing aroma coming from a small yellow building. The quaint little house had been renovated into a commercial store. The wooden sign nailed to the building read: THE BODHI TREE BOOK AND TEA SHOP. I followed the scent and walked into a magical room filled with books and crystals, plants, and hanging chimes.

The Bodhi Tree was funky—a let-your-hair-down kind of place where people could walk in day or night and be assured of soft classical music playing in the background. As you strolled through the store, the fragrance of *nag champa* incense filled your senses, enticing you to stay while you searched for the book of your dreams. Hot tea and honey were kept warm in copper teakettles for customers to sip on as they meandered through the airy aisles. And the salespeople were never pushy. They'd let you sit for hours, let you get lost in the pages you were reading for as long as you wanted. I felt so comfortable in this bliss-filled haven; I could have made myself cozy in a corner and lived there forever.

Ambling among the aisles that first day, I felt this magnetic attraction to the Eastern Religion/Philosophy section. I gazed at the crowded shelves. Studying the titles, wondering which book would call out to me, I noticed a yellow-bound cover with a black square on its spine. The longer I stared at the book, the more it began to illuminate, almost sparkle. My eyes widened as I examined the words: *The I Ching, or Book of Changes,* written in gold italics. Compelled to take the book off the shelf, I began to leaf through its pages. The words seemed strangely familiar, expansive. I found a seat on a pillowed wooden bench. And as I sat there scanning the thin sheets with their tiny print, the manager appeared at my side.

"Not everyone can grasp these teachings. They're very subtle."

I looked up at her, surprised that anyone had noticed me, let alone noticed me reading this book. Her face was both kind and austere. Her blonde hair, in a high ponytail, swayed to and fro as she spoke. Then she stooped down to my eye level, and with her hands on her knees said, "The *I Ching* is an ancient Chinese text whose origins can be traced back thousands of years. It was used as a decision-making tool by famous emperors and sages. Today people use it all over the world."

"Really?" I was totally impressed with her knowledge, and the fact that she was sharing it with *me*.

"The *I Ching*," she went on, "is based on the philosophies of Taoism and Confucianism. It offers us a way to see into difficult situations, especially those emotionally charged ones where at times our rational knowledge fails us. It helps us to get in touch with both our inner and outer worlds, allowing us to make more accurate decisions. The *I Ching* can do this because it's an oracle."

"What's an oracle?" I asked, embarrassed that I wasn't as well versed in the subject.

"An oracle translates a problem or question you're having into an image, like your dreams do. It helps you change the way you think about your situation and connects you with the inner forces that are shaping it."

I stood up, because my behind hurt—and I wanted to continue this discussion on my feet. She rose, too. Face-to-face, she continued: "The magic happens when you ask the *I Ching* a question and it reveals the answer. But what's really fascinating is when it answers a question you didn't even know was in your heart."

Intrigued by the woman's intensity, I opened the book to the foreword, written by Carl Jung, the renowned psychoanalyst. I didn't want to be rude, but I couldn't help myself. I started to read silently:

> The *I Ching* insists upon self-knowledge throughout. The method by which this is to be achieved is open to every kind of misuse, and is therefore not for the frivolous-minded and immature; nor is it for intellectuals and rationalists. It is appropriate only for thoughtful and reflective people who like to think about what they do and what happens to them—a predilection not to be confused with the morbid brooding of the hypochondriac . . .
>
> The *I Ching* does not offer itself with proofs and results; it does not vaunt itself, nor is it easy to approach. Like a part of nature, it waits until it is discovered. It offers neither facts nor

power, but for lovers of self-knowledge, of wisdom—if there be such—it seems to be the right book.

The manager had left. I closed the oracle and walked immediately to the counter to buy the book. Money was tight, but there was no way I was walking out of there without it.

The manager came back over to me as I waited in line. "You're going to love this book, trust me. I don't make a decision without it." She handed me a flyer. "Here's some information on how to ask your question. It's up to you to interpret the *I Ching's* answer. It just takes practice. If you go to the back of the book, it explains how to throw the coins."

I shook her hand and thanked her profusely.

"One last thing," she added. "Feel free to ask a question and open the book randomly to any page. It's a different experience than throwing the coins. Oh, and don't be turned off by the male-centric presentation. It was written millennia ago."

Minutes after opening my apartment door, I grabbed an apple from the fridge, the only thing left that was fresh, plopped onto my bed, and did my very best to read the *I Ching* from beginning to end. This, of course, was an insane proposition since it contained over seven hundred pages. But I continued reading until three in the morning and still couldn't put the thick yellow book down. The commentaries on the sixty-four archetypal images, referred to as *hexagrams*, were beyond fascinating. I wanted to learn about all sixty-four—push myself to read the entire text—but I had to stop, give my eyes a break, absorb what I'd read so far. Finally, I closed the book, closed my eyes, and lay there in awe of the honesty and depth of these pages.

I'd never read anything that explained so clearly how we, as human beings, could live consciously in the world, how we could create a life of integrity and balance. I'd always jumped into things without thought of consequences, like everyone else I knew. It wasn't until *after* the experience that I'd "get it" and think: *Why did I ever do that?* But something in this book, something in the very act of *reading* this book, showed me that if I didn't slow down and think about every single action I took, before I took it, my life would never improve. Once I started throwing the coins, asking the right questions, and getting answers beyond my limited understanding, I began to see the sheer brilliance of this book.

I shared my discovery with Rachel. She thought it was the best thing since batik. It wasn't long before we became *I Ching* addicts, spending hours on the phone talking about our latest question and the meaning of the "throw," the answer. The *I Ching* became a very useful advisor, helping us resolve all kinds of problems and questions in our lives. It also confirmed what we, at times, did not want to admit was true. We did not take the *I Ching* lightly, nor did we use it without due respect. Opening its pages became a sacred, religious event . . .

Finally, she's off the phone.

"Hello?"

"I've been trying to reach you for an hour. I'm going ballistic. Can you spare a few minutes before I jump into the San Andreas Fault?"

"I'm polishing up the brass on Cleopatra's breastplates."

She's in rare form.

"Tomorrow I get to work with the serpent. There's a birthday party for one of the board members of American Express. He apparently loves looking at women who fondle dangerous animals."

"Is the snake going to be drugged?" I asked.

"Of course it's going to be drugged. *I'm* the one who's gonna bite if he gets out of line. So? Tell me what happened with the interviews?"

"Well, I went on an African safari, I was a mouse in a magazine maze, and I met a horny toad with disgustingly long nostril hairs who came way too close to raping me."

"Karma," Rachel stated matter-of-factly.

"Oh, here we go!"

"Negative past-life actions. You obviously did something in a former life that's bringing these situations to you now."

"Great! I have to suffer *now* because of something I did in another life?"

"Are you kidding? By the sound of it, you could have been Hitler or Attila the Hun or the bride of Dracula. If you don't burn up these karmas *now*," Rachel went on, chomping on a carrot, "you'll have to come back a few more times till you do."

"Well, *that* really motivates me to go on living! Anyway—I'm supposed to meet this woman tomorrow. She sounds like she's sixty. Maybe the ad wasn't such a good idea. Only . . . I just received my last eviction notice, and Martha called yesterday saying she couldn't afford me anymore, and I have a grand total of seventy dollars to my name. I'm drinking way too much caffeine, and I've gained fifteen pounds."

"I know. I've seen you. You look like hell."

"Thanks for your support!"

"Look, Sandra, we've been through this a zillion times. Slow down—the decision isn't in your hands. Allow the universe to pull you in the right direction. Maybe this woman's the right one. How do you know? You haven't even met her. Why don't you come over and we'll throw the *I Ching*?"

"I'm not going anywhere. I'm catatonic."

"All right. Give me half an hour. I'll come over there. But first I have to stop at the store, buy some snake treats."

"Thank you, thank you, thank you."

I cleaned up the apartment. Well, I threw the dirty clothes that were sitting in the middle of the room under the chair and dusted the furniture with paper towels. I pushed books and magazines into the closet and rinsed off the pile of dishes sitting in the sink. I lit my favorite blueberry candle, a stick of nag champa incense, and twenty or so assorted other candles set in small pieces of tinfoil around the room. I placed the two pillows from my bed on the floor in front of the old oak table and fluffed them up so they'd look nice and new. After carefully, gingerly, closing the Indian-bedspread curtains, for fear they might fall off the pole, I sat down on the creaky rocking chair.

I couldn't stop fidgeting. Instead of going to the fridge again to eat something I didn't need, I picked up *The Collected Poems of Emily Dickinson* from the side table and tried to focus on Emily's words while I waited for Rachel. Emily was so lucky. She could be a recluse, write poetry all day, and never have to worry about earning a living.

Rachel arrived at my door in less than twenty minutes. Without saying a word, knowing how important it was to maintain silence before we threw the coins, we simply hugged, sat down on the pillows, and took a few deep breaths. Slowly, silently, respectfully, I brought out the *I Ching*, the tiny brocade pouch with the coins, and a legal-size writing pad from under my bed, and placed them all on the table. I paused a moment, to respect the fundamental nature of the oracle, and then opened the pouch, allowing the three dimes to cascade onto the tabletop.

In ancient times, it was customary to throw yarrow stalks when consulting the *I Ching*. As sacred gifts of the vegetable kingdom, these stalks were considered to be related to the source of life and, when held firmly in one's palm, would take on the qualities of one's individual vibration. Since yarrow stalks were not easy to find, especially in L.A., coins (pennies, nickels, or dimes) were suggested.

Rachel stopped chewing her gum and watched intently as I placed the dimes in the sweaty palm of my hand. I closed my eyes, knowing *how* I phrased the question was as important as the question itself. Then I focused my entire being on the question: *Should I meet this woman, Emma?* I repeated the question silently again and again, shook the dimes, and then threw the silver coins onto the tabletop. Depending on the configuration of the six throws necessary to form the hexagram, the numeric value assigned to each head or tail would signify either a broken or an unbroken line.

The first throw was an eight, two heads and a tail:

— —

A broken line. Rachel drew the two dashes on the yellow legal pad. The second throw was a seven, one head and two tails:

———

A straight line. Rachel drew the straight solid line.
The third throw was another seven:

———

The fourth, fifth, and sixth throws were all eights, broken
lines:

— —

After Rachel had drawn all the lines, one above the other starting from the bottom, I looked up the identifying hexagram in the
back of the book. It was number 46:

46. Shêng / Pushing Upward

Above: K'un, The Receptive, Earth
Below: Sun, The Gentle, Wind, Wood

> *This pushing upward is associated with effort, just as a*
> *plant needs energy for pushing upward through the earth. That*
> *is why this hexagram, although it is connected with success, is*
> *associated with effort of the will . . .* Pushing Upward *indicates*
> *. . . a vertical ascent—a direct rise from obscurity and lowliness*
> *to power and influence . . . The individual . . . must go to see*
> *authoritative people. Fear not . . . success is assured. But he*
> *must set to work, for activity . . . brings good fortune.*

We looked at each other, eyes wide in disbelief, and then Rachel, in her inimitable style, popped a huge bubble.

CHAPTER  4

The images help us to know the things,
and the oracle helps us to know the future.

I contemplated the Pushing Upward commentary for many hours and realized that calling Emma was not only necessary for my growth, but an inevitable part of my destiny. *Fear not,* it said. *One must go to see authoritative people. Success is assured. A direct rise from obscurity and lowliness to power and influence.* How could I doubt such a positive throw? How could I question that the next chapter of Sandra Billings' life was going to be a rising ascension, instead of a plummet downward?

The next morning, I kept checking the time. I figured nine o'clock was a reasonable hour, so I picked up the receiver and called Emma.

"Hello?"

"Hi, this is Sandra. I hope I didn't wake you."

"Not at all. I'm out of bed early."

"Well, um, I'd like to meet you today, if that's okay?"

She paused. "Yes, that will be fine."

"Can we meet this morning?" I asked anxiously.

"This morning?" She paused again. "Certainly. What time?"

"How's eleven-thirty?" I wanted to jump in my car as soon as I hung up. But I didn't want to sound too pushy.

"Eleven-thirty is good. I'm staying at the Westbrook Retirement Home in West Hollywood. Do you know where that is?"

"Uh . . . yeah, I think so. It's on Sunset, near the karate school, right?"

"Yes, a few blocks past the school, only on the right. There is a parking lot behind the building. I'm in room seventeen."

"Behind the building. Number seventeen. Got it. Okay. See you at eleven-thirty."

The Westbrook Retirement Home? I must be legally insane. Beads of sweat formed instantly on my forehead. Maybe her apartment was being painted, and she was staying at "the home" temporarily. Maybe she was visiting a friend. My throat clamped down in a viselike grip.

I was never good at waiting. What was I going to do for two and a half hours? Riding high on my nervousness and my inability to think of anything to do that might be constructive while I waited, I appeased my feelings of insecurity by devouring the three remaining orange Creamsicles that were in the freezer, along with two white-powdered doughnuts and some chocolate-chip cookie dough heated up in the toaster oven. There's *nothing* better than soft, undercooked chocolate-chip cookie dough to make one's nerves relax. Nothing!

As usual, I felt bloated afterward and didn't want to gain any weight, so I went to the bathroom, stuck my finger down my throat, and threw up everything I had just eaten. When there was nothing left in my stomach but what was given to me at birth, I brushed my teeth and grabbed the bottle of eye drops from the medicine cabinet. Hiding the red veins where the whites of my eyes used to be had become an art form I had mastered. I applied white pancake shadow, eyeliner, and mascara to camouflage the puffiness around my eyes, and smudged apricot rouge onto my cheeks. My lips glistened from the last of my lip gloss, and when I saw my reflection in the mirror, I looked just like one of those puffy-lipped models from *Vogue* magazine. Well, almost. My hair was in dire need of a cut, and I had to remember not to let Emma see my cracked nails.

At 11:30 A.M., punctually and a bit apprehensively, I arrived at the Westbrook Retirement Home. I walked down the long corridor and could practically taste the musty air, feel the pores in my skin wanting to close up from the toxicity and lack of oxygen. Passing the industrial steel kitchen, I smelled canned carrots, peas, and potatoes, and felt sorry for anyone having to live on these soggy vegetables. I was surprised they used anything canned. With what they must be charging folks to stay in this pricey establishment, they could certainly afford fresh food, and a French chef to cook it.

I turned the corner and came face-to-face with several elderly residents standing by their doors, staring at me as I approached. I glanced at one woman who was wearing a beautiful flowered dress with matching orange slippers and thick black designer glasses. She reached out her withered hand, wanting to know if I was a relative or friend coming to have a chat over tea. I smiled, held her hand for a moment, and then gently let go.

Part of me was frightened by the loneliness in their eyes, their desperate need for human contact. Another part of me wanted to take them all home and give them the care and attention they deserved, or I imagined myself being a journalist, asking them millions of questions about their pasts. I bet they had some intriguing stories that would have made great novels. But I steeled myself to keep walking past the needy eyes and hoped that the queasiness residing in the pit of my stomach would soon dissolve.

Uncertain whether my unease was related to my recent food binge or to my anticipation of the appointed meeting, I turned the corner and began to count the numbers on the doors: 21, 19. Here it was. Number 17. Hmmm. I could still turn around and leave. Instead, I tugged at my clothes, straightened my posture, took a very deep breath, and knocked on the bland beige door.

From inside, Emma called out, "Just a minute . . . I'll be right there."

The door opened and I stood there, speechless. In front of me, barely breast-high, was a petite old woman. Huge, ocean-blue eyes looked up at me, luminous, like a little girl's. Magnified eyes, exaggerated by fashionable horn-rimmed glasses, sparkled like the midday sun. The woman's skin was soft yet taut, translucent, like glass. There were no age marks or flaws. And sitting in the middle of her face was the most stately nose I'd ever seen. Her teeth were incredibly white and even. Beautiful silver-white hair, parted with precision to one side, lay gently along one cheek; the other side was combed back behind her chiseled ear. Aged and yet somehow elegant arms hung at her sides, while the rest of her body remained undefined, hidden beneath her oversize sleeveless dress.

Classy; childlike; ancient. I could have stared at her for hours. This woman, who I had imagined might be in her fifties or sixties from our telephone conversation, was no less than eighty. But as I stood there looking down at her shiny hair and radiant blue eyes, her age was irrelevant. There was an air about her, a mysterious demeanor. I was utterly captivated by this woman now standing before me.

"Come in," she said.

"Thank you," I replied, after locating my tongue.

She motioned for me to sit on the dreadful, and I mean *dreadful,* brown brocade couch. She took a seat directly across from me on the yellow overstuffed chair. Also dreadful. Not wanting to take my eyes off of her, yet curious to take in these surroundings, I glanced around the room. The table next to her chair was stacked with scripts. *That's interesting!* My eyes moved to the outdated furniture and accessories that lined the uninviting square room. Even the off-off-white walls looked dingy. I would have sworn on a stack of Bibles that none of the furniture in this room belonged to this woman. Polyester couches? Tacky plaid chairs and cheap, thin carpet? This lady was clearly not in her element. Priceless antiques, French provincial settees, expensive crystal placed in fine-crafted armoires should surround her. And yet, when my eyes returned to the gentlewoman, she looked surprisingly comfortable, content, among these foreign objects. But of course she would.

Emma, it was somehow clear to me, grew roots wherever she was. In her aged body, she sat in the canary yellow chair as if she were an extension of Earth itself. That's what I wanted . . . to experience every waking moment of my life with astute awareness: to walk in the world as if I were a part of it, entitled to all its offerings. Solid. Steady. Not in constant fear, like the ground was caving in beneath my feet and if I said the wrong thing or made a mistake, I'd fall off. Not scared of the present or of what the future might bring.

Our eyes met. We stared at each other for what seemed like a lifetime, and then the woman from the newspaper ad began to speak to me in this melodic voice that I could have fallen asleep to, had there been music in the background and a feather pillow for my head. But beneath the consoling sound that made me think of the beautiful voices of high-class ladies was a no-frills, no-nonsense woman who cut promptly to the chase.

"My husband, Josef, died a little over a year ago. A few months later, my best friend, Sarah, died. I suffered a mild heart attack shortly afterward. My friend Zelda wanted professional care around me until I regained my strength. She insisted I come to Westbrook. I'll be returning to my apartment in a week. It's quite spacious . . . two large bedrooms, a large living room. It requires very little cleaning, perhaps a little dusting and vacuuming once a week. Do you own a car?"

"Yeah, um, yes . . . it's an old Fiat, but it gets me around."

"Good. We can visit the farmers' market. Josef and I used to go there quite often. How old are you?"

"Twenty-one." She offered me a plate of cookies, to which I replied, "No, thank you."

"You're not from Los Angeles, are you? You have very good manners. Where were you raised?"

"Birmingham, Michigan. It's a small suburb outside Detroit."

"I've never been to Detroit. What's it like?"

"Well, it has lots of cars. It *is* the car capital of the universe, and of course, it's where Motown began. I used to sneak out to Hitsville. That was Motown's headquarters. What a scene that was! Every Saturday night, hundreds of people would sing and dance outside the studio, in the streets, on top of cars. All the recording artists would show up and . . ."

I kept babbling. I could have gone on for hours. Being in Emma's presence seemed to pull it out of me. Probably because I'd never met anyone who listened with such interest.

". . . I do miss my friends, though."

"Not your family?"

"Not really."

She changed the subject. It must have been the tone in my voice. "Why did you move to California?"

"The weather, and, of course, the theater. I was going to move to New York, but I had enough brutal winters living in Michigan, thank you very much."

I was about to ask her, *Have you always lived in California?* but she interrupted with another question: "Did you study theater in college?"

"For about a minute. Well, for a year. I wanted to major in the-ater, but I wasn't interested in the required courses, like math or economics. So I left and headed for California. I wanted to study with really great teachers."

"How long have you been in L.A.?"

"About two years. You see, I always wanted to be an actress. Well, ever since I can remember. And since I've been here, I *have* studied with the best—Stella Adler, when she came to L.A., Sher-man Marks, Walter Sheldon. To pay for classes *and* bills, I've worked practically every legitimate job Los Angeles has to offer. I am so ready to audition. But if I don't keep working, I won't be able to eat, audition, or get my SAG card—the Screen Actors Guild membership card. I thought if I placed an ad in the paper, found someone to live with, I could start auditioning . . . fortunately, I'll be getting a little money from unemployment."

The next set of words jumped out of my mouth without warn-ing: "I could help around the apartment. You know, do some cleaning, shop, cook meals." *Cook meals? Did I just say that?* I'd never cooked a meal for anyone in my life. Maybe in home eco-nomics when the whole class had to make omelets for the next class period, but it was a collective effort and we were forced to do it. Other than that, I'd never cooked anything.

"You're very sensitive. I'm sure you are a wonderful actress. Do you know Bert Klein?"

"Should I?" I felt so embarrassed not knowing this person who was clearly of major importance.

"His father was the late Harvey Klein, the movie mogul. His mother, Sarah, was my best friend who passed away. Well, he is practically a son to me." She looked over at the table with the scripts piled high. "He sends me his scripts to review. If you decide to move in, I am sure you will meet him. I know several people in the entertainment field."

She's not only nice—she's connected. I must have burned up a lot of karma these last few days. Rachel's going to flip when she hears this.

"You know," she went on, in a kind of reverie, "Josef, my husband, was an exceptional painter. He was one of New York's celebrated American Eight. We used to have dinner parties with such interesting people, stars and dignitaries. Nehru came one time," she added with a sigh. "Maybe one day I will have the strength to entertain again."

"If you want to invite your friends over, I could help."

"We won't have to worry about the dishes," she added with a twinkle in her eye. "I only use paper plates."

That was it! Between her highly rational dining customs and her theatrical connections, who was I to turn down such an irresistible invitation? Before I left the Westbrook Retirement Home, an agreement was made between the two generations. Emma would cover my room and board and pay for gas, and I would drive her wherever she needed to go, help clean up the apartment, and cook (on occasion). The scheduled date to move in was Saturday. Next Saturday. A week and a day from today.

I left room number 17 remembering the *I Ching's* words:

> Pushing Upward *has supreme success.*
> *The individual . . . must go to see authoritative people.*
> *Fear not . . . success is assured.*

cHapTer 5

The superior man discriminates between high and low . . .

That night I had acting class. Walter Sheldon's two-year advanced scene-study class was coming to an end. Twenty-five students walked in that night wanting to convey our gratefulness, to thank Walter for his dedication and sincere desire to teach us the art and science of acting. Carla, one of the students, brought a cake. I wanted to buy Walter a big, expensive gift. A cool-looking tie or one of those eccentric wool berets he always wore. But all I could afford were candles. It was the least I could do for the man who had taught me more about this craft than any acting book, class, or person I had ever studied with.

Walter was sixty-two years young, short, with a full head of salt-and-pepper hair and thick tortoiseshell glasses. He was always squinting those sky-blue eyes, and a perpetual half smile never left his lips. During the two years I'd known him, he'd never uttered a bad word about anyone. And the stories he would tell! We would stay until the wee hours of the morning, our heads collapsing on the desks, pleading with him to end the class. But no matter how much we begged, he'd ignore our pleas. We'd stay, because no matter how extended his embellishments were, we'd always walk away with a pearl at the end of the night.

My favorite gem was the one he told us about Marlon Brando. As the story went, Brando disliked doing long theater runs. He got bored easily. While performing on Broadway one year, he had an idea that would not only keep him motivated, but it would keep his character fresh. Every night, before the curtain rose, he would ask the stage manager to hide a nickel somewhere on the stage. Marlon would spend the entire evening looking for that nickel. No one had a clue what he was searching for. The audience simply thought the character was nervous or on edge. For Brando, the brilliant maneuver of the hunt kept him interested and at the top of his game.

Tonight I was presenting a monologue from Athol Fugard's *Hello and Goodbye,* a scene I'd been working on for weeks. It was a brilliant play set in the kitchen of a railway house in South Africa in the sixties. The play revealed the wounded lives of a brother and sister who had not seen each other in years. Hester, the sister, returns to the backcountry of South Africa after living in Johannesburg as a prostitute. She comes back in search of an elusive inheritance and, with her brother Johnny, begins to unpack the memories and truths of their empty and damaged lives.

I'd spent weeks working on this scene and selected it because of the depth of Hester's character, my fascination with South Africa, and my own rage at apartheid. I loved the intensity of the scene, imagining myself as a prostitute, confronting an unhappy childhood, feeling the anticipation of financial freedom, and discovering what it must have been like to come home to a place that hadn't changed in fourteen years.

The memories I drew upon had to be real, raw. There was no room for pretending or pretension. Authenticity was key in Walter's class. He demanded it. Another reason I respected him. I called my mother in Michigan, and asked her to send me pictures of the first house we'd lived in. I'd forgotten how the ivy crawled up the side of the small two-story structure and how the maple tree cast a shadow on the entryway. The more I looked at the photo, the more memories surfaced: my father's beatings, my brother's bullying, my mother's enabling . . . and the escape into the joy of putting on backyard plays. My favorite weekend activity.

Hester, my character, had to walk ten miles from the train to her house. There was no other way to get there. To prepare for the scene, I stuffed clothes and toiletries into two suitcases and walked ten miles around Westwood Village, just to see where the soreness would be, where Hester would be hurting when she arrived. The pain settled into the back of my shoulders, the right side of my neck, and in the joints of my fingers. I had to remember each one of these discomforts and bring them to the surface, seamlessly, in class. That was my job as an actress: to be aligned with the body, the emotions, and the intellect of the character.

I drove to Inglewood, a high-crime area in L.A., and closely watched one of the prostitutes walking up and down La Brea. Sitting in my Fiat across the street, I studied how this woman walked, how she spoke to the men driving by, walking by—half-smiling, keeping her head and eyes down. I watched her insecurity, and the limp in her right leg that she pretended didn't exist. I named her Claire and imagined that she'd been born in Alabama to a poor single mother . . . she had been made fun of and beaten up by classmates every day after school because she was poor and because of her height, now six feet. Her bitterness moved her to California, where she thought she could improve her life, climb a make-believe ladder, only to find that the rungs kept breaking. Here she was now, in Inglewood, walking at night, hungry to please the cannibals of the street, just to have something to eat herself.

I brought the stuffed suitcases to Walter's class. Before presenting the scene I played "Stairway to Heaven" by Led Zeppelin on a friend's cassette player, to set the mood. When I reached the perfect emotional pitch, I picked up the suitcases and walked to the center of the room, put the suitcases down on the imaginary dirt road, and brought back the discomfort of carrying the bags for ten miles. I surveyed the imaginary house Hester had grown up in. The one she hadn't seen in years. And as she walked, and as the class and Walter observed, I saw the ivy crawling up the side of my childhood home. While I repeated her words—"Please let it be different, and strange, even if I get lost and got to ask my way. I won't mind. But to think of it all still the same, the way it was, and me coming back to find it like that . . . ! Sick! It made me sick on the stomach"—I reconnected with the prostitute from Inglewood, and how she might have felt going back to Alabama and finding out nothing had changed in *her* neighborhood.

When Hester spoke the words "Those windy days with nothing to do; the dust in the street! Even the color of things—so clear, man, it could have been yesterday," I imagined her sitting on a cement step when she was young, having nothing to do but follow the dust. And as the wind blew the particles into the foam frothing from the river, I imagined her breathing in the heat, smelling the oppression. I felt each beat, without rushing a moment. I became Hester from South Africa, and nailed the accent.

When the scene was over, I stood there, waiting for Walter's critique. Instead, everyone stood up and applauded. Calvin, this guy who had a major crush on me and had loaned me the cassette player, gave me a paper flower. Walter gave me an *A++*.

I'd promised Larry Santino, a guy I was kinda dating, that I'd watch *his* scene, cheer him on as he presented an excerpt from David Rabe's play *The Basic Training of Pavlo Hummel*. The play was a good choice for Larry in that Pavlo Hummel was close to his age. In addition, both came from New York, and both were graced with low intelligence. It could have been a terrific character study for Larry had he taken his craft more seriously, developed the subtext, the provocation for the character's actions, researched the Vietnam War, or taken time to speak to veterans who'd experienced firsthand the psychological effects of war. If only he had embraced Pavlo's heart, studied Pavlo's gait, grasped the significance of Pavlo's hopeless stare. But he hadn't. The only thing we saw was Larry Santino, dressed and pressed in a soldier's uniform, pretending to be Pavlo Hummel. I knew I was going to have to varnish the truth when he asked me about his performance; otherwise his ego would be bruised and our evening would be ruined. As cute as Larry was, as great a body as had been bestowed upon him, he was extremely insecure about his acting, and he had every reason to be.

We'd met the first day of Walter Sheldon's class. It was only seconds after I'd sat down that this cute guy in a white T-shirt, cutoffs, and a Yankees baseball cap took the seat next to me. By the time his thirty-five-second introduction was over, I knew his name, where he was from, the teachers he'd studied with, and that his wink—the one he made with his right eye—was a sign of affection and a prelude to an invitation to have coffee with him after class.

Larry wasn't very bright or well mannered. These flaws in his character assured me of how short-lived the relationship was going to be. Nevertheless, Larry did have other attributes that made getting involved romantically an easy decision. He had the greatest lips on the planet; thick, dark wavy hair; and an exceedingly hairy chest. To me, there's nothing better than burrowing into a mound of hair when I'm depressed, or diving into a mass of hair when I'm horny. I once mentioned my hair fetish to Rachel. She told me I must have been a female ape in a past life, searching for my hairy male counterpart. She might have been right.

Most of all, I loved the way Larry kissed. His plump tongue always knew just what to do inside my mouth; his succulent lips and long, expressive fingers knew just what to do everywhere else—a quality that more than made up for his acting deficiencies. Which is why, when Larry invited me to his apartment after class, I graciously accepted and looked forward to proceeding with . . . what he knew best.

A joint was smoldering in the ashtray on the floor by the bed, burning its last embers. Our bodies were naked, snuggled beneath the covers. Giggling rippled out from under Larry's sheets, and only if you were lying next to us or if your head was directly above ours could you have heard him whisper the words: "I was great, wasn't I?"

"In class or in bed?" I replied.

"Very funny, bush hair."

"You were *great* in bed. *Okay* in class . . . why do you do that?"

"Do what?"

"Look out into the audience when you're supposed to be in character. You break the fourth wall every time you look out. You lose the audience's trust."

"I sucked, right?"

"You didn't suck. There were a couple of lines where I really believed you. Like, when you described how the cops couldn't catch up to you and the sirens were screaming, and how you jumped out of the Porsche and walked away, cool-like. You were really into it."

Larry lay there gloating, as if he'd just contributed something significant to a nation of needy people. I lay there next to him witnessing the swell of his unjustified ego, wondering how anyone could walk through life and remain so unconscious. As my conflicting thoughts about Larry drifted back and forth, I suddenly stepped into my own reality and stumbled upon an alarming idea that shot me bolt upright.

"I'm moving in with a stranger on Saturday. What am I doing?"

Larry took hold of my shoulder and pulled me down. It was his Italian Brooklyn accent that always ruined the ensuing moment or made me laugh out of context. "Why don't you move in here? We got plenty a room."

"Are you serious? You've got two roommates and one bedroom. You don't even have a dresser. Where would I put my clothes?"

"We could put 'em under the bed."

"Your mattress is on the floor." I reached for the ashtray for one last toke, but the joint had burned out. "I'm just feeling paranoid."

"What if she's schizophrenic? In the daytime, she's warm and loving, but when the sun goes down, she becomes a gargoyle, and flies around your room in the middle of the night, nests on your head . . ."

"I have no sense of humor right now!" I jumped off the bed, picked up my clothes off the floor, and bolted into the bathroom.

"How big's her place?" he hollered through the door. "It could be one room, for all you know."

"She told me her husband was a famous artist from New York. I'm sure the place is very palatial." I emerged from the bathroom. "I'm leaving. Are you going to help me move or not?"

Larry didn't answer. He pretended not to hear me, and intentionally slipped his head under the covers.

"Well?"

"I guess."

"Never mind."

"All right, all right. I'll help you move."

CHapter 6

*If one clings to the strong man,
one loses the little boy.*

Larry was only thirty-five minutes late when he sauntered into my apartment wearing his cutoffs and a pink T-shirt. I opened the door and found him leaning against the frame, Jimmy Dean–style. An unlit cigarette dangled from his luscious lips. He was expecting me to kiss him. Was he kidding? By the time he'd honored me with his presence, most of my things had been packed, crammed into every crevice of the Fiat. Since early that morning I had been lugging suitcases out to the trunk, stacking boxes in the backseat, laying clothes over taped boxes. Pillows and bedcovers were shoved in wherever they could fit, and the bags under my arms full of toiletries . . . I wasn't sure where they were going. No doubt squished between the bucket seats. And he wanted my *lips?*

I looked at his tanned, muscular arms and legs, and wondered why God hadn't finished the job and given him a functional brain. I asked him to wait while I made one last apartment check. He leaned his back against the Fiat, happy to oblige, as long as he could enhance his tan and not expend any effort.

As I headed back to the apartment for the last time, I knew I wasn't going to miss this place. I wasn't going to miss the torn rug that smelled of cat piss or the six-inch-square freezer that only had room for two Creamsicles and a chicken potpie, or the blotchy yellow walls, or the toilet that never completely flushed. I might miss the times I'd spent learning lines, pacing the living room as I rehearsed monologue after monologue, and sitting in the bathtub trying to get rid of my Michigan accent. I had to admit, I'd grown as an actor here. A tear fell, and it surprised me as I took my final glance. *I guess I _will_ miss this place.*

Larry and I squeezed our bodies into the two tiny spaces left in the Fearless Fiat's front seat and drove to Emma's apartment building. Hardly able to see out the back window, I endured the slow lane for the first time in my life. It wasn't bad. I guess there *was* a reason for the lane. Larry barely said a word, which was a pleasant surprise. Perhaps he knew more than I gave him credit for.

Curson Avenue, Emma's street, was located in mid-city L.A. It was lined with garden apartments and condominiums, oak trees and maple trees, and real green grass. There were only a few small houses scattered on the street; the rest of the block was mostly five- and six-story buildings with people in their seventies and eighties sitting on their front balconies talking, laughing, rocking away the hours. As we drove down the street, two kids played Frisbee on the grass, and the passing friendly mailman tried his hand at throwing the disk. It was a real neighborhood, and it'd been a long time since I'd lived in one. I welcomed the unaccustomed sounds.

Emma's building was in a gray square stucco structure. There were balconies attached, but no interesting curves or tiers. Symmetrical rectangular windows lined the front of the edifice, exposing identical off-white curtains in every frame. And each tenant had the same boxes of tulips sitting on their windowsills. I couldn't tell if they were plastic or real. That was the least of my worries. I maneuvered the Fiat as best I could, close to the curb, and sat there for a moment, flashing back on why I was making this daring move. And then I remembered.

Fortunately, Larry remained silent as I breathed in my new street.

"Okay, let's do it."

"You're sure you don't want to live with me?" Larry asked, apparently thinking, absurdly, that I might change my mind.

"Let's go."

Arms filled with boxes, hands clutching loose pairs of shoes by straps and shoestrings, clothes falling off hangers and drooping off our forearms, we approached the lobby's elevator. There on a sign were two of the most beautiful words I'd seen since I'd last lived in the comfort of my parents' domain: LAUNDRY ROOM. I stopped in mid-breath. "Larry, look! I don't have to drive twenty minutes to a hot, humid, money-eating Laundromat any longer." Larry, having no concept of the depths of my relief, grunted and pulled me inside the elevator. I pressed the number 3.

Emma's building was one of those garden apartments where all the doors opened to the outdoors. There were no dark, musty halls to walk through, no perfumed carpets that tried to hide the smells—yet another unfortunate situation I had become too accustomed to. At Emma's apartment, the inner wooden door was open. I set down the suitcase, laid the bundle of clothes and shoes on top, and knocked softly on the outer screen door. Emma greeted us with a wide smile and invited us in.

"Hi, Emma. This is Larry Santino, a friend from acting class."

"Hello, Larry. It's a pleasure to meet you." Her clear blue eyes took him in. If she wasn't impressed, she was too ladylike to be rude. "Why don't you come in, relax a little, then bring the rest of your things upstairs. I've made some iced tea for you."

"Oh, thank you," I replied, waiting for Larry to do the same. Emma waited, too.

"Please, sit down. You must be exhausted from the move."

We sat and watched Emma walk with a kind of deliberateness that revealed she'd been able to move much faster some time ago, but now, since her husband's passing and her heart attack, she had slowed down. The woman from the ad placed one foot before the other solidly on the carpet and headed toward the kitchen to get her guests some tea.

I looked around, taking in the sights of my new home. The living room had that distinct grandmother aroma: cooked fish combined with the scent of evergreen air freshener. Old-fashioned plastic rug runners started in the living room and rolled out to the kitchen, then to the bathroom, to protect the atrocious turquoise carpet from wear. The green polyester couch was also covered with a thick protective plastic. Stained maple end tables must have been with Emma since her wedding day. The too-heavy-for-the-apartment mahogany dining-room table and armoire showcasing her old white china could not have arrived much after. An old record player and a small-screen TV were placed in the corner. Strangely, there was one piece of furniture that stood out among the others. It was a beautiful green satin Victorian high-back chair. Emma's name was written all over it, even down to the faint impression of her buttocks in the seat.

Emma returned to the living room with a shaky tray and two glasses of iced tea. After serving us, she sat down in her high-back. "Did you have far to travel?"

"It only took us half an hour from Westwood. The real challenge was not causing an accident."

Emma looked right into my eyes, and smiled.

"Would you like a tour of your new home?"

I took a sip of the cold tea, experienced brain freeze, and nodded yes.

Larry poked me in the spine with his elbow and whispered facetiously, "Very palatial!"

"Very funny!" I elbowed him back.

So what if the furniture was not as elegant as I had imagined and the rooms were small? So what if there were no Persian rugs or French provincial furniture or priceless antiques? Somehow, I could already sense that it wasn't the *things* in this place that were about to change me. It was a feeling—an underlying feeling of expansion and the premonition that anything in the world, anything in the realm of possibility, could happen to me here. This feeling seemed much more important than what my eyes were seeing or what my nose was inhaling.

We followed Emma down the hallway. Paintings hung everywhere! Large paintings, small paintings, paintings in antique frames, paintings in modern frames. There were portraits and still lifes, landscapes and abstracts, each one more alluring, more animated, than the next, each one revealing a unique story. I realized then that this place, her home, where she had lived and breathed for years, was where she had nurtured Josef and where he had imbibed all her love and had woven the sum total of their love into his creations. I couldn't imagine that I was being given the opportunity to live here, to drink in this energy, to bathe in it.

One painting mesmerized me: it was of three middle-aged men sitting at a table in a dark bar. The intense brushstrokes of deeply penetrating browns and burgundies brought such depth to the characters that the figures truly came alive. I stopped at the next picture to study the rich colors of the robust country farmer, proud of the land he cultivated, when Emma's voice, close beside me, said, "He was a great painter, wasn't he?"

"Yes, he was," I replied.

And your encouragement—that made sure of it, I thought.

The woman standing beside me was quiet. A moment of stillness turned into forever while everything around me intensified—colors, sounds, touch. I could hear dust fly and smell the dried paint on the canvas and the various woods that framed the paintings. And in that moment of stillness, there was an understanding between us that went beyond words or thoughts. As we stood there in front of Josef's paintings, we were two vessels open to the mystery of what had brought us together. Open to the challenge of what the future might bring. Emma was a formidable woman indeed. She had plenty to teach me, and I had plenty to learn. I was about to be . . . Pushing Upward.

"Holy crap. I gotta go!" Larry's interjection startled me. He was looking at his Mickey Mouse wristwatch. "I'm s'posed ta meet my brother at the Sunset Diner in ten minutes."

"Emma, do you mind if we bring my things up now?"

"Go ahead, dear."

"Larry, where'd you leave your manners?" He didn't answer as we headed down the elevator and piled the rest of my bags and loose shoes in each other's arms. After Larry dropped my favorite dress on the ground, I had no words. I picked up the garment, and we took the elevator back up to my new home—in silence.

I was pretty certain about saying good-bye to Larry—forever. Saying good-bye meant an end to a significant chapter of my life, a major shift from surface encounters to what I hoped would be substantive, fulfilling relationships. I couldn't wait to meet intelligent, talented people who knew where they were going and were willing to work hard to get there. People I could learn from and respect. I didn't know *when* I'd meet these people; I just knew I was going to. It was all part of this impending excursion I was about to take off on. And like all great adventures, there was no telling how different the traveler would be when the trip was over, or where the changes would lead.

After all my belongings were stacked high on my new bed, I gave a hug to the boy who had warmed my lips and caressed my body on nights I couldn't stand to be alone. And as I pulled away from his tight embrace, I remembered how effortless it was to lie next to him, how sweet it was to kiss his mouth. And even though his jokes were insanely stupid and he was a horrid actor, I was going to miss the guy with the Yankees baseball cap and the perfect tan.

"Hey, call me later." Then he turned to Emma and smiled. "Thanks for the tea. Nice meetin' ya." Not a clue how belated he was with his good manners.

Emma smiled back. "It was nice meeting you, Larry."

сндртеr  7

Shock comes—oh, oh!
Then follow laughing words—ha, ha!

Sleeping in a new bed usually meant a restless night's sleep, and major adjustments for my psyche the following morning. But for some reason I slept quite soundly amid my new surroundings and woke up to two robins singing on the edge of my windowsill. Listening to their lyrical sounds and feeling the sun's rays on my exhausted body, I was at peace in this tiny room filled with Josef's paintings and books, its walls glowing, cupping the morning sun. I didn't mind Josef's presence, either, his memory surrounding me. It added a kind of security, a knowing that I was being looked after, cared for. This cocoon, enveloping me as I lay on the bed, seemed to be protecting me from all the possible demons lurking outside. For the first time, I think, in my life, I felt no anxiety, no apprehension about what the next minute might or might not bring.

Maybe this is what heaven is like. I held that thought and slid down beneath the covers, sinking into the soft goose-down pillows, where my mind could wander without interruption. Free to turn to one side of the bed or the other, embracing my pillow.

Feeling the soft white sheets on my freshly shaved legs as they moved this way and that with total freedom. I was completely content. *If I had my way, I'd hide under these covers forever.*

Lest I forget how short *forever* could be . . . without warning came the recollection of the dream I'd had the night before, and off and on for years. The images were dark. They wouldn't come clear. There were two shadows. Two shadowy male figures stood there, laughing, more menacing than gleeful. They were looming larger. Coming closer . . . there was a third figure I couldn't make out. My stomach felt queasy as the memory surfaced.

How foolish of me to think I could remain in this state of bliss for more than a few minutes, let alone eternity. As soon as I thought I couldn't, I didn't. The internal demons of doubt were back. I threw off the covers. *Oh God, what if Emma turns out to be weird? What if we don't get along and I have to move out?* The thought of moving again put my brain on overload.

I pulled the covers back over me, shivering. My arm slid out from the side. I reached under the bed, and brought the *I Ching* up to my breast. My fingers returned to the floor, groping around for the silk pouch, the pencil and pad. I sat up, pulled open the pouch strings, took out the dimes, and held them tightly. I closed my eyes and tried to think of the right question.

Dear God, is everything going to be okay?

No, that wasn't the question.

Will I have to leave?

I didn't even want to *go* there. *Think, Sandra.*

Okay: What is it I need to know about this relationship?

That's it. I threw the coins six times, wrote down each of the six broken lines on the legal pad, and looked up the hexagram in the back of the oracle. It was hexagram number 2:

2. K'un /The Receptive

Above: K'un, The Receptive, Earth
Below: K'un, The Receptive, Earth

The person in question is not in an independent position.

That was the truth.

This means that he must achieve something.

Achieve something. Like what?

It is not his task to try to lead at this time—that would only make him lose his way—but to let himself be led. If he knows how to meet fate with an attitude of acceptance, he is sure to find the right guidance. The superior man lets himself be guided; he does not go ahead blindly, but learns from the situation what is demanded of him and then follows this intimation from fate . . . in addition to the time of toil and effort, this is also a time of planning . . .

Planning? Planning what? I jumped out of bed, scooped up my clothes from the floor, and headed toward the shower. Water. Standing up, lying down, I loved it! The shower head was old, but it still had some juice. The towels were nice and thick. I clicked on the heat and was back in heaven. I even started to sing "Our House," by Crosby, Stills, Nash & Young. Quietly, of course.

Returning to the bedroom, I put on my clothes, made my new bed, opened the window, and tried to inhale my new life. The room looked smaller in the morning light, but Josef's paintings made the space seem bigger. They began to breathe, taking on a life of their own. I could have studied each painting all morning, all day. But there'd be time for that. Now, it was time to start my new life. I tiptoed out into the hallway, wondering if Emma was still asleep. I had no idea of her schedule or what time she started her day.

This was unknown territory. I saw that her bedroom door was open a crack. I peeked through the small opening, but she wasn't inside. I walked toward the living room and poked my nose around the corner, into the room. There she was, sitting in her elegant green satin high-backed chair, reading. As I studied her impressive posture, she looked like a retired law professor ruminating over the subtle refinements of a legal journal. She was, however, only reading the *New York Times*.

The Victorian high-back was by far the most outstanding piece of furniture she possessed. Crafted from rich mahogany, it curved in a half moon along the top, where clusters of grapes and leaves were carved delicately into the thick, dark wood. Hunter-green satin covered the seat and the back of the chair. The curve of the arms where the wood was molded fit perfectly beneath Emma's frail wrists, supporting her hands while she read.

"Good morning," I said, trying not to startle her.

She jumped slightly. "Oh, you startled me." She smiled away the surprise, set the paper down on her lap, lowered her bifocals, and waved me over to the chair next to her. Lovingly, she said, "Come, sit down. How was your sleep?"

"Not bad! I think I could have slept for two weeks."

"I'm glad you had a good rest, dear."

She paused and then gingerly raised herself up. It took all her strength to lift her body. Cup and saucer in hand, she walked step-by-step, head held high, purposefully, toward the kitchen. "There's coffee and bagels," she called back to me, "or cereal, if you like."

"No, thanks. I'm not hungry."

Returning from the kitchen, she focused on the trembling hot cup, evidence there was still weakness in her limbs. She sat down, carefully placing the cup of coffee and quarter piece of toasted bagel with cream cheese on the small table between us.

"So, do we need anything from the store?" I asked, hoping there was something I could do with all this energy and no immediate place to put it.

"I suppose we could use some paper goods, fish, chopped liver . . . there's no hurry." Her voice was a little shaky. She took off her bifocals. "So, tell me, Sandra. Do you have a plan?"

The question sounded stern. "A plan?"

"A plan for your career?"

"Well, I was planning to go to the Screen Actors Guild, to see if they had a list of auditions."

"Are you in shape to audition?"

"Well, yes."

"There is a swimming pool at the back of this building and a YWCA down the block."

"That's great . . . it's just that I'm on a tight budget, and I can't really afford the Y."

"I used to volunteer there. They told me *I* could use the facilities. I never have. I'll talk to them about you using them instead. There's also a track at the high school a few blocks away."

"I guess I could lose a few pounds." I laughed, knowing how true that statement was. Emma didn't reply, not so subtly implying agreement.

"You did say you wanted to be an actress, didn't you?"

"Yes, well . . ."

"Well, then you will need to be in pretty good shape. *Comprenez-vous?*"

"Pardon?"

"That is French for 'Understand?'"

"*Sí*," I said. "That's Spanish for 'Yes.'"

It was a lie. I didn't *see,* nor did I understand, that within a few weeks this little woman with white hair and bifocals would have me running miles around Fairfax High School, perched in the bleachers, making sure I jogged with proper breathing, timing me as I'd try to reach her newest goal.

"Keep your knees up and in sync with your breath!" she'd yell out. "Try it again. One more mile, but keep your pace steady."

I had no idea I was joining the Navy SEALs or signing up for boot camp. Where did Emma ever learn how to train? Each week I had to accomplish an additional half mile or she'd be disappointed, and I couldn't deal with that. It didn't faze her that other joggers were amused. Every time they passed her, they'd yell, "You tell her, Mama!" "Don't let her quit before fifty laps!"

As she sat by the apartment pool, in her cloth director's chair, the little lady with the surprising set of lungs reminded me: "Keep your shoulders high and your legs extended. Cup your hands." Using her black binoculars, she watched me swim—five laps, six laps, then ten.

"Synchronize your breath . . . with the movements of your stretch. Yes. Better. Smoother now. Be a fish."

If not done to her satisfaction, I was asked to do them again. My arms and legs cried out for a reprieve. I was freezing. My muscles ached to be submerged in a hot bath of bubbles. And this was only during the day. At night she'd have me read newspapers and the labels off canned goods out loud using a wine cork between my upper and lower front teeth. This technique was to train me to speak from my diaphragm and not my throat. After only a few weeks, I was reading the yogurt container—"Cultured pasteurized milk, honey, blueberries, pure maple syrup, all natural flavors"— like a Shakespearean actor.

And since the oracle had made it clear that it wasn't my time to lead, but to be *led*, I obeyed. She was the whip, the disciplinarian, the enemy to my lethargy. I never would have imagined how strenuous life on unemployment could be. My lazy self was beginning to resent her and this routine she thought I was in such great need of, but the hero in me wanted to push through. My inner child wanted her approval. I asked her where on earth she had learned this technique.

She said, "I read about it in the *National Enquirer* while waiting in line at the supermarket." She smiled. "Telly Savalas said it worked for him."

CHapTer

Progress like a hamster. . . .
Undertakings bring good fortune.

I was dying to talk to Rachel. It had been weeks. I needed to bring her up to date on my new life and tune in to the latest episode of hers. We decided to meet at the Self-Realization Fellowship Lake Shrine in Pacific Palisades. It had become a haven for us, as we tried to keep our balance in the midst of L.A. mayhem, and we came as often as possible. The beautiful human-made lake and temple had been dedicated to the spiritual leader and teacher Paramahansa Yogananda, who died in 1952. Yogananda was recognized as one of the greatest emissaries to the West, bringing India's ancient wisdom. Rachel and I loved soaking in the energy of this sacred place, strolling along the tranquil lake and sitting in the simple, elegant temple, where we could relax and pause . . . for more than a few seconds.

I spotted my friend as she stepped out of her broken-down Volvo. I was so happy to see her *and* her atrocious batik pants. Now with blonde hair instead of auburn, still brittle from all the perms, and the rest of her without question a few pounds heavier.

We hugged like we hadn't seen each other in centuries, and began to circle the lake. I was bursting to tell her the news.

"I now have my own acting coach, my own physical trainer, a roof over my head, and enough chicken soup to nurse me through a hundred and fifty colds. I mean, who would have thought—"

"It's great you have this support," she broke in, replying in a way that seemed mysteriously distant . . . and jittery.

I looked at her. "What's up with you?"

"Nothing. I'm okay," she said nervously. "Just moving through some stuff." She popped two sticks of spearmint gum into her mouth and took out a small rubber ball that she fisted and started to squeeze.

"What happened to your hand?"

"I sprained my arm on a slide at a kids' party the other day." She paused. "That's only part of it. The guy who hosted the party started making moves on me. I told him I had a boyfriend, just to get him off my back. But he wouldn't stop. So I split. Anyway, the doctor told me to use this ball to strengthen my wrist and my arm . . ."

"Did you tell the agency?"

"I tried. They don't want to make waves. He's a 'substantial client.'"

"What a bunch of hard-asses! Rachel, maybe the universe is telling *you* it's time for a change."

"I've been thinking about it." She nodded thoughtfully, looking out at the lake while scuffing her sandal in the dust of the path.

"Ya know," she said slowly, "the thing is, I don't know *what* the hell I'm doing with my life."

Rachel's face was turned away from me. But I could feel the knot in her throat, the holding back of tears. She was serious, and vulnerable, in a way I'd never seen her before.

"Look . . ." She took a deep breath. "I'm sorry . . . I'm just a mess right now." She ran her fingers through her fragile blonde hair. "My life just doesn't seem to have any direction. I'm not going anywhere. And to be honest, I don't have any idea where I *want* to go."

A light breeze blew wisps of hair across her face, and I reached out and tucked the strands behind her ear.

"Rachel," I asked her gently, "what is it you really *want* to do?"

She started walking again, opened her arms wide. "I have no fucking idea!"

I tried to catch up with her. "You have so many great qualities. You're smart, you're funny, you're creative. You've got great insight. You've pulled my butt out of fires more times than I can count. Look, I can't tell you what to do, but I *do* know that you can do anything you put your heart into."

I stopped walking, and looked at her intently. "But right now, you have to get out of this job. It's dangerous. Hell, topless waitressing would be safer. At least you could get free food and a good workout."

"Food is the last thing I need," Rachel remarked, with a slight grin.

"Tell me about it. I have more chicken soup than I know what to do with. Emma has me exercising so much, though, I can't keep *any* weight on."

"You're burning up calories. What do you expect? Your body's screaming for nutrients."

"I have no idea what to eat—and I'm supposed to be cooking," I admitted.

"Me neither. We never learned. The only difference between you and me is . . . I digest my food—which is why I've gained ten pounds. You . . . get rid of it! Food is an escape, for both of us."

"You're right." She was back!

We kept walking, admiring the lily pads in the lake, the swans floating gracefully on the still water. Then Rachel stopped again.

"Maybe this is a sign."

We looked at each other and both blurted out: "We have to learn to cook."

We cracked up, shook hands, and vowed to learn how to cook by the end of the month. That was the deal. Before going our separate ways, I made Rachel walk around the lake one more time, which she bitched about—which was fine with me—and then we hugged and kissed each other good-bye.

Emma had been preparing most of the meals. She never complained, mind you; neither did I. But I was beginning to feel a little guilty. Cooking was part of our original agreement. So, the next morning, I decided to initiate my vow and made a trip to a small gourmet kitchen store. I was blown away by the variety of cookbooks. Dessert books for chocolate lovers, strawberry lovers, even marshmallow lovers. There were cookbooks for crêpes; omelets; chicken and fish dishes from France, Scandinavia, Peru. Walking up and down the aisles, I felt dizzy from the choices, but finally narrowed them down to three selections: an African cookbook, a Jewish cookbook, and a Chinese cookbook. I was determined to embark on a culinary voyage, praying I was up to the task.

Emma was on the phone when I walked in. I didn't want to disturb her, so I gently put the cookbooks on the kitchen counter and tried to guess who she was talking to. Like I couldn't figure it out by the script on her lap and the way she expressed herself, with childlike exuberance. Clearly, it was Bert. Bert's father was the movie mogul who was married to Sarah, Emma's best friend who had died right after her husband. This was apparently the moment when Bert adopted Emma as his surrogate mother and she adopted him as her surrogate son. He was now a producer. He called Emma practically every day and sent her scripts to study and critique. She would spend hours not only reading these scripts, but writing extensive notes in their margins, detailing her evaluations. Her long pauses when she spoke to him implied, to me at least, that he confided in her and valued her comments. Where she learned the discernment to break down each scene, understand the nuances of every character, I had no idea.

Without even knowing him, I didn't like Bert. He took up way too much of her time.

While I waited for her to end the conversation, I flipped through the cookbooks. *Ohhh, Hunan chow mein! Yummy!* I hunted through the fridge, but there was no baby bok choy, whatever that was, or water chestnuts. Emma had no wok. I picked up the African book. *Mmm. Fufu,* boiled plantain; *masamba,* greens; and *pastel com diablo dentro,* "pastry with the devil inside"—the picture looked divine! I poked around the cupboards, but we were out of tuna and there were no sweet potatoes. *Drag-ola!* I picked up the Jewish cookbook, leafed through the pages. *"Ahhh,* potato pancakes!*"* I exclaimed, too loudly.

"Hello," Emma called out.

"Hello! I'm going to make lunch today," I said overzealously, hoping she'd realize how excited I was and get off the phone.

"I'll be off in a few minutes, dear. I was going to make fruit salad. My friend Zelda is coming for lunch."

"I'll make enough for Zelda, too." Emma returned to the phone, and I forged ahead, making sure we had all the ingredients: eggs, potatoes, onions, milk. But I couldn't find the potatoes. I kept rummaging through the drawers, now making more noise than I should.

Emma said good-bye and put down the phone. "What are you making?"

She was probably terrified that what I was making was a mess. I didn't blame her.

"Potato pancakes," I said, pulling out pots and pans, still looking for the potatoes. "Do you like them?" I asked, not giving her a chance to respond. "You don't have to get up. Just tell me where you keep the potatoes." I was going to prove to her that I could do this on my own.

"I'll show you." She came into the kitchen and went directly to the pantry I'd just ransacked. "They're right here, dear." She took out six potatoes from a brown bag in the back corner and placed them on the counter.

"No wonder I couldn't find them."

"How many does the recipe call for?" Emma asked, trying to be helpful.

I looked at the book. "One onion per four medium-size potatoes."

Emma handed me six more potatoes from the bag.

"Twelve potatoes? That's a lot."

"You'll see how quickly they're absorbed."

"We'll need three onions." She reached back into the pantry and took out four onions.

"Thank you . . . you can sit down now. It's my turn to cook."

"Can I peel the potatoes?" Emma asked coyly.

I thought about it a minute. "Okay. But I'm doing the rest."

Emma peeled the skins while I shredded the peeled potatoes.

"Why not grate the potatoes into a bowl of water, then strain off the water and add in the onions?" Emma suggested.

"But it says here to keep the potatoes in water *before* you grate them."

"You don't want the potatoes to brown after they're grated. While they're sitting, you can grate the onions. Didn't your mother ever make potato pancakes?"

"No one was allowed in the kitchen when my mother cooked. She said it made her nervous." I didn't tell Emma, but my mother didn't like it when people intruded upon her private asylum. The kitchen was where she went to escape . . . from everything. When my mother's hands kneaded the batter in the mixing bowls, she could forget about my father's drinking. While she stuffed the turkey (and herself), she could forget that her own mother had committed suicide. She'd probably never cooked with her mom, either. But one thing was for sure: Nobody made potato pancakes like Estelle Billings. Nobody! They were like crispy hash browns but thicker and sweeter, especially when doused in sour cream. I remember eating ten to fifteen of those puffy little critters whenever my mother made them.

"How many eggs does the recipe call for?" Emma asked, waking me from my reverie. I checked the book again.

"Three, I think . . . yep, three."

The intervening years disappeared as she handed me the eggs and showed me how to break them, using the round part of the spoon and then dropping the yellow eye and the clear liquid into the bowl, *plop.* I stirred the mixture. Seeing my own hands in the mixing bowl brought tears to my eyes as I stood there, next to this woman. I didn't realize how much I'd missed not cooking with my own mother, not being initiated into the secret of how to bring those formless globs of goop into the perfect cookie or pancake or whatever she was making. I always wanted to be one of those globs that received all of her attention. I always wanted to *be* the batter, because that batter seemed to get a lot more of my mother's love and attention than I ever did.

"We need to drain the mix, form small balls, and then flatten them with the spatula once they're in the skillet," Emma said, a note of compassion in her voice. Understanding, and probably not for the first time, that I might be more fragile than she was. "Be careful not to drain out too much moisture, otherwise the pancake will be too dry," she added.

I watched Emma's hands dive into the batter, add a little flour, and cup the mixture with her thin, veined fingers as she squeezed out the excess liquid and placed the drained mix in the oiled skillet. They weren't my mother's hands; they were Emma's. But at least they were here, guiding me, showing me not only how to make this dish, but how to drop my fear and nervousness with respect to this alien room called the kitchen and accept the possibility of intimacy, even if it was with a semi-stranger.

"Should we taste one?" Emma asked, excitedly.

"One? Let's taste *ten!*"

"Taste as many as you like. It'll be a few minutes before Zelda's here. I must warn you, Zelda is going through an awful time. She is about to get a divorce."

"That's too bad. Have you known Zelda long?"

"I have known Zelda and Max, her husband, for many years. We met in Berlin when we were young. She has been a dear friend. I am worried about her. She is being very self-destructive, drinking too much, and medicating herself."

"I'm sorry to hear about her marriage. I think I'll leave you ladies to gossip on your own. I'm going for a long walk and then meeting some friends at Schwab's to see if I can get discovered. Lana Turner supposedly got discovered there. Why not me?"

Both our hands reached for the refrigerator door at the same time. Her soft hand taking hold of mine brought shivers to my skin. Our eyes met, and the woman from the newspaper ad smiled. My eyes filled with tears. I had never experienced this kind of patience, this sweetness, anywhere, from anyone.

CHAPTER 9

The light has sunk into the earth. . . .
He veils his light, yet still shines.

Coming to consciousness the next morning, I swam up through layers of memory:

> *I'm twelve. It's two in the morning, and I hear someone sobbing. I don't know where the cries are coming from. So I get up from my bed and walk softly down the stairs. As I reach the bottom step, I hear the tinkling of silverware, and sobs from the kitchen. I walk closer and see my mother in her pink nightgown at the table eating a bowl of cereal and three English muffins. She always eats when she can't sleep.*
>
> *A newly lit cigarette is sitting in the ashtray. Six cigarette butts lie shriveled next to it. Her hair, thin and lifeless from all the dyeing, stands straight up on one side. And one can see, from any direction, the half inch of grayed new hair growth, springing from her roots.*
>
> *"Hey, Mom, why are you crying?"*

She's surprised I'm there. As she turns toward me, I see that her forehead is cut above her eyebrow in a half-moon, and bleeding.

"What happened to your face?"

"Your father hit me. It's nothing."

"What do you mean, 'It's nothing'?"

"He does it accidentally when he's asleep. It's that stupid watch he won't take off before he goes to bed."

My mom lies all the time. But she is telling the truth this time. My father has so much pent-up anger; I guess he's able to unconsciously let it go in his sleep.

Masterful at changing the subject when she doesn't want to talk about something, she asks, "Why can't you and your brother get along?"

"Because he's a jerk, Mom. That's why."

I think about the fight Steven and I had gotten into the day before because he hid my history book, knowing I had a test. I wanted to kill him, and almost scratched his eyes out. Mom defended him before she even heard my side of the story. So, part of me feels sorry for the fact that she's crying, and another part doesn't.

I've seen her cry lots of times, but not like this. And I always ask what's wrong. But she never wants to talk about it. Only this time, at 2:25 A.M., for some reason, she decides to tell me.

"I miss my mother, so much. I don't know why she had to kill herself! Why she had to take those pills. I thought they were going to make her better, but they killed her. Didn't her family mean anything to her? Didn't she think I needed her?"

I don't know what to do. It's scary to see her like this. All I can think to say is, "You didn't know, Mom . . . It's—it's not your fault." I rubbed her shoulder, wishing I could remove her pain. But she just sat there sobbing. I sat with her as long as I could. I didn't know what else to do.

"I gotta go back to bed, Mom. I have school tomorrow."

"Can I have a hug?" she asks, as if she were the twelve-year-old.

I give her a big, long one. And then I leave, because there's nothing more I can do for the woman whose mother killed herself—for the woman who is killing herself now—except feel sorry for her. And I can do that from anywhere.

I stopped at a pay phone on my way to the Screen Actors Guild that morning and placed a call to my mother, collect. She rarely accepted, but she did today. After a few months at Emma's, I was hoping I'd be able to distance myself from Estelle Billings, not fall into the usual emotional web and react. Stop questioning why she had allowed my father to drink himself into a stupor every night and whip us, why she'd turned her head when Steven terrorized me, and why her social life was more important than her children. At least I would give it a try. Besides, I was in a good mood.

"Hi, Mom."

She sounded preoccupied. "Sandra, is that you? What's wrong?"

"Nothing's wrong. I just wanted . . ."

I heard noise in the background. She must have been having one of her bridge games, because she yelled to someone in the room: "This'll just be a minute." Then she returned to the phone. "Sandra, this is not a good time. I've got a tournament here. What's going on?"

"I just wanted to tell you that I moved in with an elderly lady. She's really nice. We made potato pancakes yesterday, and . . . I thought of you."

"Is she paying you?"

"Why should she pay me?" I snapped back.

"Are you taking care of her? Is she an invalid?"

"No."

"Then, why are you there?"

There were a thousand reasons why I was there, but I didn't voice any of them.

"I hope you didn't call for money, because we don't have any to spare, and your father would kill me if he knew I accepted this call."

"I didn't call for money, Mom."

"You're working, aren't you? Please tell me you're working."

I should have said yes. But I told her that I needed a break, and wanted to start auditioning.

"For God's sake, Sandra—that was high school. *Anne Frank?* Can you forget that? What have you acted in? What have they paid you for? Can you please give us some peace of mind and go back to school and get a degree, or at least get a job? First you say hateful things to us . . ."

"Mom, I said I was sorry. I took it back."

"You say these hateful things, and leave us with all that ugliness—you can't just erase it, you know, and then walk away. Can you at least give me the gift of not having to worry about you?"

"I'm fine. I just called to tell you—"

"Call next week. Not collect. I have to go. These women are waiting."

She hung up. So did I.

CHAPTER 10

One must not expect perseverance too soon.

I had driven by the blue stucco structure thousands of times, but I'd never dared to enter. It seemed impenetrable . . . the Screen Actors Guild carried a lot of weight. Not just in my eyes, but in the eyes of every actor living in L.A. and New York. The Guild became either a protective shield or an iron wall impossible to break through. The drill was, you couldn't get into a film or a TV show without having your SAG card and an agent. Most agents would not sign actors unless they had their SAG card, and the only auditions available without a SAG card were those that were posted "non-union." The problem was, non-union plays were not highly regarded by the reviewers—which meant that the reviewers rarely showed up. Therefore, no matter how talented you were, if it wasn't a union production, your work would most likely not be seen or written up. It was a vicious circle, a conundrum I was determined to break through.

Entering the Guild today was like walking into a Fellini film. Midgets and clowns walked in one direction; a couple in formal wear, and on stilts, walked in another. Magnificent female bodies sculpted to perfection slithered by me, while young children

dragged by their mothers screamed to leave. I moved past the per-
formers, until I found the bulletin board where posters and flyers
announced upcoming auditions. The board was stuffed—one flyer
on top of the other. There were auditions for fifty-year-old fat men,
one-legged teenagers, five-year-old redheads. Not one flyer called
for a twenty-one-year-old female.

After scouring the board to make sure I hadn't missed anything, I decided to go to the information desk and question the
white-haired man sitting behind it. "Are all the postings listed on
this board?" I asked him.

"Most of the professional auditions are not publicly announced. They are found through an agent," he explained.

"If you have an agent," I replied sharply. "Do you have a list
of agents?"

"Yes, we do," he said, "but we only give it out to members."

"I see. And how is a nonmember supposed to *become* a member without this list?"

"I receive no pleasure in saying I can't give you this list. I go
through this several times a day."

"Well, then"—I switched quickly from brazen to demure—
"can't you break the mold, this one time, and give *me* the list?"
I smiled and pouted like I used to for my father, when I wanted
my way. "You could liberate yourself. A burden would be removed
from your heart, and you'd be helping someone launch an entire
career. When I'm rich and famous, standing on that stage receiving my Oscar, I'll say, 'I have many people to thank for this award,
but one very special man . . .' What's your name?"

"Kenny McBride." He winked.

"'. . . If it weren't for Kenny McBride, I wouldn't be here tonight
accepting this great award. It's all because of Kenny, the man from
the Screen Actors Guild.'" I bowed. He applauded.

"Thank you, thank you," I said to my fan. "Now, wouldn't it
be grand to hear your name announced on national television?"

The old man, I would bet once an actor himself, smiled but
made no comment. I could see his mind spinning: *Should I? She's
such a nice girl. Who would know?* He turned his head to see if anyone was looking. No one was around. *Go for it!* I yelled silently. His

hand reached for the handle of the file cabinet. *He's going to pull out the list. I know it. He knows how unfair the system is.* His hand was poised over the file. *Yes, yes.* But he stopped midway and placed his hand helplessly in his lap. The old man, stuck behind the desk, said, "I can't help you."

"Oh God," I said under my breath, then louder, "I understand, you have rules. I wouldn't want you to get into trouble or lose your job or anything."

I exited the double doors, annoyed that my charm hadn't worked. *No wonder actors play violent, explosive roles; end up in jail; or drink themselves into oblivion. Look what they have to go through—just to get a SAG card.*

I needed a long walk down Hollywood Boulevard to help me cool down from yet another of life's injustices. I started slow and began to walk faster and faster. I thought that the faster I walked, the more steam I would blow off. But the rage only intensified when I passed store windows displaying new dresses and accessories I couldn't afford. I stopped at a window and eyeballed a peach-colored blouse, knowing how fabulous the color would look on me. But all I could think about was my car-insurance payment due next week—where my first unemployment check would go.

Feeling very dejected now, I headed back. A block before my car, I stopped in a bodega, hoping to find some magazines that catalogued non-Equity listings of local auditions, anything that would give me a clue as to where auditions might be held. But there was nothing. Zippo. The nice Indian storekeeper behind the counter, gold teeth glittering, asked if I needed any help. Too bad he hadn't been warned. The girl standing before him was looking for a fight.

"I'm looking for *Variety* magazine." He gave me a blank stare. Speaking very slowly, I asked him again: "Do—you—have—any—*Variety*—magazines?"

"We run out of that magazine five minutes after they deliver it. Every day this happens, every day," he replied.

"Oh, great!" I retorted, hardly able to restrain myself. I walked over to the candy counter, hoping to find a Heath bar.

"How about Heath bars, do you have any of those?" He ignored me, and walked toward another customer.

"Hello! Are you listening?" Obviously not! I was a waste of his time. Wanting to debate anything with anyone, needing to win something from someone, I kept at him: "Do you have any macadamia nuts or peanut butter and jelly in a jar? How about Jiffy Pop? Do you have Jiffy Pop?"

He continued to ignore me, so I went over to him, interrupting his conversation with a customer, and asked point-blank: "Exactly what time does *Variety* get here? In the morning or the afternoon?"

"It comes different times, different days. I cannot tell you what time, and you are being very rude."

"I'm being rude? I came in here wanting to buy candy, magazines, nuts . . . but your store didn't have one thing I needed. I think *that's* pretty rude."

I turned to leave, but I wasn't done. I decided to buy some Mars bars, a bag of chips, and a pint of vanilla ice cream. Returning to my Fiat, I pushed the seat back as far as it could go, and made myself comfortable in my blue bubble of protection. I turned on my favorite jazz station and chomped on the potato chips first. Munching away, I looked out the window. Everyone seemed so content, laughing, gossiping, sharing secrets, bumping hips as they sashayed into the store to buy their goodies.

I opened the Mars bar next. Gee, what would it be like to be married and have someone around all the time to listen to my problems, my stupid jokes? Someone who would hold me and make the world go away . . .

I opened the container of half-melted ice cream. When the plastic spoon hit the bottom of the pint and not a lick was left, I poured the last remains of chip crumbs into my mouth, squashed the bag into a nice tight ball, and fixed my mascara in the rearview mirror. Then I picked up the empty wrappers and carried them out to the big black Dumpster. Returning to the bodega, I asked the proprietor if there was a public restroom on the premises. Indignantly, he handed me a key attached to a long wooden paddle and told me curtly that the bathroom was outside, around the side of the building.

Once inside the bathroom, with its atrocious reek of urine and pine cleaner, sickly sweet, I felt peculiarly safe. The rusty sink, graffiti-scrawled walls, and crumpled paper towels grossed me out. But at least I could be alone, do what I needed to do. I locked the door and began the ritual of wiping off the toilet seat, rolling out about fifty toilet-paper squares, and laying them on the tile floor to protect my knees from the caked dirt. When everything was nice and neat, I knelt down before the bowl, stuck my finger down my throat, and vomited as much as I could. And then I did it again and again. On the third purge, I nicked my upper palate with my fingernail. Blood appeared on my finger. Not much, but enough to warrant pulling myself up to the sink and turning on the faucet. I cupped my hand and drank some of the iron-colored water from the rusty tap in hopes of easing the sting.

The pain subsided. I felt dehydrated and couldn't wait to guzzle down some decent liquid. *Ahh,* a fresh start. A new body! After gathering all the toilet paper from the floor and stuffing it into the already-stuffed garbage can, I stepped over to the sink again, reached for the pink syrupy soap, and washed my hands. I thought about what Rachel said about using food to escape emotions. But the act was over.

Before unlocking the door, I reached inside my purse and wrote the words *I'm sorry* with lipstick on the mirror, and I then returned the key. I told the Indian man there was no more toilet paper. So he'd go inside, read the message, and forgive me.

Then I drove to Rachel's apartment to cry or scream or just sit on her couch and watch her chew gum. But when I got to her street, her car was nowhere in sight. Feeling raw, worn-out, and bleary-eyed, I had nothing else to do but go home, crawl under the covers, and throw the *I Ching*.

CHAPTER

Restlessness as an enduring condition brings misfortune.

I was too agitated to hear any clear answers from the *I Ching* when I returned from my binge-and-purge session. So, first thing the next morning, I brought out my pad and silk pouch and threw the coins. The question was: *How do I stop this debilitating habit?* The answer:

5. Hsü /Waiting (Nourishment)

Above: K'an, The Abysmal, Water
Below: Ch'ien, The Creative, Heaven

All beings have need of nourishment . . . But the gift of food comes in its own time, and for this one must wait.

"Gift" of food. *The way I use it, it's a curse. And I'm tired of waiting. That's all I do.*

This hexagram shows the clouds in the heavens, giving rain to refresh all that grows and to provide mankind with food and drink. The rain will come in its own time. We cannot make it come; we have to wait for it . . .

Strength in the face of danger does not plunge ahead but bides its time, whereas weakness in the face of danger grows agitated and has not the patience to wait . . .

It is only when we have the courage to face things exactly as they are, without any sort of self-deception or illusion, that a light will develop out of events, by which the path to success will be recognized.

I closed the book. I needed a shower, but it was still very early and I didn't want to wake Emma. Moving very quietly, I tiptoed out into the hall.

I was reaching for the bathroom doorknob when I heard someone talking and, I thought—I wasn't sure, because the sounds were muffled—crying. I stood there, listening, trying to decipher the words. It didn't sound like Emma, but it was coming from her room. Her bedroom door was slightly ajar. I moved a little closer. Through the slim opening, I saw Emma standing there, alone, facing a painting on her wall, talking to it.

"I'm so sorry, my *Liebling*." I'd never heard that word before. It must have been German. "I wanted to save you," she murmured to the painting. "I never wanted you to suffer. The sickness had a force. It took hold of you . . ." She sighed. And then touched the picture gently with her fingers.

To give her some space, I slipped into the bathroom and took my shower. Clearly, Emma was still mourning Josef. She must really miss him. I dressed and came out looking for her. Her bedroom was open, and empty. She wasn't sitting in her high-back, either. Instead, I found her in the kitchen, doubled over, in the middle of the floor. It scared the bejeezus out of me! I couldn't tell *what* she was doing because her head was down and her buttocks were raised high in an absurd position that looked like some exotic *hatha yoga* posture. "Is everything all right, Emma?"

She turned, sponge in hand. "There's honey on the floor, and I'm tired of having my slippers stick to it."

"Allow me. I'm an expert at honey removal." Relieved that she was okay, and glad to be useful, I took out a butter knife from the drawer, joined her kneeling on the floor, and began to scrape up the hardened honey. I felt somewhat ashamed, since I was the one who had dripped it in the first place and had forgotten to clean it up.

"There you go. You just needed a little muscle." I smiled, hesitantly. I helped her up from the floor, wanting to keep the conversation light. "How was your lunch with Zelda, by the way?" I had been so preoccupied that I hadn't gotten a chance to ask her about it before.

"Fine," she said, pausing to think about how much she actually wanted to divulge from her schmooze with her friend. "Zelda found Max in bed with a young girl and nearly lost her mind. She's not doing too well . . . Do you have any plans for the rest of the day?"

"No," I said, as I ran the sponge under soapy water until the stickiness was gone. "But it sounds like you do."

"What do you think about going to Santa Monica, to the beach?"

"Well, I think you're wasting a lot of time standing there when you could be getting ready."

Emma grinned, giddy as a seven-year-old. "I'll pack some snacks for us and gather my things."

"Excellent. I'll go clean my car so there's room for you to sit."

It was a beautiful day. There were no smog alerts, the sun wasn't blazing, and there weren't millions of cars jostling bumper to bumper down Pacific Coast Highway.

Ah-h-h-h, yes! This was the reason I'd left Michigan and moved to California. This was the reason I'd bought this dilapidated old Fiat convertible. To drive in the salty sea air, admire the ocean's beauty, and hear the waves crashing against each other. As we drove up the highway along the beach, I looked over to see how Emma was doing. She was squinting into the wind as it caressed her face. She was somewhere else, as if I didn't know where. Before

I had a chance to ask her if she had sunglasses, she reached into her purse and pulled them out. Before I could ask her if she had a scarf for her hair, she pulled out a *babushka* and tried to tie it under her chin.

The wind was fierce. Just before the scarf blew out of her hands and into the air, like a kite without a string, I caught it, pulled the car over, and stopped. And that's when we had another moment. It was brief. But as I tied the bow under her chin, I felt her melt, let go, and open her heart . . . to me once again. It was another rare, delicate fraction of a moment, but it felt like an earthquake. After the bow was tied, we looked at each other, acknowledging the sweetness, the improbability of our relationship, and then we both smiled.

Cooler on the skin and darker in color than the beaches along the lake in Michigan, the sand near the Santa Monica pier was refreshing. Emma and I walked a bit before finding our spot, and then together we spread out the blanket. Emma placed her purse atop one corner. I placed the basket of food on another. She took off her babushka and folded it neatly inside her purse, slipped off her sandals, and opened her wobbly director's chair. She straightened it out, making sure the legs were balanced, and then she slowly sat down.

The woman from the newspaper ad reached inside her purse and pulled out a small plastic tube of sunblock. I tried not to be conspicuous, but I couldn't help but stare as she carefully applied pressure to the cylinder so only the most minuscule amount of lotion squeezed out of the tiny hole. I observed how carefully she applied the few drops of cream to her wise, aged face and how her blue pastel sundress appeared lighter in the sun, like her eyes; how erect her back was, as she sat in the concave chair. She applied a few more drops to her legs, the tops of her feet and toes. How methodical she was. Merging her entire being into the smallest task. Never rushing. Steady as a sailboat in placid water. This was how she did things. Every move had a purpose. Every word had a charge. And yet, what I observed most about Emma was her silence—a powerful tool that I would come to know as her weapon.

She handed me the tube, and I squirted out what was left into my palm. Only I turned my palm over too fast, and dropped most of the lotion on the blanket. I tried to salvage what I could, quickly smearing the remainder on my face and shoulders before it could melt and drip onto the sand. And while I made a mess, wasting the small amount of protection left, I asked myself: What was *my* hurry? What had happened to *my* patience?

"Are you hungry?" Emma asked.

"I'm going to jog soon to build up an appetite."

We sat there listening to the waves. And as I sat next to this woman, whom I had come to admire, I realized how little I knew of her past.

"Emma, where did you grow up?"

She edged out the answer. "Europe . . . in Germany mostly, during the Great War."

"What was your childhood like?"

She became uncomfortable, shifted her posture, and paused. "Suffice it to say, I felt little hope. There was a war going on, and people were not themselves—even when they tried to be."

There were volumes in her words. I tried to imagine the thoughts she wasn't sharing. Her life must have been hard during the Depression. Standing in breadlines for hours; welcoming back truckloads of wounded men from the war; observing antiwar demonstrations, Brownshirts looking for Jews in the streets as Nazism began to rise.

"Did you have brothers or sisters?"

"I was an only child."

Hungry for answers, I kept probing: "Where did you meet Josef?"

"I met him in Berlin at an art gallery, where he was exhibiting. Zelda introduced us. We married there, in Berlin, and moved to Paris to avoid the tension. After a while, U.S. galleries became interested in his work, so we moved to the States. He was quite famous in New York circles."

"Did you have a career?"

"I loved journalism, and I wanted to be a writer. But those plans changed when I married Josef."

"Why did they change?" *I* felt like the journalist now.

"I worked as a news correspondent and supported Josef while he finished art school. I was going to be promoted, only the new job entailed quite a bit of traveling. I didn't want to be living in hotel rooms, consumed by a career. I know women don't think that way today, but I was fulfilled looking after Josef, and . . ."

It seemed she had something else to say. I was curious, but I wasn't going to press her. "Why did you leave New York?"

She thought for a moment. "The winters became too harsh for Josef. He loved painting outdoors." She went on, looking out to the sea. "He used to paint on the beach for hours at Martha's Vineyard. We'd go there in the summer. He'd only come in for a phone call and then return to his paints until dusk. At night we'd dance."

"Alone on the beach. How romantic! You'd watch him paint the whole time?"

"There would be such stillness in the air, as if the birds and even the water stood still for his brush. They understood the perfection he wanted to capture on canvas . . . He told me once that he never could have painted a tree if I weren't in his life."

"He was a lucky man."

"*I* was the lucky one, my dear."

The wind stilled and the waves subsided. I wanted to hear more. But before I had formed another question, she brought out the *New York Times* from under her director's chair, shook out the pages, and began to read, as if the previous moment had never taken place.

I got up. "I think I'll go for a run. Are you going to be all right?"

"I'll be fine, dear."

I ran down to the edge of the ocean to feel the cool, clear liquid wrap around my ankles. I cupped some water and poured it over my head. Then I took off, the wind blowing my wet face dry, synchronizing my breath with the weight of each foot pressing its image into the sand. I increased my speed, lifted my knees higher. Just like Emma had commanded. As I ran, I realized how much I loved it. How free and liberated I felt. As I ran closer to the water, feeling the cold liquid between my toes, I felt like a colt, unrestrained, galloping in the wind, propelled by streamlined legs. I could feel the muscles in my thighs tightening with each stride, my spine lengthening and straightening, vertebra by vertebra. Back straight, chest expanded. I imagined being the consummate athlete, focused on honing every joint and muscle for the ultimate competition. Not only because it felt good physically, but as an actor it strengthened my physical and mental instrument for any character I might portray.

As I sprinted along the hard-packed sand, watching the waves rush in, I had to remind myself how lucky I was to have someone in my life rooting for me, wanting me to succeed as much as I did. The only other person who had ever had faith in me was Bella.

Bella was our housekeeper in Michigan. Her room was in the basement, between the Ping-Pong table and the washer and dryer. She was tough and old and thick around the waist, her skin the color of dark espresso. My love for that woman went way deeper than color, deeper than blood. She was the rock that stabilized my life, the glue that held my spirit together.

Bella was always there, rescuing me from everything I tried to avoid but couldn't. Like the time Steven stole my diorama for the science fair, and turned it in as his own! Oh man, I wanted to really kill him that time. I'd worked so hard on that project, and he knew how much I wanted to win. When I found out *he* had won with *my* project, I went straight to Daddy.

Steven got whipped really bad that night; I knew he'd try to get back at me. The next night when our parents were out, I hid under my bed. But he found me—and chased me around the house until he caught hold of my hair and dragged me into his dark room, literally nailed me and my sweater to the door, and then left me there for what seemed like hours. He thought we were even, but I finally tore my sweater loose, ran after him kicking and screaming, pinching and clawing, and trying to gouge out as much skin from his arm as I could. To even the score, he locked me in the bathroom with his ball python. I busted the door off its hinges and ran around the house screaming profanities, grabbed the heaviest table lamp in the house so I *could* kill him.

He screamed back, "You'll never get me! And one day, you'll wish you never squealed a day in your life!"

I kept after him with the lamp. Bella came up from the basement to intervene. She took hold of me; led me downstairs to her room; and let me weep on her big, cushy breasts. She read the Bible to me and told me stories about her dead husband: How much abuse *he'd* taken from white co-workers at the factory. How they would throw beer cans at him from their cars after work and make fun of the way he walked. He'd had had polio when he was younger, which caused him to limp.

"You don't never have to worry about revenge," she told me. "God does a much better job than you ever could. A few weeks after those men harassed my husband," she explained, "they got drunk and slid off the road. Their truck lit up like a matchstick the minute they crashed in the ditch.

"Now, I don't wish no harm to nobody," she said. "But we all get comin' to us what we put out. God takes care of everybody in *His* time, not *our* time. And you know what else?" She could go on and on about God. "He always provides signs along the path, if we listen with the right ears and see with the right eyes. Sometimes He shows 'em to us real fast"—she snapped her broad black fingers—"and sometimes He waits, sees how much faith you got. And if you think you're too busy or too good to listen to what He's tellin' you, believe me, child, the good Lord will find a way to remind you. You never know how God's signs are gonna come, neither. Sometimes He's real sneaky and speaks through the lips of strangers. Sometimes He speaks through *you*."

Bella had died from a heart attack a year ago. I couldn't afford to go back for the funeral, but I thought about her a lot, prayed her soul would go to heaven and that God would take care of her when she got there. I'm sure He did. Since her death, I'd always prayed that someday an angel would fall from the sky and care for me like she did. Now I couldn't help but think, *I believe I've met that angel.*

I was miles down the beach before I turned around and jogged back to Emma. I found her sleeping, snoring quite loudly, with her babushka pushed back on her head. Newspaper pages were scattered all around her chair. I picked up the papers and looked tenderly at her. The woman with her own secrets looked so vulnerable. I shook off the sand from my towel and gently laid it across her knees so her legs wouldn't burn. Then I took her towel and wrapped it around her pink shoulders. I was about to pull down her babushka to protect her nose, when her eyes opened.

"What time is it?" she asked.

"It's close to seven. We should get going."

Her mouth opened wide in a yawn. "How far did you run today?"

I yawned, too. "Five miles. But I wasn't as tired as last week."

"By next week, you'll be running six miles."

We ate some grapes, and packed up our things. I bundled our picnic supplies into the trunk while Emma settled herself into the car with her sunglasses and her babushka. I climbed into my seat, and as I put the key in the ignition, she turned and smiled at me. "Thank you for our day at the beach. It was a lovely way to spend my birthday."

I looked at her in shock. Emma just smiled. Without another word, she waved dismissively and settled more deeply into her seat. I made a mental note: *Buy Emma a card or make her a special meal.* It was the least I could do. We drove home in silence, happily exhausted from the ride, the sun, and the wind.

Over the weeks that followed, I used Emma's membership at the Y, swam laps, used the stationary bike and the treadmill. I lifted weights to build the muscles in my arms, and took many, many saunas to sweat out the toxicity from a lifetime of sugar consumption. I made my mandatory appearances at the unemployment office and hung out in coffee shops where other unemployed actors also lurked looking for leads to auditions.

Emma seemed pleased with all of my efforts. At the same time, without her saying anything, I could feel her always egging me on, urging me forward. And every night, as I crawled into bed, I felt strangely content in the acceptance that my efforts were never enough for this tiny enforcer. The fact was, I seemed to thrive on the challenge.

chapter 12

*. . . it is just when the Creative is coming to dominance
that the dark yin force is most powerful in its external effects.*

"Emma, where are you?" I called out, as I searched the apartment, exhausted from a run. But she wasn't in the kitchen, the living room, her bedroom, or the bathroom. She was nowhere to be found.

Did she go for a walk? Did someone pick her up? She would have left a note. Hmm. I'll wait an hour and then call the police. To keep myself busy, I started to organize my room, make sure the socks were in the sock drawer, the bras in the bra drawer. I hadn't spent five minutes arranging anything in this room since I'd moved in. While I sorted through my slightly worn-out slips and undies, I noticed a tiny drawer between the two larger ones that I hadn't opened yet. It was only three inches wide, big enough for a few pieces of jewelry. *Maybe,* I thought, *I could place a few bracelets and rings inside.* I tried pulling the drawer out, but it kept sticking along the edges. Finally it unstuck, and inside was a clear plastic bag, with a lace-edged handkerchief. The name ALEXANDRA was embroidered in blue script, neatly sewn on one corner. *If I don't forget, I'll ask Emma about this when she comes back . . . whenever that might be.* In the meantime, I decided to use another drawer for my jewelry and went on with my chores.

I was getting edgy wondering where Emma was, so I grabbed an apple from the fridge and called Rachel. I hadn't seen her for a month. But just a recording greeted me: "The number you have reached is no longer in service. The party has requested no forwarding number."

What? I dialed the number again to be sure. Same recording. *Has she moved? Did she quit her job and take off for an extended vacation to Bali or Nigeria? Maybe she went to visit her cousin, Cannoli. Or she's taking some space.* She did that—a lot. We'd get really close and all of a sudden, *poof!* She'd disappear for weeks. I wouldn't know if she had the flu or if she'd been kidnapped. Then, just like that, she'd call, as if no time had passed. It was never a big deal for her. But it drove me nuts . . . and she knew it. If I didn't hear from her soon, I told myself, I was going to leave her a note saying, "I had a skydiving accident, and if you don't call soon, amnesia will have set in and I won't remember who you are."

I went back to my room, lay down on the bed, and was just about to close my eyes and escape from my present state of bored frustration—when my eyes became fixated on a painting hanging directly across from me. It was a picture I'd seen every day, but never really looked at. For some reason, the small painting of the ocean, the expansive view of the pale beach dramatically juxtaposed against the vibrant aquamarine water, pulled me in now. It took hold of me, beckoned me to slide into it. And as my eyes became transfixed by the scene, I could feel myself at that beach, the hot sand, the clear water dancing on my toes. Squinting at the orange-and-blue sky surrounding the brilliant sun, I could feel the warmth of the rays. As I lay there, this warmth gently released all the tight muscles, one after the other, until I fell into a deep sleep . . .

"Ah-hem."

I jumped straight up off the bed, I swear, three inches. It was Emma clearing her throat. I had no idea how long I had slept or how long she had been standing there. "I didn't mean to disturb you," she said. "I circled a few auditions you might be interested in." She handed me a copy of *Variety*.

"Where were you?" I asked with a tinge of anger, still shaken from the deep sleep and her surprise entrance.

Trying to catch her breath, she said, "I went with Bert to the cemetery this morning. It was the anniversary of his mother's death."

"Oh . . . that's right. You were very close."

"Yes, she was my closest friend. We brushed off the grave and left her favorite flowers."

"That was so sweet of you . . . to go with him. He's really lucky to have you . . . be there for him . . . Where did you get this?" I asked, referring to the *Variety* magazine. Still groggy, struggling to wake up. "I've been looking all over for this magazine!"

"I started a subscription for you a few weeks ago."

"But I thought they only listed auditions for Equity members?"

"That's not true."

Big black Magic Marker circles were drawn all over the page. I read the circled entries out loud: "'Non-Equity auditions: Young female jock needed, age twenty. Must work with tamed tigers for zoo movie.' You aren't serious?"

"It's never too late to learn a new trade." She smiled.

"'Female teens needed for new horror film produced by USC seniors.' No, thanks. I've paid my dues doing student films. And I hate scary movies." I kept looking. "Oh, this is interesting. 'Nineteen-year-old female needed for new play.' It takes place in Georgia. Tryouts are next week.

"'Oh, mah, how ah simply *love* to feel the ga-*lor*-i-ous Califohnyah sun on mah peachy white body.'" Testing my Southern accent.

"Not too bad, but it wouldn't hurt to go to the library and listen to a Southern phonics tape and solidify that drawl," Emma remarked as she stepped away from the door and headed toward her bedroom.

"Well, maybe ah'll jus' mosey on ovah thayah and do that," I called after her.

I didn't go to the library to listen to a Southern phonics tape, as Emma had suggested. I purchased one instead, and played it on my friend Calvin's cassette player every day for a week while I exercised, while I walked from room to room through the apartment. I used my new Southern drawl on everyone I came in contact with: people on the street, people I met in stores, people I talked to on the phone. Every song that rang out on the radio was accompanied by this Southern gal's voice.

On the morning of the audition, I ran to Thrifty Drugs to buy some ruby-red nail polish and matching lipstick, a few pink bows for my puffed-up hair, and some atrocious perfume that I wouldn't dare put on until I knew more about the character, but which I stuffed in my purse just in case. I found a long, full pink skirt at a secondhand store, and matched it with a short pink cardigan. Then I covered my cheeks with blush. I was going to show those producers exactly who they were dealing with. Before leaving the apartment, I did a few turns in front of Emma for her critique. She practically coughed up her tea when she saw me. Then she smiled, and gave me a thumbs-up. I was out the door to prove to myself—and the world—I had the goods.

The Southern phonics cassette blasted over the traffic noise all the way to Pasadena. I went over and over my accent until I pulled up to the theater, sashayed in, and took one look around the hall. Sixteen girls were waiting for their names to be called, and every one of them had blonde hair, blue eyes, and humongous breasts. I was in a Barbie-doll nightmare. Auditioning would be a total waste of my time.

Halfway back out the door, about to make my grand Southern exit, it hit me: how great I'd felt walking *into* this place—so sure of myself, so confident that I could blow every actress auditioning for this role out of the water. And now, looking at all these blondes, I was a total wreck. *Hmm . . . what are my choices? I could leave—or I could use this explosive emotion for the audition.*

I decided to use the rage and not let my dark hair and absence of substantial breasts get in the way. I turned around and walked back to where the girls were standing—all the while repeating the words: *I am an actress. I am going to act as if my breasts are the most magnificent, sculpted breasts God ever created.* In my sexiest, most seductive saunter, pushing out my lips and my chest as far as they could go, I strolled on over to the man sitting behind the sign-in table and said in my breathiest Southern accent, fluttering my lids, "Hi. I'm Sandra Billings. I'm here to audition for . . ."

The nice-looking middle-aged man matter-of-factly handed me a few sheets of dialogue and said, "I hope you don't mind waitin' awhile; there's a few girls ahead a you."

"Ah don't mind." I fluttered my fingers *bye-bye* and slowly turned, not moving my eyes from his lips while I ambled over to an empty seat. Giggling to myself, pleased my accent had worked, I read the sides he'd given me and began to explore the subtext for Jasmine, the character. The play was awful. I was tempted to leave. But it was time to build my auditioning muscle.

An hour passed, and most of the Barbie dolls had been called. When there was only me and one last blonde left in the room, a man with a long goatee asked me if I would follow him. I did. He took me through a narrow hallway and onto the stage. The lights were dimmed. The only object on the stage was a chair. The man with the goatee asked if I was ready.

"Yes," I replied.

He said, "A man is gonna come out of the wings. He'll be playing your husband. Just go with it . . ." Another man, sitting near him, whose face I couldn't see, asked me to have a seat and begin my reading.

I took a moment, centered myself, and in my very best Southern drawl, I read the lines for Jasmine. Then I stood up, ran to the phone for help (per the script directions), and—collapsed convincingly on the cold stage floor: Jasmine was shot by her jealous husband. All I could hear after I fell were two sets of hands applauding from the audience.

I got up, and then the invisible man asked me: "Would you mind wearing a wig and reading the scene again?"

"*Ah,* sure," I said.

I put on the wig and read the part again. The two men applauded, louder this time. Then one of the men asked me to remove my cardigan.

"Now?" I asked, taken aback by his request.

"Yes, please."

"*Ahhh,* well . . ."

"Work with me, Sandra. Start removing your sweater and ease yourself into feeling the nakedness of the character."

They must have noticed my sculpted breasts and wanted to see more.

I began to undo the first button, trying to listen to my own thoughts—evaluate whether or not I felt comfortable with this.

"To be true to Jasmine," he continued, "you must feel naked, *be* naked. She's just come out of the shower. She doesn't know her husband has a gun. Get into Jasmine's head. What is she thinking?"

I undid the second button. I was just about to move my fingers to the third when I stopped. I couldn't go any further. This play wasn't close to being an artistic endeavor; the script was an embarrassment to the English language, and it was the pinnacle of exploitation!

"I'm sorry, I can't do this." I buttoned up my sweater.

"But we liked your reading. You're one hell of an actress."

"Well, you know. This hair"—I removed the wig and put it on the chair—"may go with this reading, but my naked body is not going to be exposed to you *or* your audience. Not for *this* . . . script." I handed the sides back to the goateed man and made my grand Southern exit, back to the hallway and out the door.

God, it felt good to storm out of there!

The next few weeks I literally had to force myself out of bed, out the door, out of the apartment. I was determined to find other actors who might know where non-union auditions were being held. On a mission, I would stomp into coffee shops and diners and talk to other actors, only to realize they were no better off than I was. We were all struggling to find a role, an agent, and an entrée into getting our SAG card.

I heard about a few auditions from one generous actor and drove to Hollywood, Culver City, downtown L.A., the Valley, and

Ventura County. I tried out for the role of a pregnant teen, a deaf girl who drowns herself, a lawyer who gets pushed off the George Washington Bridge. I humbled myself and went back to USC to audition for a student film—something I'd sworn I'd never do again—a comedy about two goofy waitresses. But no matter where I went, no matter how well I read, I was either too tall, too short, or too brunette.

One evening, just back from a tryout for the lead role as a schizophrenic nurse, Emma came into my room and told me she'd seen an ad in *Variety*. The character was a suicidal teenage rock star. I was confident I could portray this one.

The next day, I drove an hour and a half through heavy traffic to Pacific Palisades and arrived early, so I could review the script. So did fifty other girls. I did my best to concentrate, focus on the character's lines, but it was impossible. Twenty actresses of different shapes and sizes kept talking and giggling, their voices reverberating throughout the cavernous lobby. I tried to block out the sound, but the lobby was an echo chamber. Then, without warning, there was silence—the waves of voices died away, and a hush fell over the anteroom. All ears pricked to attention as we listened to two girls describing what they had heard: The director's daughter had already been given the lead role. The producers were auditioning only to satisfy the union.

The rumor was undoubtedly true. Very depressed now, I didn't know if I should run through a red light, find a bridge and jump off like the character I had auditioned for, or drive head-on into the Pacific Ocean. I decided to stop at a local diner and buy three doughnuts, two muffins, and a chocolate-chip cookie and return to Emma's, knowing I could get rid of everything I had just eaten.

Emma was on the phone with Bert when I walked in. I didn't make eye contact. I walked by her chair and went straight to the bathroom, only to find a plumber in overalls sitting on the floor with a wrench in his hands, working on the sink. There'd be no water for hours, he told me. My stomach was about to burst. I walked into my room, but I couldn't settle myself: I was too distended, too agitated. Back to the living room; Emma was still on the phone. I opened the apartment door, strode to the elevator, took a ride to the basement, and then came back up and paced around the living room again, hoping she'd get the hint.

"In scene four," Emma was telling Bert, "why not have the protagonist attend the horse race? No one is expecting him to be there. In scene five, I think it's best that he disappear altogether. Bert, have you thought about . . ."

Filled with rage, not knowing where to go, I went to the kitchen, got a glass of orange juice, drank half of it, and poured the rest down the drain; stalked to my room and threw down my purse; looked into the bathroom to see if the plumber had made any progress; and walked back to the living room, and finally heard her say "Good-bye."

I really should have warned her to duck. My words were speeding darts with flame-tips, and they were shooting out at record velocity:

"I just drove to Pacific Palisades. It took me three hours to audition for a lead role that I was perfect for—*perfect!* I could have given the best reading of my life. But it was already cast. Can you believe that? I've studied for years with the best acting teachers in Los Angeles. I've taken improv classes, scene study, character-development classes. I was in every play my high school ever put on—with great reviews, I might add. After years of study, I have refined my ability to pick up a script and within moments, *moments,* move into the fullness of the character. I've been trained to sniff out emotional and physical attributes, understand the character's motivation. And yet—I am incapable of getting a part. What the hell is wrong with this picture?" Tears were flowing. I kept pacing the small living room.

Emma put down Bert's script, lowered her chin so her eyes could focus on me over the rims of her bifocals, and watched me move restlessly from one end of the living room to the other. "Why do you allow these daggers of doubt to puncture your heart? Just let them bounce off you like pellets of water. Only then can you be fearless."

What was she talking about?

"You can't see this now. But these rejections will make you strong; they'll build your character."

"Character, shmaracter, I just want to work! What am I sup-posed to do with all this energy? How many miles can I run? How many laps can I swim? How many push-ups and leg raises can I master? I'm so sick of nepotism and prejudice, and if you don't have the perfect breasts and cobalt-blue eyes or thighs without cellulite, you're nothing, nothing. Why am I still drawing these low-life people to me? These slimeballs, who get their rocks off by looking at women with big tits and . . . sorry, Emma. But I thought my bad karma was over. I found *you,* didn't I? I thought by moving in here, my life would change . . .

"You know what I'm going to do?" The pacing was starting to feel a little theatrical, but I continued: "I'm going to sell my Fiat and move to Zihuatanejo. I heard it's magnificent there. Cheap! Very cheap! I'll move into a hut and eat fruit and nuts all day. I'll meet a beautiful rich Latino and fall madly in love. I won't have to worry about my hair or the color of my eyes *or* the size of my bosoms—Latinos love small-busted women . . . *When's the plumber going to be finished?"* My tirade ended in a whisper.

"Soon. Sit down."

I did as she asked.

"Do you think you're the only artist who has ever been rejected?"

"No, but I'm *always* being rejected."

"Do you know how many times Josef's paintings were snubbed by art galleries and shows? How many art critics rejected his work? In Germany, France, and the States? He never complained, not once. Do you know what he did instead? He came home and took out his paints. He experimented with new colors, tried new tech-niques. He read books and studied other artists. He didn't waste his energy on anger; he channeled it into perfecting himself and his work."

"I study all the time. I just need a break."

"You'll get your break. What you need is equipoise."

"Excuse me?"

"A firm posture."

"You mean I don't stand straight?" I straightened my spine as much as I could.

"No, dear. I'm referring to your inner posture. How steady do you hold your emotions? Are your heart, your mind, and your spirit in alignment? Are you poised so that whatever happens to you, you are not thrown off balance?"

"That's the problem. I never feel balanced." I felt sick to my stomach.

"Do you get pleasure out of feeling sorry for yourself? Do you like feeling like a victim? Where are those emotions coming from? It's not only your thoughts that you need to change. You have to change your attitude, then the circumstances in your life will change. Stop seeing everyone as your enemy. You don't have to labor at being an actress. You already are one. Work on your inner life."

Emma's big blue eyes pierced right through me. I couldn't stop crying. I felt so ashamed; I didn't want her to stop caring or give up on me. I didn't want to appear as a failure. Mostly I was ashamed because the *only* thing I wanted right now was to get rid of the muffins.

"Emma, I need to go to the gym."

"What's at the gym? A bathroom?"

How did she know?

"What is it that's making you eat?"

"I don't know," I told her. And I was too ill to talk about it. I got up and went to the Y.

CHapter  13

If we wish to achieve an effect,
we must first investigate the nature of the forces in question . . .

Moving to Zihuatanejo was not part of my destiny, not yet any-way. A flyer hanging at the local deli spared me the fantasy of a futile life. The flyer read:

> EXPERIENCED ACTRESS NEEDED
> For LaPapa
> Call for an appointment
> 555-6546

LaPapa was a popular bicoastal theater company, with branch-es in New York and Los Angeles. They were a small group, well known for being avant-garde, seeking out obscure new playwrights and presenting their works as readings or as full-fledged produc-tions. They were non-union, but they had a great reputation. The name LaPapa had come up several times in conversation on the tryout circuit, most memorably when I'd spoken to actors who had auditioned for the company and didn't make the cut.

This was just the challenge I needed. I had to prove to Emma, and to myself, that my posture could be steady; my heart, mind, and spirit could be balanced—poised, so that whatever happened to me, I wouldn't be thrown off center. I could no longer afford to see these directors and casting people as my enemy. Emma was right. I had to break the cycle.

The only way to combat the psychological obstacles and emotional barriers that might stand in my way for a successful audition was to understand what the obstacles were. In other words, it was time to consult the oracle.

Rather than ask a particular question, I took out the three dimes from the silk pouch and simply *thought* the word *LaPapa*. Then I threw the coins. The hexagram that came up was:

64. Wei Chi / Before Completion

Above: Li, The Clinging, Fire
Below: K'an, The Abysmal, Water

> *The conditions are difficult. The task is great and full of responsibility . . . But it is a task that promises success, because there is a goal that can unite the forces now tending in different directions. At first, however, one must move warily, like an old fox walking over ice . . . His ears are constantly alert to the cracking of the ice, as he carefully and circumspectly searches out the safest spots. A young fox who as yet has not acquired this caution goes ahead boldly, and it may happen that he falls in and gets his tail wet when he is almost across the water.*

Oh Jesus, that was all I needed.

> *Deliberation and caution are the prerequisites of success.*

I thought about the implications of conditions being difficult, and the proverbial fox whose ears are constantly alert to the cracking of the ice, as I drove to LaPapa's rehearsal space. As I parked the car across the street and walked to the entrance, I found myself

repeating: *Carefully and circumspectly searching out the safest spots
. . . deliberation and caution are the prerequisites of success.* I hadn't
told Emma about the audition—in case I came home with more
bad news.

They'd told me, when I called, that the only reason I was able to
get an audition was because of a cancellation. It was a sign. They'd
instructed me to prepare a five-minute monologue, contemporary
or classical. So I chose a scene from Shakespeare's *A Midsummer
Night's Dream.* Helena's monologue was still in my brain from six
months before, when I'd had to perform it for a critique in acting
class. I loved the piece, understood the subtext, and was still familiar with the lines. I was anxious to strut my stuff.

LaPapa, 2nd floor, it said on the mailbox. I walked up two flights
of the creaky old stairs, paint chips falling off the walls; opened
the door to the landing; and walked down the long hallway. There
was a handwritten three-by-five card pinned on the door: You are
here, LaPapa. Underneath the card was a flyer: Barbara's Ballet &
Baton. The door was closed, so I knocked. No one answered, so I
turned the knob. It was unlocked. I peeked in and entered. There
was no stage, not even a platform, only ten chairs in a circle, with
another chair placed in the middle. A long, wide, oversize mirror
hung along one wall, and a wooden barre stretched the length of
the room in front of the mirror.

My audition was scheduled for ten. I was two minutes early.
I pulled my costume out of my bag and stood there nervously
smoothing out the wrinkles, and then returned the costume to
the bag. I waited about fifteen minutes before a woman in her for-
ties walked in and introduced herself as Celia, a third-year member of LaPapa. She asked me to have a seat on the wooden chair in
the center of the circle. One by one, the rest of the company entered in silence and sat down in the remaining chairs, encircling
me. We all sat there, waiting. For what, I wasn't sure, until the
door opened and a woman entered. I presumed she was the director. She had no smile, no words of welcome. She simply walked
over to where I was sitting, circled around my chair three times,
and asked me if I was prepared to communicate my name.

"I believe so," I replied, surprised to see how much attention this woman commanded.

"Good." Her hands folded across her chest, she continued to circle around me. "Why don't you tell us your name and then stand up."

"Sandra Billings."

"And what are you going to do for us, Sandra Billings?"

"Well," I said, my voice quavering as I stood. I needed space, and a window wide enough for me to crawl out of.

I held on to the chair firmly. "I'm going to do a scene from *A Midsummer Night's Dream*. I will play Helena, and I have a costume." I reached down and brought out the costume.

"A costume? That's very inventive," the director said. "The costume won't be necessary."

"Oh, okay." I bundled the costume back in my bag; I was *very* nervous now. *Remember the fox, Sandra; remember the fox.*

"Are you game for being spontaneous, Sandra Billings?"

"Well, that depends."

"How about we set up a little improv for you, based on Shakespeare's play?"

"Well, I'd have to—"

"We're going to ask the audience for some suggestions. You decide what to do with the information. All right, Sandra Billings?" She left me no time to answer. "Let's give Sandra the name of an animal."

Someone yelled out from the left: "Monkey!"

"Fabulous!" the director exclaimed. "How about an emotion?"

"Jealousy!" someone yelled from the right.

"Thank you. And now, a location for Helena?"

A young male with a Southern drawl hollered, from the front of the circle, "Supermarket!"

"Wonderful."

The director seemed to be in egotistical heaven, and the group played along with her little game. I refused to feel intimidated. I sat down, closed my eyes, and prayed to the Lord of Compassion, *any* Lord of Compassion, that I become nothing but an open vessel to receive the suggestions and let go of the results. After centering myself, I stood up, faced the director squarely, and said, "I will perform Helena, from Shakespeare's *A Midsummer Night's Dream*, as a jealous monkey, revealing my undying love to my beloved Demetrius while pursuing him through the supermarket."

I proceeded to get down on all fours and make monkey sounds while I commenced with the dialogue: "'You draw me, you hardhearted' . . . hee, hee . . . 'adamant . . .'"

I scratched my head and underarms while jumping around the imaginary supermarket. I was the monkey, grabbing make-believe bananas off imaginary counters, tearing food down from the shelves along the invisible aisles. And as the monkey, I went around the circle scratching everyone's heads. Then I brought one of the male members onto the make-believe stage to play the part of Demetrius. I began to scratch *his* head and underarms. Seeing one of the female members staring at my beloved Demetrius, I became the irate, jealous lover and pushed her off her chair. All the while passionately reciting Shakespeare's words:

"'But yet you draw not iron, for my heart is true as steel' . . . hee, hee, hee."

The LaPapa ensemble thought the audition was hilarious, and without further deliberation the director, Ginger Pompidou, asked me to join their elite community.

I was ecstatic! *I got in!* I flew down the stairs and couldn't wait to tell Emma, call Rachel. I wanted to scream out to the universe: *"I GOT IN!"* All those classes, and scripts, and monologues. All the jogging and swimming and wine corks! God, it felt good to be acknowledged.

When I got home and told Emma, who was at the time making spaghetti for a few guests she'd invited over for lunch, she was not at all surprised. She listened attentively.

"You should have seen me, Emma; I was steady as a rock. I kept my equipoise throughout the entire audition. Even when they threw me hurdles, I jumped through them like a trained circus tiger. Or was I the proverbial fox 'whose ears are constantly alert to the cracking of the ice'?" She looked at me as if I were from another galaxy. "Emma, you would have been proud." I helped her bring the salad and soup bowls into the living room and placed them on the snack tables she'd already set up.

"I *am* proud," she said. "But I know how talented you are. Patience is a virtue."

"Rachel. I have to call her." I ran over to the phone and dialed her number. But there was no answer. No strange recording anymore . . . but no answer either.

This is very weird. I'll have to investigate this later. I followed Emma back into the kitchen and helped her carry the serving dishes into the dining room. I was happy to help, *thrilled* to help. I could have cooked an entire meal from scratch, painted the apartment building, inside and out, climbed the Himalayas. But I had to stay grounded. Emma was having one of those serve-yourself-from-the-buffet-table lunches, and the least I could do was lend my support.

So I brought out the gold silverware and the paper plates, and shared every microscopic detail of the audition with her. She asked about the other cast members and how they'd reacted to the audition. She wanted to know when there'd be a production, how often the group would meet. I told her I wasn't sure. "But I think every day," I added.

"Every day?" She was surprised and didn't seem pleased. But she didn't say another word. The doorbell rang. Her first guest had arrived.

"Who's coming over?" I asked, anxious to know whom she'd invited.

"Just some friends."

Cool, I thought. Maybe Bert, the producer, had been invited, or Zelda, or some of her celebrity friends she'd talked about when we first met at the retirement home. Maybe some famous producers and directors were coming so she could brag about my theatrical triumph. But when Joe the mailman walked in without his uniform, and Max and Louise Silverman, an elderly couple from the second floor, came bustling into the kitchen, the anticipation of meeting new and exciting people pretty much dwindled. The doorbell rang two more times before her five guests had arrived, and with each entrance, I knew my chances of meeting someone "from the industry," or anyone creative or unconventional—anyone I could relate to—were diminishing. Besides Joe the mailman and Max and Louise, there was Suzanne, an eighteen-year-old flute player from the fifth floor, and Marion, a recent widow from down the block.

The conversation was a little awkward as we moved around the table filling our plates—at least for me. I didn't know these neighbors. I'd never more than bumped into the mailman or ventured onto another floor. I had to admit, even to myself, that I didn't care to expend the slightest bit of effort to *get* to know these people. They hadn't made movies or produced any Broadway shows. They were ordinary folks, with ordinary concerns and plebeian occupations.

It wasn't until we were all sitting in the living room, dipping our bread into our spaghetti sauce and the olive-oil dressing from Emma's endive salad, that I realized that these people had all somehow connected to this eighty-year-old woman, just as I had. And as I sat there, chewing on the toasty crust of the garlic bread, I realized what the connection was.

We were all in need of this woman's approval, dependent on her support and encouragement. We were all the same.

"Suzanne is a marvelous flutist," Emma said, as she filled Max's glass with wine. "She will be performing at the University of Southern California next month." Suzanne turned pink at Emma's announcement, but mustered the courage to provide us with the precise date and time of the performance. Tending to Louise's request for more sparkling cider and Max's need for another napkin, Emma drew in Joe by asking him to repeat the ludicrous mailman joke he'd told her the other day.

As she played hostess to each guest, catering to his or her needs, filling cups with liquid love, I watched, fascinated. She seemed to be teaching me, showing me how to tend to people's hearts, no matter who they were, no matter what their social status or profession was. As closely as I watched and as hard as I listened, I could feel a fire inside me, burning away my ego and my ignorance. The more I realized how consumed I'd been with my previous expectations—convinced of how superior I was and disappointed that these friends of hers were so, well, pedestrian—the more I burned.

What was implicit in Emma's teaching that afternoon was how one word could transform an emotional interior, how the smallest gesture of thoughtfulness could lighten someone's heart. How giving was a better trade than taking. And . . . how this was a lesson I needed to remember—and a lesson I continually forgot.

chapter 14

. . . in such times of progress and successful development it is necessary to work and make the best use of the time.

Over the next few weeks, LaPapa's troupe members read tons of scripts sent to us by playwrights from around the world. After reading each submission, the company was to decide if they liked one of the plays enough to produce it, in which case they'd invite the author to come to Los Angeles and watch the actors from La-Papa present a staged reading. If the author was happy with the direction thus far, we would cast the parts and prepare for a live performance. Since LaPapa had a significant presence in L.A. and New York, the author would be guaranteed a full house and lots of media coverage. While searching for the ultimate script, Ginger had us warm up each day by doing improvs.

I'd attended many theater classes and weekend clinics where I'd been asked to do improvisational theater games to stretch the mind and emotions. Improvs that were thought out with intelligence and foresight that helped me go beyond set parameters, go beyond any mental limitations. And I did them because I'd felt safe, protected under the directors' guidance.

Yet, Ginger dared each member to go onstage, one at a time, and re-create an extremely private moment—a moment that re-vealed something we would, under normal circumstances, be too embarrassed to share in public, something we did by ourselves when no one else was around. She told us it was an exercise in fearlessness. Now, if Ginger were the kind of director I felt safe with, I wouldn't have minded, but I didn't trust her as far as I could throw a Ping-Pong ball.

One actor put himself in front of an imaginary mirror and dressed up in drag. Another actor made us believe he was home, pulling down the shades in his living room, dimming the lights, lying down in his bed, and masturbating under a blanket. One of the dancers did leg stretches while she sensually massaged her breasts and other body parts. When it was my turn, I went through the motions of taking off my clothes, walking into a small stall shower, turning the water on, and singing "Let It Be" at the top of my lungs. Our director made no comment. Everyone else seemed to like it.

Two troupe members, the Carolina twins, refused to do the ex-ercise, and Ginger flipped out. She took their refusal as a personal insult: "You think you're too superior to do this exercise?" she screamed. "You two better get off your high horses and join the little people. What the hell are you doing here if you can't execute what you're asked? Wasting my time, and everybody else's! How do you think you're going to make it in this town without humil-ity! When you're hired as actors, you do what you're asked. You think because you're from a ritzy section of Charleston and have that . . . *hair* . . . that you're beyond reproach?"

She went on and on, getting hoarser and hoarser, until she sputtered out and sent everyone home, except me. I was the cho-sen one to stay. I wasn't sure I appreciated the honor. Trailed by the tail of her cape, Ginger made a grand pirouette, and in her Queen of Sheba voice pronounced, "Follow me, Sandra Billings. I want to show you why actors must be cautious in my presence."

Dubiously, I followed her around the corner to another room she called "home." Home was dismal and smelled of mildew. Even with the lights turned on, the room was dark and spooky. The windows were covered with black cloth. Pieces of velvet fabric were draped over a queen-size waterbed. Frayed shawls hung on the walls. Everything was musty. Ginger sat down on the oversize gray velvet chair and offered me the option of the floor or the bed. I somehow felt exposed, vulnerable, standing in the empty space before her chair. Warily, I chose the rippling waterbed. I sat watching her while she clutched the arms of her chair tightly and worked herself back into a heavy fume.

"Who the fuck do these actors think they are? I don't have time for their arrogant bullshit. I have a company to run, a tight ship to steer." She stood up, dramatically, and paced the floor, her arms flailing, her cape flying. "I'm not asking them to do anything Peter Brook and Stanislavsky wouldn't have asked *their* companies to do. Great directors expect unflinching obedience."

Is she out of her mind? Placing herself in the same sentence with these directors!

Ginger reached under the chair and pulled out a box filled with colored powders and tiny brown bottles. She began to mix and measure pinches of powder from one bottle into the other, muttering. Adding a gooey glue-like substance to one bottle, scented oil to another. One of her potions, no doubt! She added a splash of yucky green liquid to top them off. "This will show those Southern crackers who they're playing with."

She placed the mysterious mixtures on top of the bureau and began to recite unidentifiable incantations, moving her hands around and around in small semicircles above her head, chanting in some strange language, dancing to a bizarre, primal rhythm. All this to activate the magic potion, I guess!

"There are good spells and bad spells," she said, after completing her dark, mysterious worship. She approached the bed. "You just have to know the right amounts to create the right chemistry. The liquid must solidify before the spell takes effect."

Ceremony completed, she plunked down next to me, sliding her heavy body close to mine. Before I could move away she began massaging my shoulders with her masculine hands. I froze. One hand slowly, deliberately, made its way to my breast, the other massaged the back of my neck. Her thick, muscular body exuded an odor I could barely bear to inhale.

"Ginger," I said, edging away, desperately reaching for a verbal diversion, "how long does the liquid take to solidify?"

"About two hours." She moved closer.

"*Uhm* . . ." I tried to sidle sideways again, an awkward maneuver on the rising and falling waterbed. "What's going to happen to the twins as a result of this mixture?"

"You'll see, my *naïf.*" She crowded even closer.

"I, ah, think you have me all wrong. I like you and everything, but I'm not a . . . you know." I shifted, to edge farther away. But her fingers reached for my hair and twirled a few strands.

"That's too bad. We'd make quite a team. I like you," she continued in her low-pitched tone, probably meant as seductive. "You have so little ego. Most people don't let me in. But you do. You're open and trusting. It's why I picked you. Your face is young, your eyes are old, and I can feel your rage. It's a great combination. I could make you a star, if you'll let me. If you'll have me."

"Look, ah, I live with an older woman who is waiting for me to make dinner," I said nervously, trying to wedge myself off the bed, "like I promised." I looked at my watch. "Oh my God, it's seven-thirty. I really do have to go."

I leapt from the floating bed and headed toward the door, while she sat there swinging a feather boa around her head, threatening me in booming tones with a terminal curse—I think it was loss of hair—if I left.

I left anyway.

Emma jumped when I walked in the door, and pretended to look busy—she must have been sleeping in her high-back—and hurriedly picked up the script lying open on her lap. Newspapers and crossword puzzles were piled on the table next to her. She'd already eaten, she told me, but there was some chicken soup on the stove.

"What a day!" I blew out a sigh.

In her childlike voice, she replied, "Come sit down; tell me about it."

Emma wanted to hear the minutiae of my day. So I sat down and began to pour it out. From the time I walked into the theater early that morning down to Ginger's potions and the threat of losing my hair. She loved hearing the stories and asked questions about every member of the company. How I felt about each one and how they reacted to Ginger's direction. She asked about the overall climate of the company and if the New York LaPapa was different from the L.A. LaPapa. I didn't know the answer to that, but promised to ask. She *would* have made a great journalist. She was all about the details.

It was clear that she needed to be pried away from the high-back she had been glued to the last few weeks, so I said, "Hey, Emma, we have the day off tomorrow. How would you like to take a trip to the farmers' market?"

She turned to me and smiled. It was heartwarming and instantly melted my heart.

Now there are farmers' markets, and there are farmers' markets. This particular one was by far the most extraordinary ethnic enclave in the U.S., as it served the Conservative, Reform, and Orthodox Jews in the L.A. area. Sidewalks for two city blocks were jam-packed with short men wearing *yarmulkes; zaftig* women clad in ankle-length billowy skirts; and children with long, corkscrewing side curls. Everyone was rushing, bumping into each other, for what seemed to me no apparent reason. The scene was frenetic. People crowded around store windows, pushing and shoving . . . yelling at the top of their lungs, even when they stood right next to you. It was a microcosm of the Big Apple, where it seemed most of these people were from. Perhaps, on these tiny side streets off Fairfax Avenue, they were able to re-create the city they loved and missed.

The stores all sold the exact same items: kosher canned goods, chopped liver, toys, bathing suits, underwear, umbrellas, cheese, pickles. How they all sold the same products and stayed in business, I couldn't figure out. Yiddish and Hebrew notices were taped on the windows, posters of Israeli cities leaned propped against soup cans, and regardless of which of the stores you walked into, it smelled the same—like kosher hot dogs and sauerkraut.

Emma seemed totally in her element. Among this whirling activity, she came alive. And I mean *alive!* Her eyes moved from one side of the store to the other, looking at all the items she didn't need. I secretly loved watching her in action, her frail body straining to its full height as she screamed her order to the chubby yarmulke'ed clerks behind the high deli and meat counters: "I'll have two dozen bagels, a pound and a half of cream cheese with chives, and a pound of Nova. But I want to taste the Nova before you cut. I'll take six pieces of gefilte fish, a pound of potato salad, and two pieces of salmon. When did the salmon come in?" she asked with traces of a Brooklyn accent that I'd never heard before today. "Yesterday," the clerk said, so she didn't get any. Only if the salmon came in that morning would she buy. Emma liked her fish fresh, and she wanted her money's worth.

Shopping completed, she turned with the flair of a duchess, counted out change to the impatient cashier, and waited calmly for me to open the door. I was her humble servant, happy to follow the royal elder around. It was the least I could do. Besides, who else had the *chutzpah,* the class, and the ability to blend them both so well? Today Emma's spirit had been revealed. Her true essence was boldly displayed without hesitation or reserve. Unleashed from the confined space of her tiny apartment, Emma was a wondrous spectacle to observe, indeed.

I walked away from our little shopping spree at the farmers' market—once again, with a whole new understanding of who Emma was. And found myself wondering just how limited my vision was—of Emma . . . and myself.

CHapTer  15

*Going quickly when one's tasks are finished
Is without blame.*

My patience was running thin. We had yet to find a script we could all agree on. My tolerance for Ginger and her "magic" antics had reached saturation level. God, how I wanted to leave La Papa! Walk away from the witchy tyrant's clutches. But something inside me said, *Don't leave just yet!* I didn't have to throw the *I Ching* on this one. I listened to that little voice inside me and was surprised to see a confirmation so quickly. The next day the entire group unanimously selected a play: *Miss Pinsky Plays Ragtime,* by Israel Sheldrake. LaPapa was finally going to put on a show.

I was cast as Miss Pinsky, a sixty-five-year-old woman who held forth on the negative aspects of sexual exploitation. By using a funny nasal voice, I beat out the other members clamoring for the role and got the part! I didn't think Emma would be jubilant with my achievement, since the role was more of a comical caricature than a three-dimensional person with deep psychological challenges. But when I told her about Miss Pinsky and showed her the script, she was so excited that she began working on the character's costume, mannerisms, and emotional subtext, as if the play were opening at the West End in London.

"There's a god-awful pea-green dress in my closet that would be ideal for Miss Pinsky," she said, with a wry smile.

I looked at her strangely as she motioned to me to go and fetch the dress from her room. I followed the direction of her hand and leafed through the row of vintage dresses hanging in her closet. I found the one she described for me—a classic 1950s sheath—and brought it out.

"Yes, that's the one! Put it on. There's also a wig in the purple hatbox on the top shelf of the closet. Zelda bought it for me for a costume party last year."

"Did you ever have to wear it?"

"Heavens, no. Even if I lost all my hair, I wouldn't be caught dead in that thing."

"This is *so* cool! It must have cost a fortune."

I put the wig on over my hair and looked in the mirror. "You think I should wear this?" It was a dull gray bouffant wig, a style popular in the sixties.

"Of course you should. How else are you going to stand out? Look at the competition in this city. If you act like everybody else, who's going to notice you?"

"I hardly look like anyone else, Emma."

"Just leave it, and put on the dress."

I did as I was told.

"Very good. Now, stand across the room."

I obeyed, baby-stepping, so as not to split the rear seam; the dress felt, and undoubtedly looked, like it was three sizes too small.

"Now stand over there and start at the beginning of the monologue."

"Yes, ma'am." I started the monologue.

"Allow your hand gestures to be more expressive, but be specific. And make sure your voice cracks. There is more humor in the character when the voice is shaky."

Over the next weeks, Emma spent hours coaching me, pointing out inconsistencies in my delivery, flaws in my inflections, exaggerating my hand movements, telling me when to establish eye contact with the audience and when not to. She was ruthless in her attempt to create a perfectionist out of me, and . . . well, she did a rather superb job. For two weekends we performed at the Vanguard Theater, and for two weeks Emma was the ultimate coach: in the audience for every show, watching every hand movement, making sure my voice had resonance even while it was nasal. She took laborious notes and made sure I followed through on all her suggestions. Thank God for her keen perceptions. Emma was a much better director than Ginger could ever be.

The play was a lukewarm success thanks to the *Los Angeles Times* reviewer who wrote a horrible review. He did, however, favor Miss Pinsky (due to the abundance of laughter from the audience). The success of my performance left Emma with a quiet sense of satisfaction, while I was left anxiously awaiting the next role.

Regardless of the positive reviews, I could no longer work with Ginger. I called her the day after the end of the show's run and told her I had to take a leave of absence, as an invalid woman needed twenty-four-hour attention. Not wanting to close any doors, I also told her I'd had a great time working with her and would highly recommend LaPapa to other actors and actresses I knew. It was a fabrication, but I didn't want to take any chances in case her spells did indeed work. I *needed* my hair.

CHapter  16

Difficulties and obstructions
throw a man back upon himself.

I woke up grumpy, irritable. It was far from a peaceful sleep. I'd had that recurring dream again. The one accompanied by shadows and a sense of menace. The vagueness of the images was upsetting, too. The only thing I remembered, on waking, was the fact that I didn't want to be there, but somehow I couldn't get away, a looming figure was coming closer to me . . . and . . . I was a young child.

The dream left me jumpy, anxious. I sat up in bed feeling off-kilter. To add to my disgruntled state, there was no reason for me *to* get up. LaPapa was over. There were no pending auditions. There were certainly no men banging down my door for dates!

Ah . . . a boyfriend. Someone to cuddle with, go to the zoo with, or hike up the Santa Monica Mountains and have a picnic with.

I'm not asking for much here—whoever happens to be listening. Besides . . . I have all this energy now from working out and eating well. What am I supposed to do with it? I have never been good at waiting or pausing for things to happen. The in-between stages make me crazy!

I got up and did some sit-ups next to the bed.

The fact is, no matter what I do or don't do, where I go or don't go, I feel agitated and insecure. I work on maintaining a positive attitude. I try to absorb Emma's words, the I Ching's virtues of patience. I try to remain egoless and empty and cautious.

I made the bed, picked up the clothes from the floor, and put them in the hamper.

I try to "let go" and surrender, but it takes years for even the greatest saints to give up their attachments—years! Besides, they don't have to worry about being thin or having a perfect body.

I took my jeans and shirt into the bathroom.

These great beings can go off to some remote place and sit under a tree until they reach enlightenment or travel barefoot through the Himalayas until they renounce their attachments. I don't have that luxury. I have to live in Los Angeles, earn a living, make car payments, and jump through hoops to get a SAG card.

I turned on a blasting hot shower and stepped in.

I had to work on gluttony and resentment, and I had miles to swim before I crossed that ocean of enlightenment.

Try giving up a habit so ingrained in your nature that you wouldn't know how to exist without it. Try giving up anger, jealousy, and sarcasm. And those were just a few of the biggies I hadn't begun to tackle. The state of Buddhahood was far from being real for *me.*

I turned off the water, stepped out of the shower in time to hear the phone: *Ring . . . ring.* I quickly pulled on my jeans and shirt.

Ring.

"Do you want me to get that, Emma?" I yelled. No reply.

Ring.

"Emma, are you going to get that?" No answer.

I dashed to the living room and picked up the receiver. "Hello?"

"You must be Sandra. This is Bert."

Well, well, well . . . Bert Klein. This must be my lucky day! Why, Emma had mentioned only the other day that Bert was about to make his mark as an independent film producer. She was so proud, so pleased that the industry was finally beginning to take her Bert seriously. "After all," she'd said, "he has worked very hard for this breakthrough."

From what I knew, this man hadn't had an ounce of struggle to overcome in his entire life. The day Bert was born his future was cast in Carrara marble. The Klein family had been established movie moguls for two generations. All Bert had to do was mention the name Klein and the yellow brick road rolled out in front of him as he drove (I'd bet) his red Mercedes through the gates of Columbia Pictures. And she was *proud* of him? Give me a breath of fresh air!

The scripts he sent were second-rate at best—low-budget films without any substance, at least the ones I'd sneaked a peek at while Emma was napping. But his lack of taste didn't matter to Emma. His family legacy, and my jealousy, made no difference. Emma saw Bert very differently from how I did.

Perhaps I'll find out why. To add to the intensity of their relationship and drive me completely nuts was the fact that, no matter how close Emma and I became, if I asked her anything about Bert, an invisible wall would come up between us. She'd throw up a No Trespassing sign in bold neon, letting me know this particular terrain was off-limits. Was I jealous? You bet. Today, however, I wanted, really wanted, to get beyond my jealousy and not be consumed by it. But hard as I tried, I hadn't reached that place in my spiritual evolution.

"Hello, Bert."

"How's the ol' career going?" he asked sarcastically.

I was ready for him. "It has its valleys."

"It's not too late to get a real-estate license, y' know."

"I'll think about a career move when I hang up."

He laughed. "I'm just jerking your chain. Is Emma there?"

"I have no idea where she is." I really didn't.

"Well, tell her I called. I have an invitation to a Halloween party for you both. I'm looking forward to meeting you."

"And I you. Thanks for the invitation; I'll give her the message."

He slammed down the receiver without a good-bye, and I plopped down . . . right into Emma's Victorian high-back. *He's a bigger creep than I'd imagined.* I tried to remove his energy from my aura, an exercise Rachel had taught me, but his vibes didn't seem to budge. Ensconced in her royal throne, I rested my head against the magnificent carved wood and green satin seat back. Feeling the smooth wood on the elegantly tapered arms, I thought, *I'm finally going to meet the man with the scripts.*

I let out an *Aaahhhh*, like a lion's roar, to release the tension from my lungs. I did it again, louder this time: *Aaahhhh.* And again: *Aaaahhhhhhh.*

As I continued the *Aaahhhh*'s, a force of energy catapulted me from Emma's chair. I shot up from the high-back, wrestled the furniture to the sides of the room, and began a ballet routine I'd memorized from dance class when I was twelve. I began with an *adagio,* extending my limbs, stretching my arms in a slow, fluid movement, followed by the quick *petit allegro.* Then I launched into my favorite—the *tour jeté*—where I ran, jumped, did a mid-air split, turned in the air, and landed in the most exquisite arabesque, looking out over my right hand, which was extended out toward the sun. I turned again and ran into a *grand jeté,* leaping straight ahead—and plummeting into the table lamp I thought I had moved far enough away. *Ouch!*

Ring.

I picked up the lamp (which thankfully had not broken), replaced the shade, and returned to Emma's chair to pick up the phone.

"Hello?" I said, breathless.

"Hola, ¿cómo estás?"

"Rachel? Is that you?

"Sí, estoy aquí."

"Oh my God. Where the *hell* have you been? I've been trying to reach you for weeks! Months!"

"¡Buenos Aires, mi hija!"

"Buenos Aires? Where are you now?"

"I'm at my apartment."

"The one I drove by umpteen times? The apartment that no longer has a phone with a working number? *That* apartment?"

Just then, Emma opened the door and teetered into the living room, also out of breath, and gave me a startled look. I wasn't sure if she was startled because I was sitting in her chair or because the living-room furniture had been pushed back against the walls. I wiggled my eyebrows, waved my fingers, and immediately got up to return the furniture back to its proper place. Emma went into the kitchen. Rachel kept talking.

"I just came back to my apartment to pick up the rest of the boxes."

"What do you mean? Where are you going?"

"It's a long story . . ."

"God, Rachel. What is going on? Can you meet for lunch today?"

"*Sí,* Restaurante Brasserie."

"Give me ten *minutos.*"

"I'll see you in ten. Ciao!"

"Ciao!"

I put down the phone, quietly thanked the universe for Rachel's return, and started toward my room. In record time, I had someplace to go. Then, remembering my manners, I stopped and peeked back into the kitchen.

"Hi, Emma. Where've you been?"

Emma headed toward her high-back, sat down, opened a large manila envelope, and pulled out a huge script. "Mr. Slabowski, one of the neighbors, stopped me at the mailbox, told me his wife was dying of cancer. He needed someone to talk to."

She put the script down on the side table and reached for her bifocals.

"Oh, I'm sorry to hear that . . . I'm, ah . . . just on my way out to meet my friend Rachel for lunch."

"How do you know this Rachel?" She looked at me curiously.

"Oh, we met at an audition when I first came out here."

"Why don't you invite her *here* for lunch?"

I started back down the hall to the bathroom, delaying a response.

"Uh, well, I haven't seen her in so long. And you know how girls are. Gab, gab, gab! You'd be so bored."

I put on some blush and lipstick and combed my hair, remembering Rachel's smile and the way her whole body shook when she laughed, as if the whole universe was contained inside her.

I'd missed her sense of humor, her sarcasm, her batik outfits. I couldn't wait to see her.

I grabbed my purse and walked to the door, knowing Emma did not want me to go.

"Have a nice time, dear."

She didn't mean it. If she had, she would have looked up at me and smiled. But she kept her eyes down and pretended to read the paper.

"I won't be gone long." Hand on the doorknob, anxious to get out, I remembered: "Oh, Emma, Bert called. He wants you to call him—something about a party he's having. 'Bye."

cHapter 17

*The high plateau is dry and unsuitable
for the wild goose.*

Whenever we dined at the Brasserie, which on our budgets we could only afford once every few months, Rachel and I always gravitated toward the room with the fireplace. It was in this room, where the lights were soft and the sounds were muffled by thick, plush carpet, and dark mahogany walls that we shared our catastrophes and our triumphs; where we cursed and cried, and recovered from our personal tragedies

I missed our intimate talks, and swept the room looking for her over a sea of heads, huge ferns, and Tiffany fixtures hanging low. Half a hundred bodies were in the Brasserie, but Rachel was nowhere to be found. I looked back at the entrance in hopes of catching her coming in late. But only men in black suits with slick dark hair stood there, executive types, looking pointedly at their watches as they waited for the maître d'. I turned back to the dining room and scanned it again.

Someone in the back, sitting behind a tall, slender Italian vase, caught my eye. I looked again. She was the right height, but the details were wrong, the moves weren't right: the way she tilted her head, the way she slid her sunglasses up over her forehead, perching them on top of her blonde hair. She wasn't twisting off broken ends from her hair, shifting her weight in the chair every second, like Rachel *always* did. This woman was calm and purposeful. She wasn't wearing batik. She was wearing a pink Ann Taylor suit with a matching silk scarf. Rachel wouldn't be caught dead in Ann Taylor. And Rachel had . . . well, I had no idea what color her hair was this week.

I moved closer, skirting the wall, not wanting the woman to notice me staring. There was something about her. With the help of a sudden brightening of light through the windows and a waiter who had moved aside to give me a better view, my pupils enlarged when I realized: she was indeed Rachel.

I wanted to become invisible, get as close as I could without her knowing I was there. I wanted to absorb all the changes from a distance. As I moved closer to her table, I noticed that her complexion was flawless. The heavy makeup she used to wear had been replaced by a natural iridescent glow, untainted by packed-on rouge. Her eyes sparkled and her nails were polished. She looked radiant. What the hell had happened to her?

She saw me and stood up. I quickly moved over to her table, bumping into the backs of chairs and a few waiters on my way. When I reached her, we embraced. We stood there looking into each other's eyes, oblivious to the traffic jam around us. We could've stood there for hours, hugging, only one of the waiters asked us to sit.

No matter how mad I'd been that she hadn't called and had disappeared for months, the bitterness dropped away the second I was in her presence.

"Oh my God, look at you. You're completely . . . transformed!"

"Look at *you!*" she replied. "You must have lost twenty pounds . . . Turn around. Your buns look really firm."

"Well, if you ran six miles a day, swam twenty laps, and sweated for an hour doing calisthenics, your buns would look really firm, too. But Rachel—come *on,* you're a whole different person."

"I'm more than *a* whole different person. I'm two people. I'm pregnant."

"What?!" I could hardly contain my excitement as we settled in our chairs. I took a second look at her waistline. There wasn't anything showing yet, but . . . well, maybe a little roundness.

Then Rachel showed me the ring. Excuse *me*, the diamond *rock* on her third finger. "Holy shit! It's beautiful!

"Thank you. It's all kind of unbelievable to me, too. Where should I begin?"

"Begin with that bump I'm not quite seeing yet."

"Well, I think I need to start *before* the bump." We both took a couple of deep breaths, picked up the menus, and looked around for a waiter. "I stopped singing telegrams and decided to go to nursing school."

"*Nursing?* When did you ever want to be a nurse?"

"It's something I started thinking about when my father died."

"Your father died? When . . . Rachel, I'm so sorry to hear . . ."

"I'm okay now, but it was a shock. I hadn't heard from him in years, and then Kathleen, his new wife, calls me and tells me my dad had a stroke."

"What a shocker! What did you do?"

"I flew to Nevada to see him. I fed the man, bathed him. He even apologized for not being in my life. We cried. And then he died the next day. Just like that. Gone. It was so bizarre. When I left their house, it was like I had no identity. No clue what I should do with my life. He left me more money than I knew what to do with. I thought about traveling—I didn't know where, I just felt like I needed to get away. I ended up going to South America. I always wanted to see the Andes and learn the Tango. I met Armando, and that's when this nursing thing came up even stronger for me."

"Why didn't you call me and tell me any of this?"

"I guess . . . I just needed to hear my own voice. I had so many decisions to make. I didn't want to burden you with my stuff."

"I love your stuff."

"I'm sorry I didn't call. I just needed the space."

The waiter came to take our order. I ordered a bacon-and-cheese omelet with French fries and a Tab. Rachel asked for a chef's salad, with no cheese, and an iced tea.

"What? No triple-cheese omelet?"

"Remember when we met at the Lake Shrine and vowed to learn how to cook? Well, I've been reading a lot about nutrition. And, let me tell you, the human body is not designed to digest animal protein, especially milk products. You wouldn't believe how many people are lactose intolerant. Almond milk is very high in protein, and tastes delicious. You should try it."

It was hard to believe that only months before, this woman had sat in this same room, ordering cheese balls rolled in walnuts, onion soup *au gratin,* a milk shake, and marshmallow-swirl ice cream for dessert.

"Thanks for the advertisement." Then, relenting, "Rachel, I'm really glad you were able to clear things up with your dad. There's no way, this side of a miracle, I could ever clean up *any* of the relationships in my family. So . . . tell me about the baby's papa!"

"It's your turn first. Tell me, how is it living with Emma? Did you learn how to cook?"

"A little. I'm still working on it. Finish your story, and then I'll tell you about Emma."

"I met Armando in Argentina. He sat down at a table next to me at an outdoor café. This hunk, with dark Mediterranean skin and sparkling brown eyes, says 'Hi' and my knees started shaking. I thought I'd fall off my chair. Anyway, we started talking, we went out, and . . . well. I totally fell in love. I find out later he not only has a place in Buenos Aires—he has a house in L.A., and in New York."

"Let me guess. He's a doctor?"

"A lawyer."

"Of course."

"Right now he's in New York working with his father. His dad has a pretty substantial law practice on both coasts, and in Argentina. He's being trained to work with the firm. You'll like him, Sandra. He's kind, sensitive, and smart."

"And rich! God, it's a storybook fantasy."

The waiter came with our food. There was silence while we ate.

"So," I asked, coming up for air halfway through my greasy omelet, "you're really happy?"

"I'm very happy. Look, I've stopped biting my nails." Rachel showed me her manicured hands.

Manicured hands! My stomach gave a little lurch. Unbelievable! Never in a million years would I have imagined that my outrageous, frizzy-haired friend would have turned into this polished creature before me now.

"We're going back to Buenos Aires in a few weeks to get married," Rachel said with a ladylike smile. "You wouldn't believe how many relatives he has."

"Aren't you going to have a wedding in the States?" I asked, hoping to celebrate the union at some point.

"Probably not." She could tell I was devastated. "We'll have some kind of party, don't worry. Okay, enough. Tell me about Emma."

I took a big gulp of my Tab, as I tried to rebuild my self-esteem and share my story. "Well, she's amazing, supportive, caring. She has this incredible eye for detail. I don't know where she gets it. Very disciplined. She certainly helped me get into shape. She's been really good for me."

"Sandra. There's something else going on here, I know it. What's underneath the words of gratitude?" Rachel might have changed in many ways, but her insight into the workings of my brain was still operative.

"Maybe I'm just used to having my own space. Don't misunderstand me; I adore the woman—but I feel trapped at the same time. It's like she knows what I'm thinking, what I'm going through, before I do. It makes me feel claustrophobic. I don't know . . . she's great in so many ways. I have no business complaining. Maybe I just need a phone in my room. There's only one in the house, and the cord is three feet long."

"Doesn't she ever go out?"

"Hardly. Today was the first time in months I was alone in the apartment for more than ten minutes. Maybe I need a job. Maybe I need to get laid." I might have said "laid" too loud. The guys at the next table winked when I looked over, signaling none too subtly they were available if I was interested.

"How is the career going?"

"Worse than my social life," I whispered.

"Are you sure this is what you want?"

"Well, there's this bartending program I'm really keen on applying for . . . seriously! Do you think I'd have put an ad in the paper, moved in with Emma, if I *wasn't* serious?"

"Then deal with this. It'll change. Everything changes. Just be patient. Stop and look in the rearview mirror for a second. Remember how frustrated you were? Think about the other prospects you could have ended up with.

"Here, take my number. As of tomorrow, we're staying in Armando's apartment in West Hollywood until I finish school." Rachel pulled out her neat little notepad and wrote down her phone number. God, she was organized. A notepad!

"I wish I could stay longer," she said. "But I just registered for a nursing program, and orientation is in a few minutes. The professor will take off an entire grade point if we miss it." Rachel rolled her eyes. *At least that is familiar.* And then, I watched my friend's fingers move around inside her purse in search of something. It was her lip gloss. Instead of smearing it on with one finger like she used to, she brought out a tortoiseshell case with a tiny brush inside. Peering into the small mirror, she carefully applied the gloss with a brush, dabbed her lips with her napkin, and then took out her keys.

My stomach clenched. I knew we'd never spend time together like we used to. "It's good to see ya, Rache."

"Have patience, kiddo. Enjoy the moment."

Rachel paid the cashier, and we walked outside and hugged.

It seemed like the embrace was a good-bye to the friendship we had known. Hopefully, there would be future ones.

Enjoy the moment! Have patience!

I leaned back against the low brick wall of the restaurant and watched my old friend in her new pink suit walk in her pink high heels to a light gray BMW. I watched her get in, turn on the ignition, and bring her sunglasses down from the top of her head to the bridge of her nose. She waved and took off into the smog.

I wandered aimlessly down the street in the direction of where I had parked my own car.

*I'm happy her life is full. I'm glad she has everything she ever want-
ed. I'm joyful that she . . .*

*You're such a liar, Sandra Billings. You're so pissed off, you're ready
to jump off the top of that insurance building across the street. Why are
you so angry? If you wanted that kind of life for yourself, you'd be looking for a husband instead of living with an eighty-year-old woman. You
wouldn't be making this sacrifice every day to become an actress. You
don't want what she has, and you know it. So, the question is: If you
don't want that kind of life, why are you having such a strong reaction?*

I started the car. A pulsating migraine came on. My mind was
consumed with doubts. My entire life seemed pathetically shallow. I pressed down the accelerator and placed my hands on the
wheel. I had no idea where I was going . . . and yet, I knew *exactly*
where I was going.

My car, now on autopilot, drove me down Sunset and into the
parking lot of La Fontaine Bakery. Inside, my eyes—with a will of
their own—roamed the acres of fresh stuffed croissants. I moved
closer, peered through the clear glass case. I *knew* if I had just one
or two of those bakery delights, I'd feel a whole lot sweeter about
Rachel's new life. And myself.

I stood there frozen. *Do I really want to do this?*

What else is going to fill this hole in the pit of my stomach?

I asked the smiling woman behind the counter for a chocolate croissant, an almond croissant, and a cheese croissant. And to
please give me the chocolate one right away. She handed me the
pastry, rich and glistening on a gleaming piece of waxed paper,
and then went to the rear of the store to fetch the other two from
trays fresh out of the oven.

I was devouring the chocolate pastry as she handed me a bag
with the other two. I handed her the cash. Before I'd reached the
door, my hand was inside the bag groping for a second croissant.
By the time I'd pulled out the keys and started the ignition, I'd
grabbed the third, the one stuffed with cheese, and was scarfing it
down as fast as my mouth could chew. By the time I rounded the
first corner en route back to the apartment, there was nothing left
but a bag of crumbs, some almond slivers, and a few pastry flakes
that had scattered onto my pants.

I burst into the apartment and headed straight for the bathroom. Thank God, Emma was asleep in her chair. I turned the bathtub on full blast to drown out the sound, shut my eyes tight, stuck my finger down my throat, and purged. When I opened my eyes, there in the bowl were roasted almond slivers still intact, pieces of chocolate, and crusty flakes floating to the surface. I could taste the eggs from lunch, the shreds and lumps of the bacon and cheese coming up from my throat.

I kept purging. Hoping the anguish of my mind would vanish with the food disappearing in the swirling of the flushing water. But nothing more came out.

I flushed the toilet and turned off the bathwater. I was done, limp. Mascara streamed down my cheeks. I tore off a few squares of toilet paper and wiped it away. I don't know what possessed me, but I knelt down on the shiny tile floor and began to pray, desperate to understand why I continued doing this.

Wrung-out, I staggered upright, rinsed out my mouth, dragged myself into the bedroom, pulled down the shades to dim the ambient light, and collapsed on the floor. Cradling my arms around my knees, I looked up at Josef's painting, the beach scene that always invited me in. I tried to lose myself in it. But all I saw was a chaotic surface of brushstrokes, a mirror of myself. I had to look away. I thought about reaching for the *I Ching*, something that might pacify my mind, help me change the direction of my thoughts. But then I thought, *Why? What's the point?* What good was my desire to reach an understanding, to lead a conscious life, when I couldn't even control my actions? What good was all the reading if it didn't sink into my bones and change me? And even when I read the lines and had a breakthrough, I kept forgetting what I'd read. It didn't last.

I couldn't sit there in this absolute emptiness. I had to do something, no matter how pointless. I reached into the bookcase and fumbled around, desperate for a distraction. I picked up a small Buddhist pamphlet and opened it to a random page. I didn't know if the book was Emma's, Josef's, or mine. It didn't matter. The chapter I opened was titled: "Sense Pleasures." Gee! What a coincidence.

Craving after sense pleasures is primarily due to insecurity and not recognizing craving in ourselves.

We don't know what we are lacking, so we look outside ourselves. We try to fill our emotional vacuum with all kinds of diversions. But invariably we find that there is no end to indulgence and pleasure-seeking. There is no lasting and absolute satisfaction from these sense pleasures because we are not free in the moment.

There is only one way to deal with insecurity.

It is to arrive at the understanding that security cannot be found anywhere or in anything. The most critical thing is to realize our own freedom in the moment.

Freedom in the moment? I'm never in the moment. I don't know what that's like. I don't even know what that *means.*

If you start to want this and that, thinking about the past or thinking about the future, you are not free. Your present moment is preoccupied with the wanting, and as a result your natural freedom in the moment is lost.

Got it.

We are naturally free. We make ourselves "un-free." It is as though you were being tied up with an invisible rope, by no one but yourself.

Oh, great.

CHAPTER

*This shows the situation of someone too weak to take
measures against decay that has its roots in the past. . . .
It is allowed to run its course.*

It wasn't like Rachel had said "I never want to see you again,"
although she might as well have. It wasn't like I'd never work in
another ensemble like LaPapa again, although I hoped the next
director would have a little more sanity. These and a few hundred
thoughts raced through my mind as Emma and I drove through
the palatial streets of Beverly Hills to Bert's Halloween party. Cars
were backed up for half a mile. Only the reflection from floodlights in the sky revealed that we were close. And not until we
started creeping up toward the house did we have a full view of
the circus of people in costumes.

"Bert never *could* have a small celebration," Emma said, shaking her head.

Gazing out the window, I had never seen so much wealth gathered in one place. Jaguars, BMWs, Mercedes-Benzes, Maseratis,
limousines—all positioned in a regimental line, chrome dazzling
under the floodlights, purring at idle along Bert's immense circular driveway. It was hard to believe people made enough money to

buy these cars when it took me two months of obsessive budgeting to afford windshield wipers.

Emma and I sat in the Fiat as we waited for the cars to edge forward in line. Listening to drunken laughter, we viewed the colorful show from our windows: the house all aglow with orange and black lights, guests dressed in expensive ornate costumes, parking attendants in outlandish masks. Two attendants opened our doors and escorted us out. One of them drove away with my car, no doubt to some faraway alleyway to hide the old clunker from the opulent scene.

We strolled like movie stars up the red carpet neatly rolled out down the grand staircase. The closer Emma and I approached the massive double doors, the louder the music screamed through the windows, the more pulsating orange and black lights shouted for attention. A tall man wearing a turquoise velvet suit and a black satin top hat opened the formidable doors as we stepped into the foyer. Between spiderwebs and skeletons rode witches on broomsticks; frightful papier-mâché faces leered, swinging from long wooden poles. Audiotapes of canned torture blared through the thick clouds of smoke permeating the marble entryway, ushering us into Bert's mansion.

The living room was packed with guests: Zorro and Mozart, Charlie Chaplin, cowboys and Indians, goblins and go-go dancers, and . . . yes, that *was* Greta Garbo dancing seductively, snuggling close to Abe Lincoln, out on the parquet dance floor. Charming men wearing black tuxedos carried trays of champagne and hors d'oeuvres. Through an onslaught of tobacco funk, you could barely make out the food set on tables draped with cobwebs of glitter and spun silk. Happy Birthday, Bert! was spelled out in neon lights that stretched from one end of the living room to the other.

Emma must have experienced Bert's lavish parties in the past; she'd spent longer than usual preparing, adorning her face with powder, rouge, lipstick, and eye shadow. Wearing her blue chiffon party dress, she looked like Glinda, the Good Witch of the North.

I, on the other hand, wore a simple pale-rose ankle-length skirt with brown boots and a sweater to match. I wasn't interested in dressing up. I wanted to feel safe in my own clothes. My own clothes allowed me to feel the subtle vibrations in the room more precisely, feel the fake quality in the air, and safeguard myself from the phony smiles. This was not a party where close friends gathered to share the joy of a newborn child. This was a room filled with hungry vultures hovering over their prey, where not even expensive costumes could disguise the fabrication.

"Do you see the birthday boy?" I asked Emma.

"Only smoke and the tops of people's headdresses," she replied, looking around.

I looked around, too, trying to see if I could guess which costumed figure might be Bert. Suddenly, Clark Gable startled us with an enthusiastic "Emma! You look fabulous. I'm so glad to see you."

"Jack, dear. It's good to see you. How have you been?"

"Exceedingly jubilant! How are you doing?"

Jack was fortyish and jumpy in his double-breasted suit, wing-tip shoes, and toupee. His speech was staccato, and his body trembled, as if he'd survived a recent earthquake with a few persistent tremors. His impersonation of Clark Gable was pretty impressive, but he'd spent way too much time roasting his body with aluminum foil on a poolside deck.

"I'm feeling old and fine, dear . . ."

"And who's this lovely angel on your right?"

"This is Sandra. Sandra, this is Jack Hanley."

Clark Gable didn't smile or shake my hand, although I had extended it. He just looked intensely into my eyes. "You're a Virgo. September 18, 1951, right?"

"June 20, 1953," I said.

"You were born in Ohio . . . and your whole family has brown hair and problems with their feet, right?"

"I was born in Michigan, but you're right about the hair and feet."

"Gemini–Cancer cusp. Interesting." He thought for a moment. "Well, *you're* going to be feeling a surge of energy now that Mercury's gone direct. The next few weeks are going to be quite productive for you. You're about to experience a positive shift in your tenth house, the house of career."

"I bet you say that to all the girls," I quipped.

"Oh, no . . . I'm not *always* accurate with people's signs, but I know my houses," he said, a little less shaky now.

"I hope you're right."

Greta Garbo was now coming our way, slithering through the crowd, waving; I wasn't quite sure to whom. In the hand that wasn't waving was a long cigarette holder and a champagne flute. Sporting a thirties-style seductive nightgown, her small boobies bouncing, her blonde shoulder-length hair—clearly a wig—swaying to and fro, she vamped up to Emma and embraced her.

They launched right into an intimate conversation as if I didn't exist, and then, finally, Emma turned and introduced me to Ms. Garbo.

"Zelda, this is Sandra. The young girl who is staying—"

"So, you're the new roomie I've heard so much about."

So, this is Zelda. Aloud, I said, "Hello, Zelda. It's nice to meet you."

Ms. Garbo was a bit tipsy, and delightful, and made me smile every time she tried to speak. Maybe it was the way she slurred her words and her attempt to stand up straight in her inebriated state. I also detected sadness behind her girlish smiles, most likely due to finding her husband in bed with a younger woman.

Emma had mentioned just the other day that she and Zelda had been friends in Berlin. Zelda's husband, Max, and Josef were also friends. They'd all moved to the States at the same time. Only, Max and Zelda moved to California first. Josef and Emma settled in New York.

Now Zelda whisked Emma away to another cluster of costumed guests. Slowly, inconspicuously, I moved over to observe the conversation, where Emma was being worshipped. At least that's what it looked like. Some reached for her hand, others kissed her cheek as if she were royalty, or expressed concern over her illness, exclaiming how elegant, how vibrant, she looked. Emma's charm, her wry sense of humor, made her seem right at home in this social setting. It was as if she had come out of years of hibernation, bubbling like the champagne in Zelda's glass, totally captivating the hearts of a knot of breathless men and women now standing around her. Only, where had all these devoted friends been all this time? They never came over to visit Emma, or called. And why hadn't Emma introduced me to her friends or let them know I was part of her recovery? Why was she being so insensitive?

As the crowd grew larger, the costumed guests hung attentively on Emma's every word. Swept up in the wave of attention, she captivated them with stories of "the good ol' days," how life was so rich when she lived in New York. How she missed the art galleries, the theater, the artists and theatrics of the crowded city. Who *was* this butterfly now spreading her wings, this creature metamorphosing right in front of me? It wasn't Emma from the farmers' market or Emma the quiet, even-tempered woman from before we entered this gala. She was shining and glittering like the bright silver disco ball twirling rapidly above her head. As kaleidoscopically as the tiny square mirrors changed their colored reflections, Emma changed her style, her mood. Seeing her come alive was a delightful surprise on the one hand, and confusing to me on the other. I wondered why she had never shared this part of herself with *me*.

In the midst of her exuberance, a short, stocky man dressed in a silk robe with a silk purple turban on his head burst through the semicircle surrounding Emma.

"There's my goddess! I've been searching the whole damn house for you."

"Bert!" Emma exclaimed and beamed at him in sheer delight. "Happy birthday, dear." She handed him a small wrapped present from her purse. Another surprise I'd known nothing about.

Well, what do you know, Bert Klein in the flesh. Blue eyes, pudgy cheeks, pampered baby-soft skin. I noticed immediately how his lips tightened when he spoke, and how his hooded eyes had an air of superiority. I stood at least three inches taller than the man. As I observed his flamboyant behavior, I remembered the brief disclosure Emma had made about him only a few weeks back: that Bert's father, Harvey, had quite a reputation in the movie industry for being verbally abusive and intimidating. And he didn't turn off the abuse once he got home, directing most of it at Bert. Bert's mother, Sarah, smothered the boy with love to compensate for Harvey's harm.

Sarah had been Emma's good friend. She'd died not long after Josef.

I supposed I could show a little compassion for the man, knowing his unmanageable unconsciousness sprang from his father's behavior and the loss of his mother. I supposed I could even respect the guy for acknowledging Emma's usefulness and intelligence, by giving her his scripts to critique. At least he appreciated her talent.

But this was not easy. Because no matter what qualities he had or what kind of hell he'd gone through in his youth, he never, ever had to worry about a job, a place to live, or money. Everything was handed to him on a silver platter. Which, as far as I was concerned, was quite a nice little buffer. I didn't want to be jealous. I had been working on this awful trait since I'd seen Rachel with her baby bump and her ring. But these demons don't leave quickly.

About to engineer my departure to the abundantly lavish buffet, I heard Emma say, "Bert, dear, I'd like you to meet Sandra; you spoke to her on the phone, remember?"

Bert made an exaggerated turn toward me. "Ah, yes, the fledging actress—soon to be cast in Hollywood's next blockbuster. Nice to meet you."

Hollywood's next blockbuster!? He certainly wasn't referring to one of his own films.

Emma pulled him aside and whispered something in his ear. He looked at me, and then, turning back to the small crowd, he made an announcement: "Excuse me for a few minutes, everyone. I have someone I want Sandra to meet. I'll be back. Don't move from this spot, Emma. When I return, you and I are going to take some whirls around the dance floor." The surrounding crowd applauded.

"Go ahead, Bert," she said. "I'll wait for you here."

I didn't get it. Emma was like a stoic chief of police when she was with me, and with Bert, she'd just gone from kindly mother to simpering schoolgirl. It made me ill watching the "seduction."

Bert slipped his arm under my elbow and escorted me against my will to the library, where several people were sitting and talking. On our way into the room he murmured that the man he was about to introduce me to, Jerry Aldridge, was an up-and-coming writer, and it would be to my advantage to get to know him.

Jerry Aldridge was sitting comfortably by himself on the seat of an elaborately draped bay window. Dressed in beige from his sweater to his toes, which oddly made him more conspicuous than the costumed guests, he looked utterly at ease sitting there. Perhaps he was imagining a passage for one of his stories, or scripts, or novels, or whatever it was he wrote. I hated to disturb him, but of course, Bert barged right in.

"Jerry, I want you to meet a friend of mine: Sandra, uh . . ."

"Billings," I reminded him.

"Of course, Billings. Sandra is an actress; we're going to have to find her a role in one of our upcoming projects."

I saw Bert wink at Jerry, as if this statement were some kind of joke at my expense. "Why don't you two get cozy." He winked again. "I'm going back to dance with the Queen of the Ball."

I could have died right there. Jerry, not betraying any notice of my mortification, rose and reached out his hand. "Hi." He smiled. "I'm Jerry Aldridge."

His voice was sweet, melodic to my ears. His eyes were big and brown and enchanting. You just knew this man didn't have an ounce of anger in his soul. You knew he was one of those male specimens who'd never raise his voice . . . even if a terrible driver cut him off. I could tell these things about people within seconds of meeting them. Jerry had such an unusual handshake for a man; his palm was soft, inviting. His light complexion and sandy-blond hair added to his warm, virtuous quality, and he sure knew how to use those puppy-dog eyes.

"Nice to meet you, Sandra Billings." The voice was so soothing, I could feel my whole body relax into this content, open posture. "Don't let Bert get to you. He's only irritating on the surface. Underneath he has a good heart."

"Oh, you've experienced his heart, have you?" I rolled my eyes in disbelief.

"On rare occasions."

We both sat down on the window seat, not too close, but close enough for me to smell his subtle cologne.

"So . . . you're a writer? What do you write?"

"Novels mostly. I just finished my first screenplay."

"Wow, a screenplay. I'm impressed."

"Don't be. It's arduous work, frustrating when you're trying to please two producers and a director. And you? Bert mentioned you were an actress. Are you performing in anything I could see you in?"

"Don't get me started." I didn't want to complain. I hardly knew the man. Why would he want to hear a dismal story at his friend's birthday party? I found myself falling into the deep brown of his eyes, forgetting where I was. I pulled myself out . . . only to be reminded of how short Jerry Aldridge was. Even sitting, I topped him by half a head in my low heels. What a shame. I knew, once he stood up again, the fantasy I was conjuring up in my mind about him would be over.

"It's a very strange business," Jerry said. "A lot of it is *who* you know. But only in the beginning. Then, it's *what* you know. When I first started, the only job I could get was writing skits for an industrial show in Vegas. We were introducing new plumbing products to a thousand distributors, trying to make toilets sound funny and appealing."

"Now, that would be an interesting writing assignment."

"It wasn't. It was awful. The designers had no idea what they wanted, and I had to take my orders from them."

"I've been in a few productions like that."

"But at least I was writing and getting paid for it."

"I've *never* been paid for my work," I said, as tears suddenly rolled down my cheeks. At last, a man who understood, who was intelligent, who listened, without any obvious intention of wanting to climb on top of me. Even if Jerry had an ulterior motive, he had the manners to be subtle about it.

He took out his handkerchief and dabbed at my tears.

"Oh God," I confessed, "I'm so embarrassed."

"Most people can't let their emotions out. It's healthy if you can release them. It's a gift."

"If this is a gift, I have truckloads of presents."

"I don't envy your situation. At least when I feel bad, I can take out my pencil and write about it. The truth is, if you're good, they'll come looking for *you*. If you're good, someone will notice."

Why did I care if he was short? Why did I always have to be attracted to dark-complected, hairy men who invariably turned out to be jerks? Why couldn't I just fall in love with a short, fair-skinned, wonderfully warm, kind person? I wiped my eyes and did the best I could to blow my nose without sounding like a party horn.

"You know," Jerry continued, "a friend of mine, Allen Cahill, is casting a new play in a couple weeks. He wanted me to audition, which is ridiculous, since I'm not an actor." He handed me a card and wrote down: "Windmill Theater, Allen Cahill, Wednesday at four."

"You'll take my place, and show up for the audition in my spot. If I'm not mistaken, I think there is a dual female role. Don't worry—I'll call him first."

"He's not going to mind?"

"He'll be fine; he's a friend. There's a condition here, though. You have to promise to call me, let me know what happens."

"I will, I will. Are you sure this is going to be okay?"

"I'm sure."

"Thanks again. I guess you didn't know it was a costume party either."

"I did." Jerry smiled. "I came as Theodore Dreiser."

"Why?" I asked.

"'Cause nobody remembers what he looked like."

"I came as Sylvia Plath."

"Good party choice."

He smiled, and then the up-and-coming writer extended his hand. Only this time, it felt like he'd wrapped his arms around my entire body, protecting me from all the foreign entities in the room.

"I have an early appointment tomorrow, so I'd better be going. It was great meeting you, Sandra. Good luck with the audition. And don't forget our agreement."

"I'm not from L.A.; I keep my word."

Jerry Aldridge pulled away, drifted out of the library and into the mass of bobbing partygoers. I drifted behind him as far as the entrance to the living room and leaned against one of the pillars that framed the doorway. For some reason, I didn't feel alone anymore, nor did the music seem so loud or the lights so garish. As Jerry departed through the front door, my body relaxed against the solid white pillar, and I stood there, observing the glitter, the jewels, the dancing bodies moving to the beat of the samba. I could feel my spine straighten, my head resting more comfortably on my shoulders. I was no longer stung by Emma's earlier indifference. Funny how my confidence had returned. I guess it was because I met someone who cared.

I had closed my eyes in an inner prayer of gratitude when someone hit me on my shoulder. I opened my eyes, turned around, and there, standing before me, decked out in skimpy wrestling shorts and a black silk robe, was none other than Larry Santino. There was no "Hello," no "How are you?" only Larry Santino, standing there half-naked, wearing boxing gloves and grinning with enthusiasm.

"Guess what?"

I just stared at him, hoping he would interpret my expression, as this was not a game I wanted to play. He never caught on.

Jumping up and down, as if he were in training, he shared his news: "I was just cast in a movie." He didn't stop for air. "Two days ago this Italian director saw me standing on Hollywood Boulevard. He came over and asked me if I wanted to play a wrestler in his film. Isn't that the shit?" He smacked me on the shoulder again. "Just like that. The guy spots my muscular physique from across the street, comes over to get a closer look, and tells me I'm the wrestler he's been looking for."

"Is he gay?" I couldn't help myself.

Larry stopped to think about it for a minute. "I don't think so." He shifted ground, transferred his weight from his right foot to his left. "Nope, he's definitely not gay. Anyway, I leave in a week for Italy. And guess what else? I'll be getting my SAG card. Ain't that a pisser?"

The wave of jealousy that rose up inside me nearly flung me to the floor. While he took a gulp from his wineglass, my face, I'm sure, turned fire-pepper red. And this was the man I used to love kissing? With great control I made myself reply matter-of-factly, "It's a pisser, Larry." Caught between not wanting to lie about how happy I was and wanting to throw my diet soda in his face, I listened to myself recommend that he do extensive research on wrestlers before leaving for Italy and to be sure to learn all the character's lines before going on the set. Then, before I could rip the robe off this wrestler and wrap it around his throat, I said, "Congratulations, Larry. I wish you all the success you deserve. Sorry I can't stay to hear more, but I must get going—*big* audition in the morning."

We said our farewells, and I walked straight toward the dessert table. My whole body was shaking with anger, envy, rage. It didn't matter that Larry Santino had no acting ability whatsoever, that he couldn't deliver a meaningful line to his mother, let alone to another actor. My feet were moving toward the colorful table resplendent with bright red strawberries and glistening yellow-custard tarts. I wanted to devour every treat on it. It was like an emotional wave riding me forward on its current. I could feel the desire rising up through my stomach and into my chest and lodging in my throat. I could hardly breathe, and I realized: *This is what addicts go through when they can't get their fix. Smokers, when they can't get their cigarette.*

With the surge came a clarity I'd never experienced before: I became extremely conscious of how much power these emotions had over me. And yet I couldn't move. I was stuck. Rooted to the spot I was standing on. I knew I couldn't eat just because I was mad. But the desire was so intense, and the urge seemed to come from someplace so much deeper than surface desire or jealousy. I didn't know how to stop the desire, or the jealousy. I just wanted to push it down.

I reached for a tart, put it in my mouth, and started to reach for another one when all of a sudden I had a flash of how I'd felt after eating those croissants, how I'd fallen on my knees and prayed for this never to happen again. I pulled my hand back, forced myself to take a step away. Shaking, I noticed a couple, dressed as police officers, detaching themselves from the mass of dancers and heading my way. I managed to find my voice as they approached and asked, "Where's the bathroom?"

"Back toward the kitchen, doll," the female police officer said as she pinched my cheek. I beelined down the hall to the narrow door, with my shoulder bag flapping against my waist. Looking around to see if anyone was coming, I let myself in and quickly locked the door.

Resting my back against the shiny blue door, I slid down to the floor. *Help me,* I silently called out. I closed my eyes and could feel myself not being able to breathe. Panic. On my knees, I began to rock back and forth, back and forth. The panic kept rising.

All I wanted to do was to get up, go back to the dessert table, and eat everything on it, stuff down all the feelings that were surfacing.

I didn't know what stopped me. I'd never had the slightest willpower. It was a force that I hadn't known was within me. From somewhere inside, I began to hear the words: *Reclaim what you've lost . . . Reclaim what you've lost.* The words kept coming up: *Reclaim what you've lost.*

Reclaim <u>*what*</u>*?* I closed my eyes and knelt there on the floor.

And then the recurring dream that had come to me, the one I couldn't figure out—the shadow in the room with the two figures—was suddenly present. With my eyes closed, the vision, although shadowy, flashed before me:

> *I'm ten years old. Mommy and Daddy are out . . . It's night-*
> *time, and I'm singing and dancing with my Ginny doll in the*
> *living room. Steven is in his bedroom with his friend Lenny. All*

of a sudden the door to his room opens, and Steven pops his head out and smiles.

He asks me if I want to come into his room to play a game. "Sure," I say, happy that Steven wants me to play with them.

I shut off the TV and go into the open door.

Steven slams the door shut. He still has a smile on his face, but it's lost the friendly quality. He walks over to me and takes my doll and throws it on the floor. He pushes me onto his bunk bed and tells me to lie down, that Lenny is going to pretend to be a doctor who does push-ups on top of me.

"What?" Why would Lenny want to do push-ups on me?

Steven says, "If you ask any questions, the game's over."

"Okay, okay." I wanted to play.

Steven tells me that Lenny is going to show me something very cool. I'm just about to ask what he's going to show me when Steven opens the door and leaves the room.

The second the door slams, Lenny unzips his pants, pulls them down to his knees, and jumps on top of me. His "Thing" pops out. It's right there, sticking straight out. It's gross.

He has me by the shoulders, holding me down. He pulls down my shorts and then my underwear. He jams my legs apart and sticks his ugly Thing inside me. I start yelling: "What are you doing? STOP IT!"

He's only got the tip of it in, but it still hurts.

He starts shoving, pushing his Thing harder inside me. It hurts so much I think I'm going to die. "NO!" I yell at the top of my lungs. "STOP! STOP!" But he doesn't stop no matter how loud I yell, and I yell a lot because I don't know what he's doing and I've never felt so much pain. I feel like I'm being ripped open. I scream louder. He covers my mouth with his wrist. Something inside of me is tearing.

In the midst of the pain, I wonder why he is working so hard. Pushing and pulling! It's then, right then, that everything stops hurting. I no longer feel anything. Everything has gone numb. I have a body, but I can't feel it.

Everything is in slow motion. I look up at Lenny, wondering what I am supposed to do, wondering how I am supposed to react, but he doesn't say anything. He just keeps pushing down and pulling up.

I notice the wooden slats above his head. I never realized how many pieces of wood it takes to hold up an upper bunk. I've never been on Steven's bed before.

Lenny doesn't open his eyes. His forehead starts to perspire, and I notice how beautiful he is. How structured and symmetrical his face is. His strong, muscular arms pushing himself up and down. Why is he so mad? Drops of his sweat fall on my face.

But I feel like I'm seeing it from a long way away, from the other end of the universe.

From outside the door, Steven yells, "Lenny! They're back! They're comin' in the front door!"

Lenny pulls out his Thing and jumps off the bed. I lie there. I can't move. Lenny pulls up my shorts and then yanks me off the bed, but I fall when he lets go of my arm. I can't stand. There's blood running down my legs. But I have no feeling there, no feeling from the waist down—like both my legs have fallen asleep. But they aren't asleep. I just can't feel them.

He pushes me out the bedroom door. Steven is there, whispering fiercely: "If you tell anybody about our little game, I'll deny it. No one's gonna believe you anyway."

The next thing I know, I'm in the bathroom, crying, trying to wipe the blood from my leg. One of my pigtails has come undone, and I don't have my doll.

I sat slumped against the bathroom wall in Bert's Hollywood mansion, ashamed, raw, stunned. My mind began to spin. For a few moments, I didn't know where I was. Was this real? Were these memories true? And if they were, why were they surfacing now? What was I supposed to do with them?

But it did happen. The memory of the incident flooded my senses. I remembered every detail. How had I forgotten? How could I have blocked it out for so many years? Not only the rape, but Lenny's *and* Steven's betrayal.

Anger rose up like a volcano. My body was on fire. I wanted to call everyone I knew and tell them what had happened. Still seething, but fragile and vulnerable, I slowly hauled myself up to a standing position. I staggered over to the sink and began to wash off the black streaks of mascara smeared down my cheeks. I brought out the tube of toothpaste from my shoulder bag and squirted some paste onto my finger, rubbed it around my gums. I could taste the zesty peppermint flavor. It made my eyes water, but it brought me back to life.

I rinsed my mouth with the water from the gold swan faucets, wiped my lips on the pretty pink towel, and washed my hands. They were shaking. They continued to shake as I put on my lipstick and straightened out the wrinkles in my sweater and skirt. I felt completely violated, embarrassed, and most of all, ashamed.

Then I took a deep breath and, as if I'd simply come into the bathroom to empty my bladder and was now ready to enjoy the festivities like all of Bert's invited guests, opened the bathroom door. Was I ready to walk out? Shaky, transparent, I made my way tentatively back up the hall. Nobody noticed me. I might have been one of the Halloween ghosts, invisible, as hollow as I felt.

Unaware of how I got there, I found myself back at the dessert table, standing above a bowl of fresh strawberries. I picked one out and took a small bite and felt the prickles on the surface as it touched the tip of my tongue. The red strawberry, glistening, was refreshing. I popped the rest of the berry into my mouth.

One was all I needed.

I walked out into the heat of the party and scanned the room looking for Emma. I spotted her in the middle of the dance floor, grinning like a child in her blue chiffon dress. Besides being Glinda, the Good Witch, she was Cinderella at the ball, with Bert holding her close, her cheek resting on his chest. I was watching *her* flashback now: Emma and Josef vacationing on Martha's Vineyard, afloat on the strains of romantic music from their cottage, dancing on the cool damp sand at the beach. I'd never seen Emma look so youthful, so at peace.

As I stood against the wall, still dazed, admiring Emma, watching other guests move to the music, I saw Zelda wave from across the room—to me, I thought. I wasn't sure. Doing her best to walk in my direction. Sliding off her heels, trying to place one foot in front of the other, wobbling, champagne sloshing out of her glass.

"Hi, Emma's roomie!" she stated, only inches away from my face. She didn't wait for a response. "Well, good for you. Good for you." She socked me on the shoulder. "You must be very brave, 'cause I coulda never just moved in with anybody, like you and Emma. Not even with Emma, and me and Emma are very close, very close." She took an unsteady gulp of her drink.

"We knew each other in Germany. You know, our fathers were very good friends, and our mothers, too . . . before all hell started . . . before Emma and Josef and me and Max got out . . . Did you know her mother killed herself?" She hiccupped. "Her father . . . whoa . . . what a bastard he was! He was a fucking drill sergeant." The word *fucking* was accompanied by a spray of saliva. "Thank God she met Josef and had a . . ." She stopped and then went on. "Emma's very psychic . . . did you know? Did she tell you my husband is divorcing me for a cute young girl with big round tits? I got Morty, though . . . where *is* Morty?"

Zelda wandered off looking for Morty. I stood there, watching her cling to the walls, trying to make progress around the room. And then I turned my attention back to Emma, dancing with Bert. This woman I was so upset with, this woman I thought was so insensitive—turned out to have more in common with me than I'd thought. I stood there trying to imagine what it must have been like for *her* to lose her mother and live with an obsessive father. It was pretty clear that the discipline she insisted I adopt came from her own childhood experience.

On the ride home, I was not the same person who'd driven to the party a few hours ago. Something had shifted inside of me. I was different. It was as if all the molecules in my body had changed. I couldn't be that person who just blurted out my experiences like a schoolgirl and expected Emma to process them for me. I couldn't talk about my encounter with Zelda or ask about her childhood. I couldn't whine about Jerry being short, or gripe about how jealous I was of Larry's film role. I couldn't even tell her about my memory of Steven and Lenny. Not tonight! Instead,

I told Emma how beautiful she'd looked dancing under the disco ball, how generous it was of Bert to open his home for this party. I told her about meeting Jerry and the possibility of an audition— without the exaggerated enthusiasm. I mentioned that I'd seen Larry, and that he was offered a wonderful role.

Still glowing, Emma listened attentively and said she noticed something quite different about my behavior. She said it was a pleasure not to hear me complain. I nodded, and thought: *I must be pushing upward.*

CHAPTER  19

Bites on dried gristly meat.
Receives metal arrows.
It furthers one to be mindful of difficulties . . .

The next morning I sat up in bed wondering what to do. The memory of the rape kept looping over and over in my brain: the details of that night, the fact that I hadn't remembered it, the *invasion* of my privacy, and my brother's betrayal. I needed to tell someone, get the weight off my heart, but who? I couldn't tell Emma, not yet anyway. And it was too early to call Rachel.

Michigan! It was two hours later there. Someone would be home.

I jumped out of bed, threw on my coat over my pajamas, laced up my gym shoes, and tiptoed past Emma's door. As the images of the memory continued to well up, I jogged to the nearest pay phone on Sunset.

The phone kept ringing. Finally, someone picked up.

"Hello." It was my mother.

"Mom, it's Sandra. I have to tell you something. Remember those nightmares I used to have? The ones with the scary shadows and . . . well, the whole thing came back to me in living color. The shadows were of Steven and his friend Lenny. Lenny raped me, Mom . . . and Steven set it up. It all came back."

"What? What are you talking about? Are you insane?"

"I know it's hard to believe. But that was what those dreams were about. Lenny got on top of me and he stuck his . . . but Steven was right there. He put him up to it. Steven was right outside the door, and—"

"What the hell are you trying to do, kill me? Because that's what you're doing!"

"It really happened, Mom. I saw the whole thing, clear as day. You have to believe me."

"You are a liar, Sandra Billings. All adolescents explore. But *you* have to take it to the extreme, don't you? You have to be the drama queen, don't you? Enough!"

"Mom, this was not something I made up! It was real."

"Well, deal with it! Just don't involve us with this . . . this filth. And, do us a favor. Forget about coming home. You're not welcome here."

She hung up.

I could hardly breathe. I sat there in the phone booth, numb, my hand still on the receiver. I wasn't surprised she didn't believe me. She'd responded true to style. Well . . . the hell with her. *I don't have a home. Home is where they believe you.*

I got up, hung up the phone, and opened the door. I had to walk. I needed to move, pull myself together. With no destination in mind, I started down Sunset. As the cars and trucks streamed by, and a light drizzle misted the air, I knew she wouldn't believe me. Who was I kidding? Did I really think she'd sympathize with me? She never had before. I kept walking and tried to unearth details about the event.

Steven knew exactly what was going to happen behind that door. And I knew why he'd done it. Steven hated me from the day I was born. He hated the fact that Daddy gave me more love and attention than he gave him. He was jealous that I had so many friends, that I was popular. He always wanted to shut me down, turn out my light. He never liked me to shine. He'd been tormenting me my whole life—but he'd been biding his time for his ultimate revenge. What an ass! But why Lenny? Because he was the only friend Steven had, and he knew I had a crush on him.

I was into a full sprint now, racing past supermarkets and clothing stores, flower shops and gas stations. The light rain kept on. I scanned over all the times my brother had sabotaged my efforts, humiliated me in front of my friends, and terrorized me. All the times I'd tried to ignore him, and wanted to kill him. All the times I had to hide my light—for fear it would be taken away.

I passed Monroe's Funeral Home, slowed my pace, and stopped. Looking into the window at my own reflection, I realized Steven and I had never, ever looked at each other with love . . . not once that I could remember—ever. Rachel would have said, "Past-life karma." And she might have been right.

A distant church bell struck nine. I had to see if Rachel was still here or if she'd left for South America again. I jogged back to the pay phone. _Please be there. Please be there._

It rang three times before she picked up.

"Hello?"

"Rache! Thank God! I have to talk to you. Something very amazing just happened."

There was a lot of noise in the background.

"Sandra?"

"Yes, it's me. Can we talk?"

"It's crazy here. I can hardly hear you."

"I _have_ to talk to you."

"Armando's sisters are here helping us with the wedding. They just flew in from San Francisco. We're getting ready to leave for Buenos Aires tomorrow."

"There's no way we can meet?"

"I'm so sorry, Sandra. I wish I could, but I just can't."

Tears welled up. I took a deep breath . . . I needed to say something . . . so I told her about Jerry and the audition instead. "An audition, can you believe it?" I wiped the tears away. "I think this is going to be a big deal."

"It sounds great, Sandra. I just don't want you to get your hopes up and—"

"Hey, Rachel!" I interrupted, mad at her for doubting me. "It's a sure thing. You should have heard this guy, Jerry. He was serious about calling the director and setting up the audition."

"Just stay in the moment. Don't jump ahead of yourself . . . look, I promise I'll call you as soon as I get back. And good luck with the audition."

I wished her luck with the wedding, placed the receiver on the cradle, and stood there in the small, narrow booth.

Now what?

Bella used to say, "God doesn't give us anything we can't handle."

It was the first time I questioned her words.

cHapter  20

The eclipse reaches totality . . .
even the small stars can be seen at noon.

Rummaging through old bags I hadn't unpacked since I moved in, I found the dress I'd been looking for. The one I'd bought at a second-hand vintage store on Melrose, near the Bodhi Tree bookstore. The dress reminded me of a Russian neighbor I knew from Michigan, which was the reason I bought it in the first place. Maybe it was the dark brown plush-smooth velvet that reminded me of her deep hazel eyes, and the pale orange stitching that reminded me of the delicate lines that formed on her skin when she smiled. The soft collar brought to mind her gentleness. The dress was big on me now, but it worked as a dress from Russia, with a belt. I took it off, shook out the mustiness, and laid it neatly on the bed.

A shower was next. As the water poured over my head, I knew I had to focus on the audition, not the memory of the nightmare. I forced myself to think about the characters in the play. Jerry didn't tell me much—other than that the production was called *The Turning of the Century,* and consisted of two one-act plays by Clifford Thorne. One of the characters I was to audition for was a young Russian actress, the other a medical student. In both cases, these women were going to be clean, really clean. Standing in the steam, the pellets stinging my skin, I imagined how their personalities could be different from one another. How one could have a stutter, or never look anyone in the eye, to convey shyness. The other could be ballsy, crass, to suggest the extreme. Of course, until I'd read some of the dialogue, I couldn't draw any conclusions. But I wanted to think of some options before seeing the script.

I tried not to think about how nervous I was. Yet as I massaged the shampoo suds into my scalp, I understood that fear has a mind of its own . . . and was something I still couldn't control. So I did my best to let it go—for the moment.

Hair toweled and blow-dried, makeup in place, I nervously slipped the dress on and secured the belt. I returned to the bedroom and sat down. For precautionary measures only, I brought out the *I Ching*, the pouch of coins, and the yellow pad. The question was:

The audition?

42. I / Increase

Above: Sun, The Gentle Wind
Below: Chên, The Arousing, Thunder

A time of blessing and enrichment has such powerful effects that even events ordinarily unfortunate must turn out to the advantage of those affected by them. These persons become free of error, and by acting in harmony with truth they gain such inner authority that they exert influence as if sanctioned by letter and seal . . .

The superior man sets his person at rest before he moves; he composes his mind before he speaks; he makes his relations firm before he asks for something. By attending to these three matters, the superior man gains complete security.

All righty! I had my marching orders.

On my way out through the living room, I thought about what I'd say to Emma. She knew I had an audition, but I hadn't given her any details. I didn't want to set up any expectations for her, any more than I had for myself. So, as she sat reading the *New York Times,* I tiptoed toward the door. Without looking at her, I could hear the rustle of the paper, and her lowering it to her breast. I glanced over to her, smiled, and waved good-bye.

"I'm going on an audition." That was all I said.

The Windmill Theater was located on the corner of Sunset and Highland, hidden from view behind the solid trunks of majestic palm trees and densely grown shrubbery. You had to turn the corner and look closely for the sign, now overgrown by vines, before you could even see the marquee—THE WINDMILL THEATER PRESENTS—and the name of the show. Two years ago I'd seen a play here and thought how deceptively small the theater looked from the outside. Once inside, though, I was surprised to see the size of the auditorium. Seating capacity was 200, quite considerable for a Los Angeles playhouse.

I walked in and the feeling of being home came over me instantly. The feeling of being safe and protected surrounded my bones, and the tension I'd held so tightly on the way there dropped away. I always felt this kind of peace, whenever I walked into a theater. I inhaled the electricity moving through the halls and felt instantly rejuvenated by the currents of expectation, of magic. It was a sign for sure.

I'd wanted to get there early, before the others, to get a feel for the place again. I walked upstairs and followed the buzz of voices to a room where a line had already formed for the auditions. Beyond the eight or so women standing ahead of me was another woman in her fifties. She had long bleached-blonde hair, a weathered face, and a firm expression. Her name tag, pinned to her violet blouse, said FLORENCE. Florence sat on a stool signing in the other actresses. I waited patiently for my turn.

"Your name, please?"

I cleared my throat and then said confidently, "Sandra Billings."

The strict-faced woman checked her list of names, but didn't find mine. She said she was sorry, perhaps there was a mistake and I had the wrong date.

"I have an appointment with Allen Cahill," I replied sternly. I took out Jerry's rumpled card to reread it, and even though I'd read it a thousand times, I read it again to the lady, to Florence, out loud.

"Jerry Aldridge set up this appointment."

While Florence searched through her papers, a film of sweat began to form on my forehead, the fingers on my right hand clutched the leather strap of my shoulder bag. I started shifting my weight from one foot to the other, scrunching my toes tightly inside my pumps, trying to think of what to say next. Florence kept searching through, around, and under a pile of papers for what seemed to be an eternity, and then she pulled out a piece of paper from underneath a notebook. A few words were scribbled on it. Her expression changed.

"Yes, Ms. Billings, there is an addendum here that was not brought to my attention. I apologize. You are scheduled to audition at five-thirty. As you can see, we're a little behind. A forty-five-minute wait at least."

"Forty-five minutes? Not a problem."

"Please, find a chair. I'll get you a script."

"Thank you, thank you very much." *Thank you, thank you, thank you, thank you, thank you.*

I sat down and tried to tune out the voices, but the hallway was narrow, with no carpet to absorb the sound. While I listened to the chattering auditioners, I realized this was the first audition I'd been to where I didn't have to wear a wig, or dress up like an old lady, or become an animal, or wear falsies. I could act my own age, look like myself, talk in my regular speaking voice.

In a loud whisper, one of the girls announced the play had been a hit in England, and Allen Cahill had won an award for his direction. It was scheduled to be the Los Angeles premiere, making it an absolute certainty that critics from all major newspapers would be attending. *And* rumor had it that Clifford Thorne himself would be attending one of the performances.

"Hi, my name is Cayman." Tall, rangy, rough-and-ready, Cayman sat down next to me with his grizzled stubble and a cowboy hat too big for his head.

"Cayman, as in Cayman Islands?" I asked.

"Yep, you got it. First try. Pretty good."

Where did this cowboy hail from? His accent was as thick as three layers of cheese on a nacho chip.

"Do you live around here?"

"Nope, just arrived from Kentucky."

"Are you serious? Actors are flying in from out of state to audition for this play?"

"Well, I'll tell ya." He slid around in his chair to face me. "There ain't too many opportunities these days for actors showcasing their work. *You* oughta know how tough it is. My agent told me about this here audition. And with Allen Cahill directing, *sheee-it,* I thought, why the hell not."

"You, ah, had to have an agent to get in?"

"Yep, you got it! You new in town, too?" He laughed, with a grunting sound from the back of his throat. "I got me a good agent, I did. She even lined me up a few movie auditions while I'm out here. Yep, I feel real lucky in this town."

Oh no, what if they ask me who my agent is? What if they say I can't audition? Why didn't Jerry tell me? I thought the planets were on my side. The astrologer said . . . I could feel the sweat breaking out, soaking the material of the dress under my arms. I stood up and paced the narrow hallway. The thought of leaving was playing in my mind when a young man handed me a mimeographed sheet of paper that requested my name, phone number, guild affiliation, and agent. I was doomed. I could leave right now, spare myself the humiliation, or fill out the sheet and lie.

I decided to lie. I wrote down Emma's name as agent. I checked the square for Equity member. If they had any questions, they could call Emma.

We were given the script and told that we had thirty minutes to study our scenes. I excused myself from Cayman and marched into the restroom, knowing it would be the only place where I'd have some quiet. I sat down in the farthest stall, locked the door, and began to skim the script, concentrating on the scenes I'd be auditioning for. All of a sudden, I realized how much time I actually spent in bathrooms. (Did I really want to analyze that? Not at the moment.)

It took only a few minutes to figure out how to play each of the roles. Jerry was right. It was a double role. The first character was a young actress who had traveled a fair distance to meet a famous Russian playwright. The other was a shy medical student who spent her days listening to her professor argue with his wife. How could I not nail these parts? Schizophrenia was second nature to me, being a Gemini.

Once secure with each character's subtext and motivation, I looked over the lines again and again. I wanted to familiarize myself with them enough to feel comfortable looking away from the page. I had learned the art of cold reading from Walter Sheldon, and endless auditions.

Thirty-seven minutes passed before my amplified name was called over the loudspeaker: "Sandra Billings, please come backstage. Sandra Billings, backstage . . . now." I closed my eyes and tried to center myself before leaving my peaceful potty haven.

The bleached-blond woman asked me to follow her. We went backstage, where another actress waited to audition, which allowed time for my nerves to take over and my mind to start worrying. I prayed that my thorax would relax enough to allow the dialogue to exit freely from my mouth. I leaned back against the black stucco wall, inhaled until my lungs were filled, and exhaled slowly. After repeating this a few times, I heard Emma's voice: *Why do you allow these daggers of doubt to puncture your heart? Just let them bounce off you like pellets of water. Only then can you be fearless.* I kept listening to her words. I remembered the *I Ching*'s words: *The superior man composes his mind before he speaks.*

"Sandra Billings, onstage, please." I jumped at the summons, regained my composure, and walked onto the stage. *Okay. This is it.* Time to take control and fill that stage.

Within seconds, I felt conscious of every move my body was making. I was in the moment, capturing the intimacies of one character and moving effortlessly to the other. On target when the actress revealed her embarrassment; on cue when the medical student was supposed to laugh and at the same time conceal the outburst; knowing when the dialogue had to speed up, when to idle. There was no separation between me and the characters; we were one. It was a cosmic, out-of-body experience.

As one of the company's actors stood in the corner feeding me lines, I imagined the character he was reading to be close, standing next to me, sitting near me. The pulse of the play was like my own heartbeat. I wanted to embellish every nuance of the character, finish the entire script, but someone in the audience said, "Thank you, Miss Billings. Thank you very much."

I'd lost all sense of time. I looked out to see if I could detect a face, but it was too dark. All I could see was a spotlight and a man coming closer, down the aisle. He walked into the light, down in front of the stage, and there, standing before me, was the most beautiful dark-complected, dark-haired, neatly bearded Greek god I'd ever seen. My legs felt wobbly. Maybe he was the stage manager coming to tell me to get off the stage and go home. Maybe he was the producer coming to tell me the same. Whoever he was, he was gorgeous—and walking my way.

"Hi, I'm Allen Cahill."

"Hi." My face turned twenty million shades of red.

"Very good audition."

"Are you sure . . . ? I mean, thank you!"

"So, you're Jerry's 'replacement'?"

"*Ahhh,* yes. He insisted that I come, and I, uh . . . let him . . . insist."

"Would you be available for a callback?"

"When do you think that might be?"

"We'll, if you're busy, we can arrange . . ."

"No, no, call whenever you want."

"Are you in another production now?"

"Not that I can think of." I caught myself. "No, not at the moment."

"We may start rehearsing right away. Is that a problem for you?"

"I can't think of a problem."

"Good, then. We'll be in touch."

God, I hope so. I managed to find the door. I somehow made my way to the exit and back past the narrow hallway where other actors and actresses were still waiting. I glided down the stairs, and by some mystical movement that propelled me forward, I reached the door that led outside, where the cool early-evening air brushed across my face and shoulders, reminding me that I was still a part of the universe, the earth, still living in Los Angeles, standing in front of the Windmill Theater.

I walked for hours down Sunset Boulevard with no hint of fatigue, in a state of euphoria. The evening gradually deepened around me to a violet dusk. Streetlights winked on, and somewhere above, the invisible stars emerged unseen. Traffic was hushed. Storefront displays shimmered, and the warmth of convivial restaurants glowed in invitation. It wasn't until after nine, when I looked at my watch, that I knew Emma would be concerned. I picked up speed and started jogging back to the Fiat.

Emma was asleep, snoring gently in her room. So I took an eternally long bath and crawled into bed. Relieved that the whole ordeal was over, still vibrating from the rush, I went through the audition again and again. Did I go too far? Did I not go far enough? Should I have spoken in a Russian accent? *Allen Cahill, Allen Cahill, Allen Cahill. What a hunk! Oh, Sandra, go to sleep.* Who could sleep? All I could think about was his face and his neatly trimmed dark beard and the way his eyes sparkled in the spotlight.

I couldn't tell from the stage. But I was pretty sure he was taller than me.

The next morning I stumbled into the bathroom without turning on a light. The glare would have blinded me for sure. Clutching the sink, fumbling for my toothbrush in the cabinet, I tore off a piece of paper that was taped to the mirror and swept it into the wastebasket. It wasn't until I started to brush my teeth that I thought there might have been a reason the paper was taped to the mirror. I pulled it back out of the basket, uncrumpled the scrunches, and read Emma's slightly shaky handwriting:

Congratulations, you got the part! They called this morning. You start tomorrow at 10:00 A.M.

I gasped, almost fainted. *They made their decision so soon? Not even a callback? I guess I <u>didn't</u> go too far. The director liked me. He really liked me! There were so many girls. Oh my God!* I sat down on the sink counter and read the paper three more times to make sure that what I read was correct, and then I yelled at the top of my lungs, "Yahoo! I did it! We did it!"

I went to Emma's bedroom door to see if she was there, but the door was open and she wasn't inside. She was in the living room, in her chair, reading, of course, the *New York Times*.

"Wahoo! We did it!" I screamed again. Then I gave her a big hug and started dancing around the living room like a lunatic, doing jumping jacks. "We have to celebrate! How are we going to celebrate? I know, let's go out for breakfast. Come on, I'll take you to Denny's. I wish I could afford the Polo Lounge at the Beverly Hills Hotel, but Denny's will have to do for now. Come on, Emma." I grabbed her arm to gently pull her up.

"This is great news, Sandra, but I can't leave the house right now. I'm expecting a call."

"Okay, okay." I stepped back and thought for a second. "How about I make you breakfast in bed?"

"I'm already up," Emma said.

"Okay! Why don't you go back to bed? I want to have the honor of making you breakfast in bed."

"That's ridiculous; I'm dressed. If you want to go through the needless trouble of preparing breakfast, I'll sit in my chair and eat it."

"Fine, sit in your chair. I am going to make you the most awesome Hawaiian French toast and coffee and scrambled eggs and fruit salad and . . . what else?"

I turned on the radio and danced around the kitchen while I prepared Emma's breakfast: pouring orange juice into wineglasses, taking out the gold silverware, and borrowing a plastic flower from one of the arrangements sitting on the windowsill to place in a vase.

While Emma sat contemplating her breakfast on a tray on her lap, I ran back to Josef's room and pulled out my Three Dog Night album. I rushed back, placed the record on her old record player, and out boomed "Joy to the World." I pushed the coffee table and chairs and ottoman to the side, and before Emma had a chance to finish her first bite, I asked: "May I have this dance?"

She smiled, slid the tray onto her side table, and lifted herself slowly from the high-back. I extended a gentlemanly arm, and we danced around the room. God, we must have looked ridiculous, this beanpole towering over this tiny woman. Neither one of us was quite sure who was leading, and neither one of us really caring.

When the song was over, I bowed from the waist, thanked her, and helped her back to her chair. Both of us out of breath, we sat in our respective seats trying to regain our composure.

"It's about time you received a decent part. Now you can show people what you can do. You have no more excuses."

I sat there smiling, speechless.

Emma reached for her breakfast tray, unfurled her napkin, and removed her glasses. "You've waited a long time for this, Sandra. Emotional perspective is very important now. You must do your best to stay centered."

"I know, I know," I said, as I got down on the floor to ground my excitement and begin my morning warm-ups. I had no idea what I was going to do for the rest of the day. Tomorrow couldn't come soon enough for me. My head was swimming with all kinds of thoughts, mostly about the fact that I'd actually gotten both parts . . . and the director.

chapter  21

Water flows to unite with water. . . .
Thus every member finds that his true interest
lies in holding together . . .

To be in a play whose characters finally had some substance, to take part in a well-written script, professionally directed . . . and work with seasoned actors who were as committed to the acting process as I was . . . well, all I could think of was, *If this is my truck, I'm taking the brakes off—'cause I'm ready for the ride.*

The first day of rehearsal was always my favorite. It was when all the cast members sat around and read the script out loud. In a relaxed ambience, we listened to each other's voices, sensed each other's style and tempo, and got a glimpse of who the characters were, even though they'd not yet taken form. Anticipation filled the cavernous space as we gathered round, excited for the process to begin. The eager cast pulled the old, beat-up metal chairs around the table and sat down. One by one, we introduced ourselves: Marlene Kennedy; Bob Driscoll; Frank Geraldi; Sandra Billings; Bill Fleishman. Each of us gave a short synopsis of our professional past. Including the director.

"Hi, my name is Allen Cahill. I'll be your director." There was applause from the cast, who obviously knew him from his TV work directing cop shows and sitcoms. He had recently played a role in a Robert Altman film, not yet titled. He went on to discuss the play—and how Clifford Thorne, the author, was able to capture the essence of czarist Russia and turn the play into a contemporary "dramedy" (drama-comedy). As he spoke, his eyes roamed from one person to the next. Until those flashing dark eyes journeyed over to me. And then, well, I tried to listen, I tried to be alert, but I couldn't concentrate on what he was saying. I sat there watching his lips and the way his mustache moved when he spoke. The only sound in the room was the rhythmic beating of my heart.

So what if he was twenty years my senior! Who was going to judge me? This was Hollywood. My body trembled with fear and delight.

We read the play from beginning to end. Then our director called a lunch break.

Everyone took off to nearby restaurants. Bill Fleishman invited me to go, and I would have, had I been able to sense my legs or stand steadily on my feet. I was emotionally spent, and felt way too exposed. I thanked him for the invitation and told him I'd brought my lunch—which I had. I waited until everyone left, and climbed off the stage. I looked around the auditorium for the perfect seat and found it, in the back row. I was happy for the silence and opened my bag lunch.

I couldn't eat. I stared at the red velvet seats, thinking of all the bodies that had sat there over the years. I glanced up and saw the sparkling chandeliers, with a few missing crystals. The floor was black, but you could see the scuff marks from the soles of recent patrons. I closed my eyes to take it all in and heard two feet walking leisurely up the aisle. I opened my eyes slightly and saw a pair of men's shoes come into the light, then trouser cuffs and wrinkled khaki pant legs, held up by a red leather belt. And as the steps came closer, my heart started leaping like a cricket hopping from one piece of grass to another.

Mr. Cahill came closer. He was holding a bag lunch, too.

"May I sit down, or would you prefer to be alone?"

"Please, have a seat," I replied.

He smelled of baby powder when he sat beside me. I wondered if this was his signature scent.

"What did *you* bring for lunch?" he asked.

"Tuna fish. It's awful. I was out of celery and onions. It's no good without the crunch, you know?"

"I know. The crunch."

We both looked at each other, but I quickly looked away.

"You're quite a committed actress."

"Because I like crunchy salad?"

"No." He laughed. "Because your audition was terrific. Jerry told me you were talented, but, I must say, you impressed a lot of people that day . . . I don't want to give you a swollen head or anything."

"It's okay, my head's been deflated for years." I took a bite out of my sandwich, wanting to look at him, but afraid he'd see . . . too much desire. "It's amazing Jerry recommended me. I mean, he'd never even seen me perform."

"He has good instincts. It's what makes him a good writer. I've read his work, which is why I trusted the guy . . . hey, I detect a Midwestern accent."

"Michigan. And you?"

"San Diego. But I've been in L.A. for twenty-three years."

I looked him in the eye this time. "Have you been a director long?"

He held my gaze for a second and then dug for more chips. "Not long enough in the theater. Too long directing TV. If I had my choice, I'd be directing theater most of the time, and a film once a year."

"If I had *my* choice, I'd just be *working.*"

I wanted our conversation to continue through rehearsal, and for the rest of the night. I wanted to be lifted into his arms and carried home to his bedroom—to be seduced, ravished, my clothes torn off. I wanted to feel his body pressed to mine, feel the sweat from our heat. And at the end of our lovemaking, I imagined myself lying beside him, breathing in his baby-powder scent, while my head lay pillowed on his chest. *How many women has Mr. Cahill had? Is he close to anyone now? Is he just another hairy Greek god, or is there potential for something long-term?* Oh, the thoughts that consumed me, until we returned to the stage!

There was no light in the kitchen when I walked in through the door, only a small reflection from the living room, and the aroma of chicken soup steaming in a pot. The dining-room table was set for one. I peeked around the corner from the kitchen into the living room and saw Emma sitting in her chair, reading the *New York Times,* looking like she was ready for sleep.

She must have heard me come in. She put down the paper, took off her glasses, and turned in my direction. "A box came today, with a card in your name. Do you know who might have sent it?"

I was afraid to guess. "I have no idea."

Emma spoke coolly, removed. "Why not open the refrigerator and take out the box."

I opened the fridge and removed the long box, setting it down on the counter by the sink. Layers of green tissue unfurled before twelve white roses came into view, their petals tightly closed.

"Holy smokes! They're beautiful!" I picked up the card: "'Dear Sandra, congratulations! I'm glad I gambled.' They're from Jerry Aldridge. What a guy. Oh, damn—ah, sorry, Emma. I forgot to call him. I'll call him from the theater."

I brought out the vase from under the sink and filled it with cool water, sliding the stems of the sleeping roses down to the bottom of the glass. I placed the bouquet on the dining-room table and looked over at Emma. "What a sweet thing to do."

She didn't let on if she was pleased or not. "Is Jerry the man from Bert's party?"

"Yes," I said, still lost in amazement.

I inhaled the scent of the petals and sat down at the table. I couldn't believe my life. How quickly it had gone from no men to two men, from no play to two roles, from being bored out of my mind to getting up every day and going to a theater.

Emma leaned forward, turned to me. "Tell me, dear. How was your first day?"

"Well." I got up and ladled soup into a bowl, grateful for it steaming on the stove. "Emma, it is *sooo* satisfying to be in a production where I'm finally working with professionals. No prima donnas. You know, actors who need to be told how great they are every second or else they can't perform. Not here. These actors don't just *say* their lines. There's meaning behind them, feeling behind them. And they listen to each other, to the director, to themselves. It used to drive me crazy when actors weren't there—I mean really *there*, you know. You'd be saying your lines, wanting them to react to you, and you knew that all they wanted you to do was finish your lines, so they could say theirs. Boy, that really irked me . . ."

I sat down near her and told her about the play and the cast, the old theater and the reading. I kept talking to make up for my absence today, and for all the weeks ahead. I talked to make up for the mother she didn't have, the father who was strict and unforgiving. I kept talking about everything that had happened, from the minute I walked into the theater, until the end of the day. I told her everything, except about Allen. I didn't want a lecture. I was too tired. I got up from my seat. "I have to get some sleep. Sweet dreams, Emma."

Despite my fatigue, I washed my soup bowl in the kitchen, walked into my room, and pulled out the *I Ching*. I needed to know what was going on with Allen, and perhaps with Jerry. I needed to know how I felt, what to do. Not able to decide what, or who, to throw it on, I flipped one of the dimes to be safe. *Heads I cast the coins on Allen, tails on Jerry.*

Heads it was. *Thank God.* I held the dimes in the palm of my hand and thought about the question: Allen *was* the question. I closed my eyes and focused on all the things that attracted me to him. And then I threw the coins.

The hexagram said:

4. Mêng / Youthful Folly

Above: Kên, Keeping Still, Mountain
Below: K'an, The Abysmal, Water

Keeping still is the attribute of the upper trigram; that of the lower is the abyss, danger. Stopping in perplexity on the brink of a dangerous abyss is a symbol of the folly of youth . . . When the spring gushes forth, it does not know at first where it will go. But its steady flow fills up the deep place blocking its progress, and success is attained.

What the hell did *that* mean?

Often the teacher, when confronted with such entangled folly, has no other course but to leave the fool to himself for a time, not sparing him the humiliation that results.

Fool? Humiliation?

This is frequently the only means of rescue.

To what?

For youthful folly it is the most hopeless thing to entangle itself in empty imaginings. The more obstinately it clings to such unreal fantasies, the more certainly will humiliation overtake it.

This throw was way off. None of this was accurate. Not a single line. *I'm throwing the coins again.*

I took the coins and placed them in my hand, closed my eyes, and shook them really hard this time. I wanted to be sure the dimes were tumbling freely. I dropped them onto the bed. Two heads and a tail. Eight. I drew a broken line on the legal pad and then picked up the coins. Three heads. Nine. I drew a straight line right above the broken line. I threw them again. Three tails, three tails, three tails again. I drew three broken lines above the straight line and then picked them up for the last time and closed my eyes. Afraid to see what the last throw would be, I dropped the coins. They came up three heads. I didn't have to draw the straight line. I knew what the hexagram was. It was number 4—again. Youthful Folly.

I'd planned on throwing the coins on Jerry, but I fell asleep.

CHAPTER  22

*After the change is made, it is necessary
to note carefully for some time after
how the improvements bear the test of actuality.*

Decked out in thick black-framed glasses, with a thin, unsure-of-himself body and a heavy New York accent that cracked everyone up whenever he delivered a line, Bill Fleishman was someone it was hard to stand next to and maintain a straight face. Even though his jokes weren't that funny, his Silly Putty face, contorted into a cartoonish character, made me break my concentration every time. He had a crush on me, for sure. But he knew, without any proclamation from me, that this heart belonged to someone other than him.

Like some frustrated, underpaid journalist from the *National Enquirer,* Bill filled me in on the history of each actor. As we sat in the audience, waiting for our scenes to be called, he gave me the scoop on Marlene Kennedy, Bob Driscoll, and Frank Geraldi, as they were called up onstage.

Marlene, he told me, had once been a sought-after child actress, repeatedly cast in soap operas and commercials. Marlene was about thirty-five now, at least that's what Bill had guessed as she paraded across the stage with her husky voice, flaming red hair, and a pair of knockers that would make Zsa Zsa seethe with jealousy. She'd been touring in *The Music Man* and *The Sound of Music,* Bill said, "before her career shifted from acting to drugs."

"She must have been quite a knockout," I said.

"She's not too shabby now," Bill responded, "even just out of rehab, divorced, and bringing up three boys on her own. This show, I bet, is her return from exile."

Bob Driscoll was chosen, without question, for his body type. He certainly couldn't act. A tall, lanky man, Bob looked awkward onstage. Perhaps the director cast him solely because of this attribute. Personally, I didn't think the man was going to last through the production. Bill didn't either.

Frank Geraldi was familiar to everyone, known worldwide as the potato-chip king. His face had graced national television commercials for years. Bill said he wouldn't be a bit surprised if most of the audience would be coming to see Frank. "That would be grand," I told him. "I hope all his fans come so they fill the chairs and then tell their family and friends."

"Ya know," Bill remarked, "our director's been through the marriage door a couple of times himself. He's got at least three kids that I know of." That was of interest to note.

Bill stopped gossiping, and we watched as our director began to work his magic. All eyes were glued as Mr. Cahill stopped the scene and asked the actors to imagine that they were in another country, another time period. He wanted them to explore different scenarios, so they wouldn't become one-dimensional. It was captivating to see what happened to each actor when they resisted versus when they surrendered and let go. There was an immediate distinction that either stopped the action or moved it forward. What an education I was getting, sitting here watching these actors play this out.

Allen Cahill knew the art, heart, and soul of directing. He knew how to pull out core emotions you didn't even know you had. And then he'd mold them without your being aware of the adjustment, allowed you to go off on tangents for long stretches of time, knowing just how far to let you roam before bringing you back to center. As much as he had a passion for control, he knew when to give it up. His innate gift for finding the subtext in each scene, adding just the right touch of spice, like a seasoned chef, to each vignette, was compelling to observe.

He was explosive and contained, sensitive and firm, always aware of what he wanted and when. And as I sat there melting in the chair, ignoring the fact that Bill Fleishman was still next to me cutting jokes, I watched this master magician in action.

We were deep into rehearsals, and I was growing impatient that Allen hadn't come over to me, other than with comments about the play. We hadn't shared any more lunches. As much as I wanted to stay detached, I craved more of those encounters. I just didn't know how to make them happen. I didn't want to be demanding. Our director seemed to be moving through a tumultuous time. I couldn't tell if it was personal or professional, but something was off.

This morning, he was deep in thought as he circled the back of the auditorium. He was pacing. I knew he wasn't thinking about the scene. The conviction in his voice was missing. Instead, he was spacey and withdrawn. There *had* to be something going on, because Mr. Cahill never once acknowledged what had happened between us. And there were just certain signs within the universal law of male-female attraction that were undeniable. Like when two humans came close and waves of electricity ignited between them so unmistakably that if you touched either person, you would get a shock. How could he not have experienced this exchange?

When we did speak, he would canvass my face, stare at my lips, search my eyes for confirmation. I knew he wanted to know if I was attracted to him, if I was interested in pursuing the relationship further. *Jesus, why doesn't he just ask?* I wondered. Maybe he was too familiar with the dangers of getting romantically involved during a production. Maybe he was shy. Maybe he was smart and cautious.

"Sorry to bother you, Ms. Billings," the stage manager said, handing me a note. "I was asked to give this to you right away."

"Thank you." My first thought was . . . something terrible had happened to Emma. I quickly unfolded the small yellow paper. Instead I read: "Can you escape for a few minutes and go for a ride? If you aren't outside at 12:15, I'll understand and call you later. I'm in a dilemma. Hope you can make it. Jerry."

Hmm. I looked at my watch. *It's almost noon, I've already rehearsed my scenes for the morning, and I'm not scheduled again until after lunch. Allen wouldn't miss me. Or maybe he would.* I took the script, grabbed my jacket, sidled quietly out of the theater, and ran to the corner café to get a salad and a Tab. Then back to the theater . . .

Jerry was there, waiting, in a blue Audi. His puppy-dog eyes smiled as he leaned over and opened the door.

"Hi, Sandra. Sorry for being so last-minute. I need a second opinion about something and thought you might like the break. Can you spare a few minutes?"

I got in the car, closed the door. "Perfect timing! I *can* use a break. How are you? Did you get the message I left? Thank you so much for the flowers. They were beautiful."

"I did get your message, and you are very welcome." Jerry started the car and off we went. I had no idea where.

"Oh, Jerry, I still can't thank you enough. If it weren't for you, I would never have known about the audition."

"Good things happen to good people. How's the play going?"

"It's wonderful, challenging, exciting. By the way, didn't I have to be an Equity member to get into this production?"

Jerry smiled again. "Actors are allowed into productions without representation or guild affiliation as long as the director is willing to sign a waiver. You can get your Equity card anytime now. As far as an agent is concerned, there'll probably be a few in the audience opening night."

"Please don't tell me that. If I start thinking about opening night and an agent, I won't be able to function."

"Bert told me you were staying with his friend Emma. I saw her on my way out of the party. She seems like a lovely woman."

"She *is* a lovely woman."

"How has Allen been treating you?"

"Oh." I choked on my Tab. "He's been a perfect gentleman . . . Where are we going?"

"I've been looking at houses, and I've narrowed it down to two. I can't make up my mind. One is very expensive, and the other is closer to being reasonable. I need help. I'm getting tired of the cold walls of condominium living. You don't know me very well, but I have two boys from a previous marriage, and I'd like them to have separate rooms to sleep in. Right now they're sleeping in the same room on futons."

"How old are they?"

"Jeremy is six; Kevin is eight. They're great. They just need some room, a yard, and a dog."

"I know what you mean. I'd like any one of those myself."

"So . . . you don't mind taking a ride? I'd like to know what you think."

"Not at all. I'm an architecture addict. My father was a builder, so I've spent a lot of time watching cement trucks pour concrete into big holes."

"Really?" He laughed his loving laugh.

"Oh yeah. I used to study his blueprints before I walked through his houses—just to test the dimensions against the drawings and get the feel for how they translated into real space."

"I'm impressed."

"Oh, please! I used to love looking at those tiny architectural models, the ones that look like little dollhouses. Do you have any idea how they make grass for the lawns of those little houses?"

"I have no idea, but I think you're going to tell me."

"They dye sawdust and put it through a strainer. To make trees, they take foam, whip it in a blender, and then dye the foam all different shades of green . . . Guess how they make bathtubs?"

"They take a normal-size tub and shrink it in a oven?"

"No, they use dental compound and make tiny little molds. And when they need a roof, they crush granulated sand with a rolling pin, spray it with black lacquer, and dry it with a hair dryer."

"Well. I had no idea I was asking a pro."

"Do you want some salad?"

"No, thanks. I have an early dinner party."

I ate my salad carefully, not spilling a crumb on his beige leather seats. He was so easy to talk to, so much fun to be around. And he was giving me a lot more attention than Mr. Cahill was at the moment. I rolled down the window and inhaled the tang of the sea air.

After a beautiful drive, Jerry and I arrived at our destination, just a few blocks from the beach. The air felt so rejuvenating that I wanted to jump into my running gear and sprint along the coast, but I looked at my watch and couldn't believe time had passed so fast.

"Jerry, we have to get moving."

"Here are the houses."

"These two? Right here, in front of us?"

"Yep, right next to each other."

"That makes it convenient. Do you have keys?"

"I tried calling the Realtor, but she wasn't there."

"Can we peek in the windows?"

"Sure. No one lives in either house."

I leapt out of the Audi and walked up to the house I found less appealing first. Years of study moved me quickly into high gear.

The first house was Spanish, with a pueblo look to it: flat roof, small chimney, and very few windows. There was an unattractive square window in the front door, and when I looked through it, I saw a hideous staircase right behind the door, taking up half the visual space. "Why do builders do that?" I muttered. "Who wants to open a door and be greeted by steps? It makes the entryway so uninviting. This house has no chance, and it's an embarrassment to Spanish architecture."

The second house had much more style. It, too, was Span-ish, but more eclectic. Graceful proportions. There were three wings, distinguished by variations in the height of the roofline, with a Renaissance-inspired entryway. The clincher for me was the stained-glass window placed perfectly under the cross-gable tile roof, and a huge lawn that swept the length of the house. I climbed atop a low rock wall and stood on tiptoe to look inside the grand picture window, and there it was: an iron spiral staircase. So dramatic! So enchanting! I turned around to tell Jerry he was crazy to consider the other house, when I lost my balance and fell straight into his arms.

"Oh, I didn't realize you were right there."

"I *am* right here."

"You certainly are."

He looked at me with such desire that I could hardly speak, and then he leaned in to kiss me. I searched my soul for a reason to give in. Was it really *my* desire? Wasn't I just using him to make Allen jealous? I looked deep into his soft brown eyes, his face, aware of his strong arms. I wanted to kiss him because he was kind and gentle and I trusted him, but I knew how I felt . . .

We kissed.

I shouldn't have. I disengaged. "You, *ahhh* . . . must be in pret-ty good shape to catch me without falling over," I said, trying to lessen the intensity of the moment. "This house has my vote." I pulled away and straightened out my shirt.

"I had a feeling you'd like that one," he said.

I looked at my watch again. "We have to get going, Jerry. I am going to be *sooo* late."

On our race back to the theater, I learned that the house I was in favor of was substantially pricier than the one I disliked. But, I explained to Jerry, there was no decision to be made. "The house that is meant for you will let you know. Trust me, you won't be able to sleep or work or anything until you arrive at the right deci-sion. It will become very clear."

He drove me back to the theater. As I reached for the door handle, Jerry said, "Thanks for coming, Sandra." He leaned over to offer me his lips. An offer I hesitated to accept, but then did.

"Can I call you at Emma's?"

"Sure. Thanks for the diversion, and the tour. Talk to you soon."

"'Bye, Sandra."

The back door to the theater was heavy-duty metal, with a squeak that would set your teeth on edge if you happened to be within range of its echoing shriek. I thought it would be easy to sneak in, make an invisible entrance, and fool everyone into thinking I'd been there all along. But the actors were onstage when the door screeched the announcement of my arrival. I walked meekly onto the stage, found a spot to place my embarrassed body within the semicircle around Allen, and listened intently to his critique of the previous scene.

I could tell our director was annoyed with me. *Hmm, maybe I was missed!* I apologized for being late, but he ignored my appeal. After he concluded his notes, he asked us to redo the scene. Fortunately, I knew the lines. Perhaps there'd be some mercy from our director after he'd seen how easily I flowed with the other actors. He only had to stop the action once to remind me of a specific blocking. But when he did, we all experienced the leaping of the lion from its cage. The anger reverberating in his voice made it only too plain to me, and everyone else, that the director was agitated—and it wasn't about the blocking.

It took the rest of the afternoon before his anger dissipated. When the hand of the clock finally pointed to seven, we were ready to leave. I couldn't wait to go home, light some incense, and crawl into bed.

Everyone waved their good-byes, and when I opened the big black door to exit the theater, there stood Allen leaning against his shiny white Porsche. Without warning, without any preliminary dialogue to soften the impact, he asked, "I hope you had a good excuse to be late today."

"I did," I said. "I had to help a friend." I didn't want to go into detail.

"How about joining me for dinner?" he asked unexpectedly.

"Dinner?" *Oh God,* I thought. *What a question.* Did I want to have dinner with him? Did I want to sit in a romantic restaurant, watch the fire burn and the wood crackle, laugh, share stories, drink wine, and cuddle? (Make a guess.) But he'd caught me off guard. I was exhausted from rehearsal, and afraid I wouldn't have anything intelligent to say. And then there was Emma. So I hesitated.

"I'd love to join you for dinner," I said, "only I live with an older woman, who I haven't spent much time with since rehearsals started. Would you mind just walking me home? I live only a few blocks away." The truth was, I had driven my car to rehearsal. But I could get up early tomorrow morning and walk to the theater.

"Sure," he said, without pausing.

The Los Angeles sky was dark, and if you stared into the blue-ness long enough, you could glimpse the barest hint of a star. The traffic was slow, and we hardly spoke as we strolled down Sunset Boulevard. I could feel his desire to be with me. I could sense his longing to be close. I didn't know if he longed to be with *me,* or simply with any woman. And as much as I wanted to know the answer, this was not the time to obsess about it. I didn't want to miss this or any other moment.

We looked into store windows, made our opinions known about the upcoming season's fashions. We talked about how much the cement sidewalks were in need of repair, and how tarnished the bell on the church had become. There was a synchronized rhythm to our speech and in the way we took each step. And yet there was a holding back. I wanted to know why. What was going on with him? Thousands of words went unspoken. The air grew thick with emotion. We rounded the corner.

Knowing I was almost home, I was bursting to ask him a million questions, I could only come out with one: "So, the play's going well, don't you think?"

"The play is going well," he responded.

"I think the play's going well, too."

"Bob Driscoll, I thought, would be stronger. He's not hitting the notes. I might have to let him go."

"Yes. I actually thought he was kind of weak for the part. It's too bad. He's a nice guy."

Then we simultaneously blurted out:

"Are you seeing anyone?"

"Are you involved with anyone now?"

We laughed at how ridiculous we sounded, like goofy teenagers trying to find out if the other one was "taken"; then he turned to me with fiery eyes. "Sandra, I just got out of a relationship that should have ended months ago, and . . . I don't want to rush into another. But I want you to know that I am attracted to you, and I would love you to . . ."

I closed my eyes because I knew this was a dream I wanted to remain immersed in. I closed my eyes because I loved his voice and the sound of it resonated more when I listened that way. It was familiar, as if I had heard this voice lifetime after lifetime. Who knew who we were before? Who cared?

He kissed me and held me, and I responded with the same fervor. He took my hand, and we walked slowly toward Emma's apartment. Then he turned to me with those dark eyes and stroked my hair with his fingers.

"Your hair—it's like a thick, rich mane."

"I was a horse in a past life."

"A magnificent mare, no doubt."

"And what were *you* while I galloped around the countryside looking for a place to escape from the demands of the Wild West?"

"Oh, I captured you"—he lightly touched my hair—"don't you remember, and turned you into my getaway steed while I robbed the local banks and trains."

"I must have been a loyal horse, dedicated to the cause. Had you always been involved in these acts of charitable accomplishment?"

"I needed the money to feed my horse."

"Selflessness is a commendable trait. Thank you for accompanying me home."

"Have dinner with me next week?"

"Why, I'd just *love* to have *dinnah* with you next week." I always seemed to break a serious emotional moment with a Southern accent.

"I'll look forward to it. Good night," he said, and as I entered the lobby of the building, my past-life proprietor disappeared down the block.

I ascended in the elevator. Not wanting to break the spell, I stood on the landing and looked down over the railing, still breathing in his baby powder and aftershave. Remembering the feel of his mustache on my lips, rubbing my lip with my tongue to savor his touch. Imagining he was still in my arms. I floated into the apartment and found Emma sitting in her chair with no book in her hand, no newspaper before her face, no script on her lap, her eyes fixed upon air.

"Hello," I said softly, not wanting to break *her* trance.

"Hello," she said, faintly, from somewhere far away.

"Want some tea?" I asked.

"No, thanks," she replied, still in her state of absorption.

I stopped to really look at her. "Are you okay, Emma?"

"Yes, I'm fine." She moved her head a little, as if to clear it. "Did you eat?"

"I'm not very hungry."

"How did rehearsal go?"

"Great, great," I said, wanting to say good night and hightail it out of there. But I couldn't leave her sitting there, not in the state she was in, looking so lonely. She'd been by herself all day, and for the past month. I sat down next to her and took a deep breath.

"Well, Bill Fleishman, I'm afraid, is going to steal the show. He is so funny! He plays this guy who sneezes constantly and gets in trouble because of his sneezing, which ultimately becomes a political showdown. But the doctor, Bob Driscoll, has mercy for the man, and . . . what am I doing? I'm not telling you any more about the play because if I do, you'll be totally bored when you see it."

I got up and rummaged in the fridge for a carrot, and began to peel it over the sink. "Did you do anything special today?" I asked from the kitchen, hoping she had something new to share.

"I heard from Josef."

"Oh, that's great. What did he have to say?"

"He's fine."

I walked back into the living room, suddenly realizing what she'd said. I looked at her in disbelief. "Excuse me, you heard from *Josef?*"

"Sometimes I stare at Josef's paintings and remember the smell of his oil paints and the sound his brushes used to make when he cleaned them. Tap, tap, tap." She looked so peaceful in her memory of him. "He'd always tap the brush like that. Tap, tap, tap. Today, I felt his presence so strongly, I heard him tapping the brushes on the can, and whistling."

"Maybe his spirit is still here, and you're sensing it. That happens, I'm sure of it. There have been lots of books written about people coming back to visit their loved ones and communicating with them on subtle levels."

I'd hit a nerve, I saw, without meaning to. So I rushed on: "The Bodhi Tree has tons of books on this topic. I'll take you there, whenever you want to go. It's a beautiful store, with all kinds of books on past-life experiences and near-death . . ."

I was babbling because I felt helpless and couldn't think of anything to say that might ease her loss. And for the first time, I saw a tear drop onto her cheek, which she quickly wiped away. She stood up without saying another word and went to her room. I waited until she closed her door, and then I went into my room to return to *my* dream.

The bedroom had now become a barometer, a psychic measuring device that would assess my state. There would be nights I'd be so angry that the room was so small, so filled with Josef's things—pictures hanging on every wall, leaning against bureaus, stacked in corners—that I felt suffocated and wanted to tear them down. Other times, I'd feel so expanded, so content to lose myself in the colorful, animated scenes, especially the painting of the pale beach and the brilliant sun reflecting on the aquamarine water.

Or I'd pretend to be any one of the figures in his paintings. I would enter their world, reach into their personae, and lose myself. But tonight there was no need to escape anywhere. I had plenty of colors on my own palette to create my own painting.

As I dreamed myself back into Allen's embrace, all this love welled up inside me . . . and all that love filled the entire room.

CHAPTER 23

The superior man sets his life in order
And examines himself.

Chaos reigned during the final weeks. Rehearsals raced by. It was a pressure I hadn't experienced since the year I spent in college, during final exams, when every minute, every second, had to be accounted for, and there was no time to waste on incidentals or pleasures. No time for TV, movies, or dates; only studying, cramming, and lots of stimulants, mostly caffeine. There might have been a few uppers—after all, I did live in Detroit. The only difference now was that the cast of characters was older, and we weren't being graded—at least with letters. Our grade would come the day after opening night when the public read the critics' reviews.

Life was intense at the Windmill Theater. But we all knew the sacrifices we made today would lead to our growth as actors, future opportunities, and a deep feeling of satisfaction. At least these were *my* objectives. Still, the cast of *The Turning of the Century* complained about having to come in early and leave late. They missed their families. Free time. A life. *I* missed the possibility of sitting on a couch with Allen in front of a fireplace, drinking wine and watching the sunset, taking long walks and holding hands, dancing beneath the stars. Just holding him and being held would be enough.

To top things off, an incident occurred that really set us back. Bob Driscoll, the man Bill and I thought couldn't act worth beans, the man Allen thought was slowing the production down, was fired. The cast had to take turns filling in for his role while Allen looked for a replacement. After interviewing several actors, he hired Kevin Hawthorne, a Broadway understudy who was, luckily for us, a *quick* study.

It was now a Friday, and we were all looking forward to a relaxing, replenishing weekend. I was looking forward to having dinner with Allen. It was our scheduled date night. But before leaving the theater, he made an announcement: "I was going to call a rehearsal for tomorrow. But I have to go to New York. You've got a two-day respite. Just don't make any plans for the following weekends; we're going to need them before opening night. See you Monday at nine."

At least we had these two days to relax. Everyone said their good-byes and took off. I went to my dressing room to prepare for our dinner date. The one Allen had promised the night he walked me home. Although he had postponed it once already, I was anticipating being with him tonight—big-time.

I was prepping—brushing my hair, sprucing up my makeup, and studying the newly formed zit on the side of my nose—when there was a knock on the door.

"May I come in?" Allen asked in a hushed voice outside the door.

"The door's open," I stage-whispered loudly back.

He stepped inside, came over to the dressing table, and sat down on the edge of it. "I know we were supposed to have dinner tonight. And I feel awful that I have to postpone this again. I wish this meeting hadn't come up, but I have to leave tonight."

"That's fine." I was feeling cocky. I put down the brush and stood up to reach for my jacket.

He grabbed my arm, gently. "Look at me. I'm as disappointed as you are. You have no idea how much I wanted to be with you tonight. Can we make it next week?"

I couldn't look at him. I turned my head from side to side to avoid his eyes. I didn't want him to see how disappointed I was. I wanted him to blow off his meeting, spend the night, the weekend, the rest of his life, with me. Tears were standing in my eyes, unbidden. I walked toward the door, opened it. "You don't want to be late for your flight, do you?"

He met me at the door. "If I didn't have to go, I wouldn't. This may be an offer to direct a film that I have been waiting a year to negotiate. I can't miss this, no matter how much I want to be with you. You can understand that, can't you?"

He turned off the light and pulled me close. We kissed.

"Believe me," he said, "There isn't anyone else I want to be with."

We kissed again.

"I believe you."

The jolt of disappointment, after the anticipation of being with Allen, left me hollow. As I got into my Fiat, I wondered why my life had to filled with these severe ups and downs that were so devastating and exhausting. *I'm constantly riding on this emotional roller coaster and can't seem to get off. I just wish the ride wasn't so intense.*

It was also intense at home. It felt like I hadn't seen Emma in I couldn't say how long. I'd come home after she'd retired for the night and leave before she got up. I had no time to clean or cook, sit with her and talk, share a smile, or laugh at her sardonic comments. We used to spend hours together, and now I was rushing in and out, treating her apartment like a hotel. We hardly spoke anymore. There was a chasm opening up between us. But what could I do? My life was moving incredibly fast. Time to share it just wasn't there. When I was home, I was memorizing lines, not just for one character, but for two. Exercising, eating, sleeping. I hadn't even told her about Allen. Not that I really wanted to. Because I knew how she'd respond. Emma seemed to be crawling into a shell, getting quieter and quieter. Once again I was at a precipice, and not quite sure how to proceed.

On my way home, I pulled into Renée's Deli. I thought I'd surprise Emma with a deli dinner we could both enjoy: some turkey, salad greens, and a few slices of Monterey Jack. Hoping the small gesture might soothe the wound of our distance and make up for the time I'd been away. There was a bouquet of flowers sitting by the counter in a bucket. I bought them, too.

Bearing gifts of food and good news—the weekend off—I burst into the apartment, where I saw Emma sitting in her chair, on the phone; I couldn't make out with whom. It wasn't Bert or Zelda. I could tell by the way she responded. As I unwrapped the food and got the mustard and mayo out of the fridge, I listened from the kitchen, to get a hint of who might be on the other end of the line.

She cut the conversation short: "It was wonderful to hear from you, Jackson. I'll see you tomorrow. Good-bye."

Who is Jackson?

"Hi, Emma." I jumped right in, wanting to set a cheerful tone. "I stopped at the deli and picked up some dinner."

"I've already eaten, dear." Her words cut into me, even with the word *dear.* "Thank you."

"Sorry I got here so late . . ." I went on nervously, hoping she'd forgive me again. "We had a long rehearsal today."

My stomach felt queasy from her abrupt response and the unstable ground I was now trying to stand on. I peeled off a few slices of turkey, rolled them into a cone, and dipped them into the mustard jar. The silence, thick with her secrets, made my mouth dry. I poured some juice to wash the turkey down.

Emma sat in her chair, pretending to read a magazine, pretending nothing was wrong or out of the ordinary. Trying to feel her out and think of something to say, I put the groceries in the fridge, and the flowers in a tall porcelain vase.

"Oh, Emma, Allen—the director—gave us the weekend off. How about going to a museum tomorrow?"

"I'll be going out with my friend Jackson tomorrow."

I was glad she was going out, visiting with friends. But again, it was the way she said it. Like a defiant schoolgirl! Something was up. Something was off. I brought the flowers into the dining room and placed them on the table.

I tried again. "Have I *met* Jackson?"

"No. He's an old friend from New York. His niece is in town. He wanted us to meet."

"Well, how about we go to the farmers' market on Sunday, pick up some groceries?" If only she'd agree, saying that it was a lovely idea.

"I'll probably rest on Sunday."

"Oh, okay."

I didn't know what else to say. I was afraid to dig any deeper. I stood there looking at her, hoping she'd open up and declare: "Let's have a chat. How was your day?"

It didn't happen. She stood up, holding on to the arms of the chair. Her shoulders set, she walked toward her bedroom. Once inside, she closed the door.

CHaPTer 24

*With the complex of events immediately before one in image form,
one could follow the courses that promised good fortune
and avoid those that promised misfortune,
before the train of events had actually begun.*

I woke up edgy and angry. My eyes were a graphic witness—red and blotchy, with huge, puffy bags. I felt as if I'd wrestled a band of boa constrictors in my sleep. My neck was stiff, and the lower part of my spine ached. But my body was not my concern. There were more pressing things to think about.

Emma.

I could only guess that she was mad at me for not being around, not sticking to our agreement. As I reached over to pull the curtains to one side, let in some light, I knew the one important thing that *had* to be done today was to clean. Something I hadn't done in weeks.

I forced myself out of bed, pulled out a pair of jeans, scooped up a T-shirt from the closet floor, and carried the clothes into the bathroom. I stripped off my pajamas, turned on the shower full force, grabbed the Comet from under the sink, and stepped in. I scrubbed the porcelain tub until the faintest ring had disappeared.

I removed the hair from the drain and rinsed the dried, cakey soap from the soap dish. I removed the shower curtain from the rings and bleached the curtain until all the disgusting mold spots were gone, and then, still naked from the shower, I poured Mop & Glo on the bathroom tiles and sponged the floor, wiped down the cabinets, sprayed Windex on the mirrors, and brushed out the toilet.

I put on my clothes and advanced to the kitchen, where I proceeded to swab the floor until every speck of dirt had vanished, and I tackled the sink until it glistened. I soaked the dish drain and the Rubbermaid pad with bleach until all remnants of dried food disappeared.

While dusting the living-room chairs and windowsills, wiping away my guilt, I admitted to myself: I hadn't followed through on my end. Wiping down the window, making sure there were no streaks, I resolved that it was time to make good on my promise. Perspiring, I headed back toward the closet to get the vacuum cleaner. The telephone ring startled me.

Out of breath, I answered it. "Hello?"

"Hi, Sandra. It's Jerry. I hope it's not too early. I wanted to catch you before you made plans for the day."

"Oh, I'm still here. Just going through my fan mail before the limo picks me up to get my hair done. How are you?"

"Great," he said with a laugh. "Listen, how would you like to go to the marina today? There's this cute little Italian restaurant . . ."

"I would *love* to go. It's just that"—I lowered my voice—"I really need to tidy up the place. I haven't been around much."

"I understand." His voice dropped.

"Thanks for the invite, Jerry."

"Listen, you take care. I'll give you a call soon."

Sigh. I placed the phone back on the table. *God, it would've been good to get out.*

Emma walked into the living room, diffidently, as if she wanted to be invisible. As if she didn't want to be noticed or spoken to. So I went on with my chores and just observed, out of the corner of my eyes. She was wearing a dress I hadn't seen before, a blue cotton print that matched her eyes. She headed straight to the kitchen and made herself some breakfast. Wanting to avoid her, at least until I knew what (if anything) I was going to say, I kept my course in the opposite direction, back to the closet for the vacuum.

While Emma had her bagel and butter, I vacuumed. While she drank her coffee, I wrapped the vac cord. While she rinsed her dishes, I dusted the coffee table and wiped the dust from the plastic couch cover. Timing my approach, I waited until she'd finished the dishes, thinking furiously of something to say.

But she just headed for the coat closet to get her sweater. In the foyer she turned and opened the door. Then, without much expression, as she headed out the door, she said, "Have a nice day, dear."

I sagged against the wall as Emma, and the tension, left the room. *Now what?* This was one of those moments I had experienced way too many times. Being stuck, without a clue what to do. Without thought, I lunged for the phone. *Jerry! Where did I put his card?* I ran to the bedroom, riffled through my purse, and called him back when I found it.

"Jerry? It's Sandra. Can we still go today?"

"Sure! I'll pick you up in an hour."

"Cool."

I gave him the address and rushed to get ready.

We spent the morning walking around Marina del Rey, strolling the boardwalk, looking at grand and expensive yachts, admiring the lavish lives of the rich and famous, the well-to-do's. I could have strolled forever among these boats with this gentle man, slipped the knot from any one of them, and off we could have gone . . . to the Caribbean or Bali. Boy, was I tempted.

"I think that's Bill Bixby's boat." Jerry waved to the man standing on the deck—security, we supposed. Jerry called out to him, "Hi, isn't that Bill Bixby's boat?"

We saw the security man frown, trying to think this through. He finally answered, "I'm not supposed to say."

Jerry roared, and I joined him. As we quieted, he stared, reading me like a page. "Is everything okay with you?"

"Can we talk about something else?" I begged. He was my escape, the diversion I needed yet again—from Emma, from guilt, from my mix of feelings about Allen.

Wanting to lighten my mood, he tried to amuse me: "An Irishman, a midget, a priest, an Italian, and a horse walk into a bar. Bartender says, 'What is this, some kind of joke?'"

I groaned. We both escaped by telling each other the worst jokes we knew. We even sang—the most awful songs. It was the freedom I needed. And then, in the spirit of our joy, he put his arm around my waist as we walked along. He held me close, hip to hip. He paused, and I felt myself become afraid because I knew he was going to kiss me.

"I'm starving." I blocked the momentum. "Instead of Italian, let's get some eggs."

We strolled toward the nearest restaurant, and I listened to him express his enthusiasm when he spoke about breaking into TV and how excited he was that his script was picked up for a Movie of the Week. We'd covered all the arts before we'd finished our omelets. And as we reached for our jackets, he asked about Allen.

"How is he doing? I heard a rumor."

My arm stopped in midreach, and my breath caught. "Oh, what rumor is that?" I asked innocently.

"He's being considered for a blockbuster film. This could really boost his directing career." He was telling the truth.

The air in my lungs was released. "Well, he's a great director. I wouldn't be surprised."

Was Jerry testing me, and my reaction? He wasn't the type to play games. So I let it go, and enjoyed the ride home: the breeze, the scenery passing by, and the ease of the afternoon that continued to flow through my heart.

Before saying good-bye to the man who somehow always brought me back to my center and made me feel safe in my skin, I asked, just to be sure: "You'll be at opening night, won't you?"

"I wouldn't miss it for the world."

Emma was sitting in *her* chair reading the *New York Times* when I returned. I went over and sat down in *my* chair. The chair I had always sat in, ever since I'd moved in, the chair that sat to the other side of the tiny round table that held Emma's lamp, her bagel and tea—the table that now separated our lives. We sat in our little worlds, only inches apart, but tonight, it felt more like galaxies.

"Did you have a nice time with Jackson?" I asked.

"Yes, we had a lovely day." That was it. That was all she said.

Emma put down the paper and removed her bifocals, as if she wanted to tell me something, but changed her mind. Maybe it was all in my mind, but one thing was for sure different now. Whenever we'd talked in the past, she would completely face me, give me her undivided attention. This evening she didn't turn my way a smidgen. She simply stared straight ahead, as if I wasn't there.

I got up and walked into the kitchen, just to stretch the time out, and poured a glass of lemonade. It wasn't until she'd picked up the newspaper again that I walked back into the living room, sat down, and blurted out the words that I'd been holding back for so long.

"Look, Emma, I know you've been spending a lot of time by yourself. And I feel awful about it. I just don't know what to do . . . other than quit the play."

She took a lifetime to answer. "I have plenty of people to keep me busy."

"It's not just weekdays that we're rehearsing. It's weekends, too."

She just listened.

"I know I haven't been cleaning or cooking very much."

"You have a play to work on, Sandra. You should focus on that."

"You have no idea, Emma. I have two parts to learn. I have to memorize the lines, the pacing, the blocking—every move. My emotions are all over the place because . . . I also have a major crush on the director, which I have been wanting to tell you about, and I . . ."

Emma shook her head ever so gently, in what looked like disappointment, and picked up the paper again.

My head was aching; I started massaging my temples. I wanted to yell, but instead asked her calmly, "Please, Emma . . . tell me why you're acting so strange and distant? Did I do something, or not do something, that upset you?"

Emma's fingers nervously clutched the arms of her high-back; her arms shook as she lifted her body from the chair until her feet were solidly planted on the gold carpet. She stood upright and placed one foot in front of the other as she headed toward her room. She stopped midroute and turned, again as if she wanted to say something to me, but couldn't. She turned again. "It's all right, Sandra. I just need to be alone for a while." And then she entered her room, and closed the door.

I sat there shivering, confused. I grabbed my purse. I couldn't breathe. I took the elevator to the garage and got into the Fiat. I turned the key so hard in the ignition that the car made a grinding noise. Pressing down on the accelerator, I nearly backed into the stucco garage wall. I yanked the car into drive, turned the tight corner around the poles, and peeled up the ramp. I left a lot of black rubber on the cement. A couple of old ladies watched with their eyes wide open in amazement.

I knew where I wanted to go: to the top of Mulholland Drive, the highest point in L.A., with one of the best views of the city. And I wanted to get there fast. I'd go there when I needed to see the world from a loftier perspective—when I couldn't put all the pieces of my life together in my brain, or when I thought about jumping off someplace tall.

I pressed the pedal to the floor and went through a red light, whizzed past broken-down shacks and Spanish estates, watching the dust shoot up in my rearview as I passed. My wheels spun, skidded corners, and jumped curbs. I kept climbing faster, running stop sign after stop sign. Cutting across the middle line, I took a sharp left . . . and, *Oh shit,* almost hit an oncoming BMW.

A hundred yards up the hill my rearview registered the man still sitting in his car shaking, wondering what had nearly hit him.

I wasn't far now from the top of the mountain, only a few hundred feet away. I ran another stop sign, as a mother and daughter were crossing the street. The young girl was dancing, twirling in circles, and laughing. The mother looked up in alarm. She must have heard me coming. I slammed on the brakes as hard as I could. Tires squealing, I swerved sideways, then sat there in a cloud of burning rubber. I'd come *that* close to hitting them.

I looked over. They were fine.

And *that* was when I pulled over and turned off the engine. Ashamed, embarrassed, I pressed my head against the steering wheel. My hands dropped their grip on the wheel, and my head fell back against the headrest.

I rolled down the window to take in some fresh air. It wasn't enough. I opened the door, climbed out of the Fiat, and walked across the road toward a broad-trunked coffee-colored eucalyptus tree.

I sat down on its roots. My spine relaxed against the tree's firm presence. I looked up at the ribboned leaves above me, stirring softly in a breeze too light to feel. I wished they were closer so I could wrap them around my body and feel them enfolding me. I closed my eyes and imagined the bark breathing life into my back, the tree supporting me with its strength, its age. With every breath, the tree responded. I could feel it exhale when I inhaled, inhale when I exhaled. I allowed my entire being to surrender into the tree's embrace.

As we kept breathing in unison, the tree and I, I reviewed the last few months of my life, to look more closely at what I had done and not done to upset Emma. As I sat there going over every single action and reaction since I'd been there, it came to me that although I had made mistakes with Emma, maybe this thing going on with Emma had more to do with *her* than it had to do with me.

cHapTer 25

A crane calling in the shade.
Its young answers it.
I have a good goblet. I will share it with you.

The next morning, I woke up hugging the soft-feathered pillow on my bed, reliving the sensation I'd had when I first arrived at this enclave of protection. It was hard to believe that time had passed so quickly. Emma's home had been a sanctuary for almost a year. There had always been a sense of tranquility that had followed me around the apartment and hovered over me while I slept. It had accompanied me to auditions and classes, everywhere I went. But now . . . I wasn't sure when it had left, but I wanted it back. I had never experienced that sense of security anywhere else. *And if it stays away, where do I find it again?*

I lifted what felt like my three-hundred-pound body off the bed and dragged myself into the kitchen. I needed an orange to feel alive again. On the fridge was a note from Emma: "I'm spending the day with Zelda. I'll be back later. E."

Oh no! I thought she was going to rest today. I thought we could talk, maybe go for a walk. Maybe she's just avoiding me. There were no oranges in the fridge, so I swigged some grapefruit juice straight from the bottle. It was fine. She wasn't there. Even when she *was* there, as long as I did my swigging behind the refrigerator door, she would never see me. Today, I could swig all I wanted.

The empty space made me nervous. So I slipped into the shower to wash away the unease. Closely watching the soap form bubbles on my arms and stream down into the small holes of the drain, I realized that Emma hadn't mentioned where she was going today with Zelda. Clearly, the details of her life were not shared with *me* anymore. Every move she made was a surprise.

I got dressed and thought about what to do the rest of the day. *I know. I'll go see a movie. Should I? Why not?*

Not even thinking to look at the clock or check the paper to see what was playing, I got into my poor little Fiat, in need of a serious wash, a tune-up, and new windshield wipers. Knowing these fixes would have to wait, like the rest of my life, I took off for the La Grande Theater.

The La Grande was a venerable fixture for L.A. movie buffs, known for its unique selection of noir, classic, and foreign films. They'd mix it up so you'd never know what genre they'd be playing, which made the theater *très* chic and very popular. Rachel and I used to go there last-minute all the time. There'd be at least one film that we'd see, and we'd always be glad we went. I was hoping that would be the case this afternoon. But it didn't matter what I watched. I just needed to get out of the apartment, out of my head, out of my life.

The movie playing today was *Harold and Maude.* I had always wanted to see this film. I'd missed it when it had come out a couple of years before. All I'd heard was that it was bizarre—which enticed me even more. Today, I had my chance. I parked the car in the lot next to the theater, ready to leave Sandra Billings' life and enter Harold and Maude's.

I bought my ticket, a moderate-size tub of popcorn, and stepped into the semi-dark theater. The middle of the twentieth row was perfect. There was one seat left. *It's a sign.* I looked around to see if there was anyone I knew. There wasn't. So I sat down and waited for the lights to dim. I couldn't wait to absorb the nuances of the characters, the cinematography, the editing, the directing. I loved critiquing every aspect of film, seeing how quickly I could psych out the director's next move. Just as I was about to launch into my popcorn, I heard someone call out my name from behind.

"Sandra, Sandra Billings!"

I turned around, and there was Carole Saunders from acting class, waving exuberantly, practically jumping up and down. Carole was a perky eighteen-year-old with way too much enthusiasm. I'd admired her chutzpah, but not her incessant need for attention or her loud, boisterous voice.

"Hi, Carole." I smiled, wiggling my fingers back at her, hoping this would be the end of our tête-à-tête.

"Where have you been?" she shrilled. "We've missed you in class. Are you still seeing Larry? I saw him the other night with a tall blonde at the Troubadour." The Troubadour was a nightclub in West Hollywood. But since you had to be twenty-one to get in there, I wondered how *she* got in.

Carole went on, "She kind of looked like a guy. The blonde, I mean. Maybe she was." She giggled. People in nearby seats tried not to listen, without much success. Thank God, the lights were dimming.

I gave Carole another wave and a little half smile. "Take care." Larry was the last person I wanted to hear about . . . or think about.

Harold and Maude started rolling. Not a minute too soon. There were no trailers at La Grande. They'd just go right smack into the film, which I loved.

Harold and Maude. What a trip! I was so glad I came.

It was a masterpiece! Harold, a death-obsessed nineteen-year-old, and Maude, a seventy-nine-year-old bubbly anarchist, meet, become best friends, and spend most of their time visiting funerals. While Harold's mother enrolls him in a dating service and tries to force him to join the Army, Maude reveals to Harold her quirky, philosophical perspective that totally opens his heart. It's like she takes him on this wild tour of what it's really like to be alive. What a ride! On the day of Maude's eightieth birthday, Harold proposes to her. And in so doing, he finds out the truth about life—at the end of hers.

That's when I really lost it. The film blew me away. It was so iconic. Never had I laughed and cried as much during a movie. I sat there in the empty auditorium, after everyone had left, and stared at the screen as the last credit rolled off and faded to black. While young boys in red vests marched in to sweep the popcorn-kerneled floor, I sat there questioning my own perceptions of life and death . . . my own understanding of the existential nature of our lives and the reasons we were here.

Why are we here? Maude seemed to have figured it out. Has Emma? Was my coming here today a random act, a coincidence? Or did the universe send me here to witness something about my own life? The film was entirely too close to home.

Finally, I went for a very long walk so I'd be too exhausted to think . . . about anything.

Tired, but free from burdened thoughts, I walked into the apartment. You can imagine my surprise when I saw Emma sitting at the dining-room table with a fiftyish African-American man I'd never seen before. I stopped in my tracks, watched him lean over the table across from Emma, his massive body shaking with a big belly laugh.

"Hello!"

The black man looked up. He was surprised, but smiled. Emma jumped. Silence, then she recovered: "Oh, Sandra, hello. Come meet my friend Jackson."

I put my purse on the sideboard and walked over to the table. I reached out my hand to Emma's guest. "Hi, I'm Sandra."

"Jackson Parker."

"Nice to meet you, Jackson."

"Jackson is an old friend from New York. He's recently moved to Los Angeles," Emma said. Her voice was restrained, but it was sweeter than it had been.

"Well, welcome to L.A.! What do you do here in this lovely city, may I ask?"

"I'm a trumpet player. Jazz mostly."

"Really? Jazz is my all-time favorite music. Miles Davis, Dizzy Gillespie, John Coltrane."

I did love jazz, and I would have talked with Jackson for hours about all the musicians I used to listen to. All the jazz festivals I used to go to. I wanted to ask if he played at the New Orleans Jazz Festival, or at Newport. Had he ever played with Yusef Lateef? But I could hardly stay on my feet.

"You look tired, Sandra," said Emma. "What time is rehearsal tomorrow?"

"Nine," I said. I wasn't sure if she was really concerned or if she wanted me to leave. Either way, I was about to keel over. I was ready to excuse myself when a beautiful girl, about eighteen, with gorgeous light brown skin, big brown eyes, and a killer smile, emerged from the bathroom and sat down next to Jackson.

"This is Jackson's niece, Sharleen," Emma said.

"Nice to meet you, Sharleen." I leaned over and shook her hand.

"Sharleen is staying with Jackson until she finds a place to live. She's offered to help out with some cleaning."

I looked at her in disbelief.

Why hadn't Emma talked to me about this? Had she planned this? There were so many words not being said. I didn't know whether to stay, or leave, or pull Emma into the hallway and ask her what the hell was going on. My stomach knotted. I decided to take a deep breath and sit for a minute. Maybe I was overreacting, blowing this out of proportion. Maybe the freeze-up was with me.

Struggling to find my bearings, and a little humility, I calmed down and turned to Sharleen. "How long have you been here?" I asked.

"A week."

"How nice. How long are you staying?"

She looked at her uncle and then at Emma. "I don't know yet."

My acting teacher used to say, "There are volumes in that line"—I now understood what he meant.

"You know, I think I *will* turn in early. Jackson, it was nice meeting you. I'd love to hear you play sometime. And Sharleen, I guess I'll be seeing you. Good night."

I picked up my purse and walked into my room.

I grabbed my robe and went into the bathroom, turned both faucets on full force, and ripped open a package of lilac bath salts. Pouring the contents into the yellow tub, I watched each bubble bounce up to the surface. After stripping off my street clothes, I let myself down into the pale lavender water. I slipped deeper and deeper into the warm bubbles, until only my chin rested on the foaming surface and the rest of my body melted into the hot, liquid womb. The water wasn't hot enough; I turned the knob with the engraved *H* and felt a liquid blast of heat hit my toes.

The water was really hot now. I closed my eyes. It was my intention to burn away all feelings of abandonment, to steam out the lifetimes of torture I obviously must have caused others to endure. Why else did I have to suffer like this now? Rachel always talked about the debts we had to pay for our previous lifetimes. No doubt I'd been an Egyptian queen who'd spent her days ordering people around. Or maybe I was a prince who'd neglected his responsibilities and jet-setted around the world. After lifetimes of greed and leisure, it must be my time to repent.

All I wanted was for the scalding water to steam away all the past, present, and future I'd ever have to face so when it came time for me to reemerge from this pool of memories, there'd be nothing left but the experience of rebirth—permanently and forever.

I poured in another packet of lilac crystals.

God forbid anything good should happen to me for more than a day, a week, a few months. I felt nauseated. My whole body was trembling. Lying there in the purple water, I watched my childhood parade in front of my closed eyes: there was my father kicking me out of his den, my mother shooing me out of the kitchen, Steven wanting me out of the solar system. Steven, the bastard! I began to kick my feet in the water until it rained onto the floor tiles. *Why did I just lie there? I was such a wimp. How could I have let Lenny tear me open and throw me out the door?*

Reclaim what you've lost! Maybe that's what the memory was all about. Reclaiming my self-respect. How do I even begin to do that? Where do I start? And now Emma was pushing me out. Worthlessness leapt up full-blown. All I could think about was a pint of vanilla ice cream.

I left the tub and wiped the drops from my face, toweled down my body, grudgingly mopped up the shallow lake that had flooded across the floor, pulled on my pajamas, and headed to my bedroom. Not mine, Emma's, Josef's. Feeling like a caged animal, I lit a match, the candle, and a stick of sandalwood incense, and sat down on the bed.

Did Emma want me to leave?

Without thinking, my hand moved to the *I Ching.* I pulled it out from under the bed and began groping for the silk pouch with its coins, and then drew back. *No. I'm not going to throw it. Why should I?* It'd been wrong about Allen. Our relationship was far from Youthful Folly. He adored me. Anyone could see that. I wasn't entangling myself in empty imaginings or unreal fantasies. He cared for me as much as I cared for him. There'd been no humiliation, as the *I Ching* had predicted. It was off, way off. I was never going to throw the coins again.

I opened my eyes and settled myself firmly back against the pillows. I rummaged through the pile of books on the night table and picked up an old Tibetan pamphlet. At random, I opened to the question-and-answer session between one of the Buddhist monks and his students, hoping to find some words of wisdom or just to settle the spin going on in my mind. I read:

> There is no such thing as a feeling of happiness that is permanent and everlasting.

No shit.

> Those feelings, thinking that if we get everything we want, we will be happy, are an unreal expectation.

I was used to unreal expectations.

> When we try to find satisfaction outside of ourselves, we end up running in circles. We will find lasting happiness only when we stop looking for it—only when we let go of our desire for it.

Yeah, yeah! Well, that'd be as easy as getting tar off lace. I'll just give up my desire for everything. Right!

I snapped the pamphlet shut. I was tired of getting answers off printed pages, off of other people's words. Tired of reading, and forgetting everything I'd read. I turned off the lamp, closed my eyes, and hoped that when I woke up, I'd be someplace else, somebody else.

cHapTer 26

The enthusiasm of the heart expresses itself involuntarily . . .

On my way to rehearsal, I knew I couldn't hide the emotions whirling around inside me. I knew from experience that if I tried to hide them, they would come across as tension—and tension, as any actor knows, is a performer's worst enemy. I had to use every ounce of emotion I was feeling—unworthiness, helplessness, vulnerability . . . all the feelings I was trying to conceal—and weave them between the lines. Integrate them seamlessly with the words from the script and allow them to be a part of my every move, my every gesture.

I watched as Allen rehearsed the scenes that didn't include me. I watched with rapt attention, so I wouldn't have to think about what I didn't want to think about. I went over my lines so they were certain to be memorized. During lunch, I stayed in my dressing room so I wouldn't have to speak, to anyone. I kept myself busy with letters to friends, composing them from the personas of the actress and the medical intern, in order to see the roles from different perspectives.

I went over and over my lines, until I heard Allen call out: "Sandra, get onstage, please. I'd like to rehearse the audition scene."

I snapped back into the present, walked up the stairs, and took center stage. Emulating the actress's fear of arriving alone in the big city of Saint Petersburg was effortless. I used the subtext of my own fear here, the pent-up panic running through my veins, the fleeting thought that I might have to leave Emma's. When the actress met her idol, the famous writer, scared to death she might make a mistake and fail the audition, I used my own frailty. I projected the uncertainty I was feeling, the apprehension about confronting Emma. It was time to find out the truth, whatever it was. It was surprisingly easy to act with humility. Exposing myself felt natural. It was easier to reveal these emotions to strangers than it would be to disclose them to the one I'd come to care for and was afraid to lose.

When rehearsal was over, I saw that Allen and the others had been moved by my performance. They sat in the theater in silence. No one made a move—not the cast, not the stage managers, not even the three middle-aged women who managed the box office and who had ventured into the auditorium, standing by the entrance with their mouths agape. Marlene ran over to me and took me aside. "You were amazing. I've never heard you say your lines with so much . . . I don't know, intention, passion. Are you going to have any juice left for the show?"

"Oh yeah. There are gallons more."

Allen called it an early night, knocking off at six-thirty instead of the usual seven. Everybody scurried off the stage to go home. I felt grateful that I'd been able to release so much tension. The exhaustion was worth it. I'd let it all out, and now I was, thank God, too tired to think. I went to my dressing room to wash my face and chill out, just sit. I could feel my nerves pulsating. I was sweaty, and beat.

There was a knock at the door.

"Come in," I said, as audibly as I could muster.

Allen walked in with a smile and a silly plastic rose. "You gave yourself quite a workout today. Hungry, my little star?"

"Oh, I could eat something small, like a buffalo."

"How about you let me take you to my place, where we can survey my fridge and see what we can come up with?"

I accepted the invitation without missing a beat. A restaurant would not have been appealing. Not tonight. I was in no mood to sit in a commercial setting or expose myself to bright lights and strangers. My senses needed pampering and caressing. My body yearned to stretch out on a huge couch with big pillows, and my ears wanted only the sound of classical music and hushed words whispered into them. My eyes needed soft lights, and my nostrils wanted to inhale the fragrance of burning firewood so I could offer all my fears into the fire and watch them blaze up and burn down into ashes. I needed to be with someone who cared, who would listen to my heart and not be afraid to share his.

I loved sitting next to Allen in his leather bucket seats, watching him take control of the car, the steering wheel. My life, if he wanted to. He must have worked hard for this Porsche and its fancy black seats.

Allen's house was tucked away in a cozy cul-de-sac where hundreds of homes cascaded down the slopes and canyons of the Hollywood Hills. As we pulled into his circular driveway, he said, "This is where I replenish myself, away from the world. It's my private hideaway."

So, this was where he'd lived with his wife of seven years—perhaps a few other wives. Although I couldn't imagine him married. Thank God he now lived here alone. He came around, opened my door, and escorted me to the house. Unlocking the front door, he bent down to scoop up the mail that had fallen through the slot, and we entered his secret retreat.

Inside, I immediately felt a sense of loneliness, emptiness, as if the house had once been filled with joy, or children laughing and playing, but now had been reduced to silence. The smell of cigar lingered in the air. Down the stairs, the living room was all earthy tones, browns and golds and reds. I was happy to see the brick fireplace and the dark, masculine furniture. Somehow they provided concrete evidence for my feeling that Allen was stable, of the earth, and I could trust him.

There were photos of his ex-wife and child, another photo of a second ex-wife and children from an earlier marriage. (Bill Fleishman was right.) The photos sat on an impressive mahogany desk, surrounded by pads of paper and a stack of scripts.

Allen opened the French doors to his deck, to air the place out. While he looked through his mail at the desk, I crossed the room to the deck to look out onto the City of Angels. Standing at the railing, admiring the view from this height, I watched lights winking on one by one, like fireflies, as dusk settled over the valley. I found myself thinking about Emma. What would she say if she saw me tonight standing on Allen Cahill's deck? Would she smile, or walk away in silence, leaving me behind to guess at her reaction? Why should I care?

I stood on the solid wood planks of the deck, looking to see if I could locate the Windmill Theater, when Allen's arms came up from behind me, his hands slowly taking hold of my waist. And then, I don't know if he turned me around or if I turned myself around, but I will never forget the sweet taste of his mouth and the fullness that sprang from his kiss. How protected I felt. Whatever was going through my mind about Emma completely melted away.

When the kiss ended, I said, "*Mmm* . . . that was a pleasant surprise."

"I'm glad," he said.

Here I was kissing the man I'd wanted to be alone with since the first minute I'd laid eyes on him, and now that I had the opportunity, I was nervous. Not quite ready for the intimacy.

"I'm starving—what's in the refrigerator?" I started to move back inside, toward the kitchen.

"Wh-where you going?" He gently took hold of my wrist before I got too far and pulled me back close against his chest, supporting my back with his hands. Our eyes close, our lips almost touching.

"I was going to get something to eat. Aren't you hungry?"

"Very." He kissed my neck.

"I mean for food."

"You were great today," he said. He kissed my forehead gently. "There was so much passion in your monologue."

"I had a lot to work with," I admitted.

"You always have a lot to work with."

"Look, Allen, you have no idea how difficult things are for me. I just think we should wait."

"Till when, after dinner? I don't think I can wait that long."

"No, until opening night."

"Opening night is three weeks away," he objected, like a child not getting the candy he wanted *now*.

"I have to know that what I'm doing is right. Not out of fear or desperation . . . I need some clarity. And if we wait, we'll have something to look forward to and celebrate."

"I can think of a lot to celebrate right now."

"If we make love tonight"—my words were saying no, but my fingers were entwining themselves in the strands of his black wavy hair—"I'll be walking around rehearsal like a zombie, and everyone will know, you know, and I won't be able to keep my hands off you."

"I don't see that as a problem."

"It's not easy for me to be patient, either."

"I think underneath that sweet smile is a very sadistic human being who derives great pleasure out of torturing the male half of the species. I will be patient. Not because I want to. But because"— he kissed my nose—"this way, I get to fantasize more. However, if it were up to me . . ."

Inside, the phone rang. Allen broke off the embrace and moved swiftly to pick it up. "Hello," he said cheerfully. There was a pause. And then his face closed in, his eyes looked down, his voice lowered discreetly.

"Hi, uh, it's wonderful to hear from you . . . I'd love to, but I have a guest over at the house. Of course . . . can I call you, later . . . ? Wonderful . . . talk to you then."

We kissed again. "Who was that, Cliff Thorne, calling in all scripts for a rewrite?" I asked jokingly, although seriously wanting to know if this was a call I should be concerned about.

"No, it was a friend who needed some information. I'll call them later."

He resumed kissing my neck. I stood there with at least four lines of thought fighting for my attention. I was curious about the call. I wanted to tell him about Emma and how difficult living with her had become. But I didn't want to appear needy and immature.

Knowing I had to figure this out on my own, I pulled myself away, took his hand, and led him into the kitchen, where we pulled together a salad from remnants of assorted vegetables and warmed up two pieces of leftover chicken. When our plates were full, I took both our dishes out to the deck and waited for him to join me.

"How about some Mozart?" he called out, looking through his LP collection.

"Mozart would be wonderful. You must have read my mind." He put on a Bach suite instead, dimmed the lights inside the house, and joined me with a bottle of Chablis and two glasses. The man was so prepared, so together.

"Would you like some?" He poured himself a glass and waited for my answer.

"Sure, I'll have a little."

We sat on the lounge chairs as Allen spoke about the play and drank his Chablis. He talked of his disappointment in directing television and his desire to direct film. He shared his excitement about the film deal he was negotiating with the producers in New York. I sat there listening to the modulations of his voice as he articulated his sentences, pronouncing every word as if I were the recipient of all his years of training, watching his lips become wet from the wine and his expressive hands gesturing with abandon.

I interrupted his soliloquy with yet another one of my adolescent fears: "You know, you're always going to have the advantage in this relationship."

"Why is that?"

"You're older. You're more experienced. You're always going to know things before I do. You'll always have the edge."

"What's fifteen, twenty years? Not much when you see the whole picture. Let me show you something." He stood up, walked inside to his desk, and brought back a pencil and a pad of paper. He sat down next to me and drew two circles on the page.

"This circle is you," he said, "and this circle is me. And all these other circles"—he covered the page with a lacework of loopy circles—"are all the other people we *have* ever and *will* ever come in contact with. Now, some of these spheres spinning around will get close to our spheres and hang out for quite a while. Other spheres will come close only for a short time and spin away. Haven't you experienced that already in your life?"

"Yes, but, because you're older—"

"The interesting thing is," he cut me off, "that we never know how long or short our spheres will come together for—"

"Some psychics know," I cut *him* off.

"The thing is, I don't know any more about what's going on with our two spheres than you do." He had the most compassionate eyes, the sweetest fatherly voice. "I don't know what's going to happen the next minute any more than you do."

"Opening night is too far away," I said.

"I thought *I* said that."

We kissed for a long time.

And while we kissed, my mind kept watch, as if I was observing from a distance, circling, hovering. I couldn't settle. I still had my doubts, regardless of his cosmic overview. I wanted to know: Was I just a convenient fling, some young gullible actress gaga over the director? Were there other women in his life? Was he involved with anyone else? I didn't want to wait to see how long our spheres would be close; I wanted to know, now. I didn't want to seem unsophisticated and ruin the mood because of my impatience. So I refrained from speaking, and kept on kissing him and touching his face and running my fingers through his thick black hair. I melted as his hands caressed my neck and my breasts. And the more I let go of my thoughts, the more I let go of my fears about him, about Emma, about the world, one after the other after the other.

We lay there on the lounge chair, holding each other in the sweet, warm night. Content in the silence, we could easily have fallen asleep. I didn't want to leave, ever. But there was rehearsal tomorrow. And hopefully Emma would still be speaking to me, waiting for my return.

Arm in arm, propping each other up from the gravity of life, from the intoxication of lips and tongues and the touching of each other's skin, Allen and I managed to make our way back to the door, dragged our bodies to the car. There was nothing to say, so we were silent as he drove me back to the city below. I found a good jazz station on his radio and melted even more as we listened to John Coltrane's *A Love Supreme*. When we reached Emma's building, we kissed again. It was impossible to leave.

"Good night, Mr. Cahill."

"Good night, Miss Billings."

CHAPTER 27

The bed is split up to the skin.
Those who persevere are destroyed.
Misfortune.

Ever since the night I was introduced to Jackson and Sharleen—the night Emma had made it known to me she didn't want me around—Emma was no longer the same person I'd met when I'd moved in over ten months ago. She had changed. Instead of smiling and acknowledging me, she walked around the apartment as if I hardly existed. She spoke only when necessary. Like if she needed something from the store or if she couldn't reach something on a shelf. I might as well have been a ghost or some unwanted guest for an overnight stay. She no longer asked questions about my day or inquired into the details of rehearsals. The farmers' market no longer enticed her. Just to test the water, I'd ask her if she'd like to go with me to pick up a few things at the store, but she'd say, "I have no interest in traveling." Her only desire was to stay home.

Screaming and yelling was something I could relate to. It was woven into the fabric of my family. It was just how we communicated. I hated to holler, but at least I knew where people stood. Silence scared the shit out of me.

I tried to imagine where Emma's behavior might be coming from. Why was she acting this way to me—and why now, when my life was at a crossroads?

The day before opening night, I felt this strong sense of urgency, almost dread. I knew I had to do something. I looked at the bedside clock. Eight o'clock. I had an hour to get to the theater. I reached under the bed and pulled out the *I Ching*, opened the silk pouch, and poured out the three dimes. Yes, I had sworn never to throw the coins again, but I needed answers that no one else could provide.

I pulled the notepad out from under the bed and hunted around for the pen, which I found hidden under a pair of jeans. Fist tight, eyes closed, I asked the oracle: *Should I move out of Emma's?* I threw the coins six times, praying that the answer would relieve me in some way. This was the *I Ching*'s response:

23. Po / Splitting Apart

Above: Kên, Keeping Still, Mountain
Below: K'un, The Receptive, Earth

This pictures a time when inferior people are pushing forward and are about to crowd out the few remaining strong and superior men. Under these circumstances, which are due to the time, it is not favorable for the superior man to undertake anything.

Oh great, this was all I needed to hear.

The right behavior in such adverse times is to be deduced from the images and their attributes.

Did it have to be so obscure?

The lower trigram stands for the earth, whose attributes are docility and devotion. The upper trigram stands for the mountain, whose attribute is stillness. This suggests that one should submit to the bad time and remain quiet.

I was so tired of remaining docile and silent. When would it be my turn to have my voice heard? When would I get the chance to take some action?

For it is a question not of man's doing but of time conditions . . . . It is impossible to counteract these conditions of the time. Hence it is not cowardice but wisdom to submit and avoid action.

How could I avoid action, remain quiet, when I was ready to bust through these walls? How could I listen to the *I Ching* when it hadn't been right about Allen? When so many signs were pointing to LEAVE. How could I continue to be tossed around by these coins?

I pushed the book aside, jumped out of bed, and threw on some clothes. I began to search the room for Bella's gift: the little blue telephone book she'd given me before I'd left Michigan. The book that'd been through every job, every move, every person I'd met since moving to L.A. I rummaged through every drawer before I found it at the back of my underwear drawer and put it in my purse. Then I walked into the living room.

Emma was sitting silently in her chair. I walked to the door, stopped, just in case she'd decide to look up, break her silence, say something to me. But there was nothing.

I left without a word, without a wave, without the slightest sign of good-bye.

The mood at the theater was hectic, frenetic. How could it be anything else? It was the day before opening night. Stagehands were busy fitting new curtains and removing old chairs. Carpet cleaners sucked up dust from old seats, and mops slopped around the aisles. People I'd never seen before were everywhere, making decisions, critiquing the lights and the curtains. All the cast was onstage while Allen went over last-minute notes. I tried to listen as he gave them, but everything seemed surreal. I was there, but I wasn't. I watched as the actors went over their blocking. I tried to remember lines and move to places where the character was supposed to go, but I kept flubbing my lines, and Allen had to stop the scene twice. We started again, but I forgot more lines. Allen's eyes were throwing bullets. I got it together for a short time when I caught his expression, and then turned, almost on cue, and tripped over the ottoman. By the time the scene was over, the entire cast was ready to pulverize me.

Bill and Marlene came up to me afterward. "What's going on with you? Are you on drugs?" Bill asked, only half-joking.

"If only I were. I'm going through a little rift. But it's about to change, soon. I promise." They may have heard me say the words, but they didn't believe me.

Allen waited until the break to invite me into his office. I followed him, knowing I was in for a scolding.

"Have a chair," he suggested. I grudgingly sat. He pulled his chair out from behind his desk and wheeled it over to sit by me. I watched his brain search for words and, at the same time, try to subdue his anger. "What the hell is going on with you? I've never seen you like this—forgetting lines, tripping over furniture, missing cues."

"I know, I know," I told him. "I'm a mess. I'll be fine . . . soon."

"How soon?" He was no longer subdued.

"Soon. Promise." I crossed my heart.

"Sandra." He pulled his chair closer and took my hand. "Why aren't you trusting me?" He sat there searching my face with those compassionate eyes of his.

"This has nothing to do with you. I'm working out some issues with Emma. The woman I live with."

"I'm here; you know that." He paused, hesitating, wondering if he should say more. And then he did: "The last thing I want to do is call in an understudy."

I could feel my face turn white, and then red, and then redder. I sat stock-still on the chair, afraid to move, afraid to speak, to breathe.

"If you need a half hour to chill, it's yours." He gave me a hug and left me alone in his office.

The door closed behind him. I sat there, numb, and then lunged for the telephone. No, I couldn't use his phone. I darted out of the office and headed for the phone booth on the other side of the stage.

Once inside the narrow, glassed-in cage, I opened Bella's book. The phone book I'd opened on so many occasions, but never thought I'd need again so soon, at least not for this. I went through the alphabet: *B, F, M,* no . . . I came to the letter *R.* Rachel's name popped out at me. Was she back from South America? I dialed her new number. The answering machine said she and Armando were out of the country and to please leave your name and number.

I left her a cryptic message: "Hi, Rache. It's Sandra. I don't know if you're back, but I wanted to know if I could stay at your place. It's a long story. Call me at the Windmill Theater. And opening night is tomorrow night, if you *are* back."

Staying at Jerry's was not even a consideration, but I wanted to call him, just to listen to his voice. Maybe he'd have some advice for me, a mental Band-Aid to put on my wound. But *his* machine said cheerily that he wouldn't be back until Thursday.

That's when I started to sweat. There had to be someone I could stay with! I flipped through more pages. *Ahh,* Francesca from acting class. It was a long shot, but I tried. Her line was busy. I wasn't surprised. Francesca was always talking . . . about everybody. She was a beautiful model who'd once tried to fix me up with a celebrity she knew. She didn't tell me until afterward that the celebrity was married. When I found out, I turned her and the celebrity down. I decided to pass on Francesca.

I wouldn't dare call Larry. It'd be too humiliating. He would totally get off on playing the noble prince, saving his old girlfriend, albeit now in distress.

Flipping through the pages, I stopped at *Schreiber.* Of course, Calvin! He was conservative, shy, and very generous. I met him in acting class. He let me borrow his tape recorder for an unlimited time. He wasn't taking the class to be an actor—he wanted to improve his presentation skills. He lectured around the world on cutting-edge computer chips and actually earned a living (something no one else in the class was doing). He had a little crush on me, but he knew it was platonic on my end. I wasn't physically attracted to him. I *was,* however, hungry, and he often treated me to dinner. Calvin wouldn't mind. His machine said he could be reached at work. So I called him at his office.

"Hi, Calvin, it's Sandra Billings. How are you?"

I could tell he was happy to hear from me. "Aren't you a star yet, Sandra Billings?" I giggled. "Where are you living? What's goin' on?"

I relaxed for a second, just hearing his questions, knowing he still cared. "Calvin, I need your help. I need a place to stay. Not for long. I'm in a situation . . . and I was wondering . . ."

"Sandra, you got it. Sure, use my place. I'm leaving for Europe tomorrow. I'll be gone most of the month. You can move in tomorrow."

"I knew there was a God," I told him.

"I always told you I was God, Sandra. You never believed me. Listen, I've moved. But I'm still in Beverly Hills. Here's the address." I wrote it down. "I'll leave a key with the doorman. His name is Mike. There's plenty of food. You better eat it or it'll go bad by the time I get back."

"Thanks, Calvin. I really appreciate this."

"Take it easy, Sandra. Everything will work out. When I come back, I'll help you find a place to live. Unless I can talk you into staying."

"Calvin. This is such a rescue . . . have a great trip. 'Bye, and thanks."

I fell back against the glass side of the booth and closed my eyes; the search was over. I could breathe easier now. But this was no time to dwell on achievements. It was ten after one. I had to boogie back to the stage. Rehearsal had started at one.

I flew back to the stage, and heard someone say something about a dress rehearsal as the cast scurried away.

"Did you call a *dress rehearsal?*" I asked Allen, almost bumping into him, out of breath.

"Actually, I did. Just clothes, no makeup," he said with a trace of annoyance.

"The costumes are finally ready?" Still catching my breath. Still anxious, but relieved.

"They're in the dressing rooms. I won't ask why you were late."

"Good."

"Go get dressed and try on the wigs. I'd like to see how they look."

"Okay, okay." I looked around to see if anyone was close, nudged him kiddingly, and said, "Don't be so pushy."

He looked around, too, obviously wanting to cover his next move, which was to lean into me. Close. I inhaled his potent after-shave, which was so intoxicating. It had a Western scent, as if he'd just stepped off his horse; it lassoed my senses, daring me to come even closer. I wondered what had happened to the baby powder. But there was no time to ask.

"I'd better get that costume on."

"Wait a minute. I'm the director. You take orders from me. It's written in the contract."

"There was never a contract, and if there was, I never signed it. I'm going to call my lawyer." I turned away toward the dressing room, but Allen grabbed my arm and pulled me toward him.

"This will only take a minute."

"Not if you move one inch closer it won't . . ."

"Are you going to be all right?"

"I'm much better now."

"Opening night is too far away," he said with intensity.

"I hope the costumes fit. I'd better go try them on." I started away again, but he once more pulled me back.

"Do you know, your eyes sparkle and your lip goes up on the left when you get upset. Did you know that?"

"No, I didn't. Did you know your . . ."

He looked around, and then we kissed. I broke away, ran back to my dressing room, pulled off my jeans, tried on the intern's costume, put on the wig, looked in the mirror, and went into shock. Oh my God, you could see, plain as day, that I wasn't wearing any underwear. Which meant everyone *else* could see that I wasn't wearing underwear.

I pulled open the door, rushed over to Marlene's dressing room to ask her if she had a slip. She wasn't there. I ran to the stage, where the entire cast was waiting for me. Embarrassed beyond comprehension, I yelled from behind the curtain, "I'm sorry. I can't come out. I have no slip, and the lights are too bright. You can see right through my legs."

"What are you talking about?" Allen yelled back.

"I'm not coming out—you'll be able to see my you-know-what." I could hear everyone laugh.

"I'm not coming out unless I have a slip."

I wasn't being a prima donna. I was mortified. I didn't want people looking at my privates while I rehearsed. "I'm going back to my dressing room to put my jeans back on. I'll be right back."

I ran to my dressing room, zipped myself back into my jeans, and ran back to the stage.

When I returned, I couldn't believe what they had done. The entire cast *and* crew had pulled down their trousers and were mooning me, butts high in the air.

"Sandra, it's not a big deal. It's not like anyone here hasn't seen a naked body before."

I laughed so hard that I dropped to my knees. I laughed so hard I cried. The more I laughed, the more I cried, the more I could feel the tension release from my body and all the knots in my neck and the tightness in my shoulders, the headache surrounding my temples, drop away. Still, I didn't want to move.

"I don't care," I managed to squeak out, still on the floor, trying to get the words out between the laughter and the tears. "You can all rehearse naked if you want. I'm not wearing that dress without a slip."

The stage manager returned after a few minutes of scrounging around the costume room and handed me a slip for which I expressed profound appreciation and took back to my dressing room to put on. When I returned to the stage, the bare-assed cast had zipped their trousers back up, and rehearsal resumed as normal. Well, as normal as could be expected.

It wasn't until I was walking home that I began to think about the conversation I wasn't looking forward to having. What would I say? How would I start? How would Emma take the news?

Thank goodness she was on the phone when I came in. I was able to walk through the living room and into the bedroom without having to say a word. I assumed she was talking to Bert, or Zelda. I wasn't sure. All I heard was, "Just to the bank and the post office; that's all I need. Thank you—see you in the morning."

I still had no idea.

The next thing I heard were pots and pans clanging in the kitchen. I waited a few minutes, trying to think about what I was going to say, but I knew it was a waste of time. *I'm just going to have to trust,* I told myself, *that whatever comes out of my mouth is what I am supposed to say.*

"Would you like me to make something for dinner?" I asked, testing the water.

"No, I'm just going to heat up some soup. Thank you."

I watched Emma walk to the freezer and take out a frozen plastic container and hold it under the hot water. Every movement was so clear, so definite. I found myself watching her move with a kind of silence that no longer frightened me, a silence in which every simple gesture had significance—as if I might not see her defrost anything again.

I sat at the table while she opened the drawer and took out a gold spoon. I didn't care if she saw me staring or not. I sat there, munching on a carrot while she sipped on her soup, knowing I might not see her sipping soup again.

She finished her soup, washed out her bowl. And then walked with utter self-possession over to her green throne, sat down, and turned on the TV. I followed her over and sat in my chair, staring at the TV, too, while I gathered the courage to speak. Finally, with every ounce of bravery I could muster, I said, "Emma, we need to talk."

She ignored me at first. Then she surprised me by turning off the TV with the remote. She must have heard it in my voice that this was not going to be a talk about the weather or dinner. She removed her bifocals and stared straight ahead. She knew something was coming.

"I think I need to move out."

She didn't respond. I waited to hear her say, "Are you crazy? What in God's name are you doing that for?" But she didn't say a word.

I waited some more. "Did you hear me, Emma?"

"When did you decide to do this?"

"Yesterday," I said, "or maybe today." My teeth were chattering.

"I see. Where will you be going?"

"A friend's house," I said defiantly. *Why does she care where I'm going?*

Another pause, only this time she shifted position in her chair. I couldn't read her, though, and found myself stumbling for the words. "I thought you *wanted* me to move out."

"What made you think that?"

Her voice was devoid of any emotion. I couldn't tell what she thought.

"Sharleen, for one. And you've been so quiet, not wanting to talk. It just seemed pretty clear that you didn't want me here."

Again . . . no response.

"I know you need help around the house and don't want to be alone all day, and I've been so busy. I don't know what else to do. I haven't been able to focus on rehearsals, and if I don't get it together . . ." I'd hoped that she would stop me and tell me to shut up and go to my room and that I was being silly.

Instead, she asked, "You've made up your mind?"

"I-I guess I have. Sharleen's planning to stay here, so you're not alone, right?" Tears were coursing down my cheeks. "That's what you were planning all along, right?"

Another pause. "When are you thinking about leaving?"

"Tomorrow." The word just came out of my mouth.

She looked surprised. "So soon? You found a place so soon?"

"Yes, I told you, a friend's apartment."

"The director's?"

"No, not Allen's."

She looked relieved. She sat back. Before she could turn the TV on again, I spoke, praying that I wouldn't burst into tears again.

"Emma, opening night is tomorrow night, and I want to re-serve seats for you and Sharleen, and Bert. I thought Bert could drive you, and then Sharleen could come back with you. You are planning to come to opening night, aren't you?"

She paused even longer this time. Then she turned to me, and I thought I'd fall off my chair. There was so much intensity and, at the same time, love and compassion in her eyes. "I will arrange it with Bert. I would like to see the show." There was even a minuscule smile that followed her words. That was it.

That was all I needed to know. She didn't hate me, and she was coming to opening night.

Emma leaned back in her chair and reached for her bifocals. She sat back in her magnificent high-back, pressed the ON button on the remote, and pretended to watch TV. I sat there, too, pretending to watch TV with her, hoping I hadn't made a mistake.

CHQPTEr 28

Thunder and lightning:
the image of BITING THROUGH.

Morning came too soon. I wasn't ready to open my eyes or experience the sun quite yet. I would have preferred to lie there and pretend that everything was fine. But I knew better.

My eyelids felt like weighted shades. My body, a beached whale. I lay motionless on the bed, wondering what time it was, unwilling to find out the answer. Instead, I looked over at the painting of the pale beach and the brilliant orange-and-blue sky and tried to lose myself in its calmness, but this was not a morning for refuge or reprieve. I had wanted to get up before eight, before Emma's alarm clock went off. That way I could pack my things and sneak out of the apartment without having to face her or talk. I lay there, debating whether to look at the clock or not. I looked. Holy shit! It was nine-thirty!

I forced the beached whale up and jumped off the bed. Gently, I opened the door. On my way to the bathroom I overheard Emma dialing a number from the living room. I walked into the bathroom, closed the door, not quite all the way, and strained to hear what she was saying. Emma always talked softly. But she was speaking even more *sotto voce* this morning. She thought I was still in bed, or she didn't want me to hear.

"Zelda? Yes, dear. I have a ride. I wanted to let you know. Jackson is picking me up, then the bank. Yes, I'll call you when I get back."

There was urgency in her voice. At least she was going out. In a few minutes she'd be gone. *Slow down, Sandra. Deep breath in, deep breath out.*

I closed the door completely and climbed into the shower, lathered up, and tried not to think about anything but the soap and the way it felt on my hands. The way the hot water beat against my skin, massaging my scalp and my shoulders and breasts. I tried desperately to stay in the moment and not allow my mind to spin off in the hundred million directions I knew it could go. I pleaded with myself: *Be here now. Just be here now!* I rinsed off the suds and dried myself with Emma's pink plush towel.

I pulled on my jeans, slipped on my T-shirt, put on my makeup, and then packed up all the bottles and creams into my travel case. When I cracked open the door, I heard Emma in the kitchen toasting her bagel. I could hear the click from the toaster oven signaling that her quarter piece of bagel was done. I could hear her take out the butter from the fridge . . . I tiptoed back to the bedroom, my nerves worse than ever, closed the door, and took all the empty boxes—the ones I'd unpacked eleven months ago—back out of the closet and began stacking my books inside them. I pulled my clothes out of the drawers and stuffed them into my suitcase.

I opened the tiny center drawer, the one I'd opened months ago. The handkerchief was still there, inside its plastic bag. The name Alexandra still embroidered in blue. I lifted the bag to see if I might have left something underneath it. I turned it over and, tucked inside, found a lock of light brown hair. Underneath was a delicate gold locket in the shape of a heart. Curious, I carefully removed the locket. I opened the clasp and found a photo of two women. One was a youthful version of Emma. Next to her, smiling, was a younger woman, not much older than I was. Who was she? I closed the locket, placed it back in the bag, and shut the drawer.

Then I heard Emma walk into the bathroom and close the door. I stopped packing, and breathing. I heard the toilet flush, the faucet turn on and then off, the bathroom door open again, and the light switch click off. I waited to hear her return to the kitchen. But she didn't. She just stood outside my door, listening to discover if I was moving, still here. We both stood on opposite sides of the door, waiting for each other to move. Not until I heard her walk away did I return to my cautious packing.

I pulled my hanging clothes out of the closet and piled them on the bed. Reaching underneath the bed, I brought up the *I Ching*, the silk pouch, and the legal-size writing pad. Holding the book, my hands began to shake. I was in awe of the power this book still had. Maybe it *was* right about Allen; maybe it *was* right about Emma.

I thought about leaving the book behind. Showing it who was in charge. But the knot in my stomach told me otherwise. I couldn't leave it. It had become a part of me—good or bad, right or wrong. I placed it on top of the other books, and closed the cardboard lid.

I did a final search around the room—every corner, the high closet shelf, the nightstand drawer, the windowsill, under the bed—making sure everything I'd brought here nearly eleven months ago was packed.

The doorbell buzzed, and I jumped.

It was Emma's ride. I heard her murmur a few things to a man, and then I heard the door close.

She had left without a good-bye, without saying, "See you later. Break a leg. Have a good show." I felt ill. Should I run after her and tell her . . . what? What was I going to tell her? *What, Sandra? Stop it. Stop torturing yourself. Keep moving. Just keep moving.*

I grabbed the clothes from the bed and threw a few more items, whatever could fit, into my suitcase. I picked up the clothes still on hangers and hauled them out to the elevator, then went back and brought out another load, and then one more. When all the clothes and all the boxes were out of the bedroom and outside the apartment, I looked around each room one last time. I was about to close the door, but instead swung it open and went back inside. I had to leave a note. I should have written the sixteen hundred pages that were bursting from my heart, but instead I jotted these words on a napkin I found:

> *Dear Emma,*
> *I'll call you from the theater to make plans for tonight. I'm so glad you'll be coming. Talk to you later.*
> *Sandra.*

Calvin's apartment was off Wilshire Boulevard, about ten miles from Emma's. And although taking Wilshire was the most direct way there, it looked like there was an accident up ahead. So I turned onto a side street, and noticed the sweetest art-deco apartment building I'd ever seen. The wooden sign in front of the small garden read: ONE-BEDROOM FOR RENT. *One day!* I promised myself. *One day I'll have a nest of my own.*

I circled the block back to Wilshire, and found Calvin's building. It was a cold, white high-rise. The front entry portico was easy to pull into, and as I parked the car at the front, I wondered if Calvin had remembered to leave the key. I left the Fiat running and ran inside to find the doorman.

A short, stocky man with bifocals sat on a stool reading a dirty girlie magazine. I was about to say, "Excuse me, your tenant Calvin Schreiber was supposed to leave me . . ." when the doorman looked up and said, "Hi, you must be Sandra," and handed me an envelope. "I've been expecting you. The key's inside."

"Thanks," I replied. "Sorry to be in such a rush, but I have an opening tonight!" I ran back to the Fiat and grabbed my suitcase and some bags. The doorman followed me out to the car and grabbed a few, too; he led me to the bank of elevators and showed me the elevator to take—the one that would take me to the twenty-sixth floor.

I slid in the key, turned the bolt, and opened Calvin's door. Before me was expensive furniture—luxurious rugs, glass-and-chrome tables, glass-and-chrome chairs, glass-and-chrome mirrors. The place was huge, and sterile, and a mess. Dishes were piled high in the sink; days-old cold, congealed pizza was still in its open box on the couch. Clothes were scattered everywhere. I wanted to go back to Emma's. I wanted to cry. I wanted to die, but there was no time. It was already ten-thirty.

I took the elevator back to the lobby, made a few more trips up with the doorman's help, and then grabbed the overnight bag that I'd packed for later, for Allen's.

"Good luck," the doorman said to my back as I got into the car. And as I drove like a madman, I repeated a prayer: *Dear God, give me strength. Just let me get through the night.*

I ran to the dressing room, placed my overnight bag in the closet, made sure all my costume changes and wigs were in place, and then darted back to the stage. Everyone was there, receiving notes. Our director wanted to run through the play twice—once without costumes, once with costumes. So that's what we did. The first rehearsal was done at lightning speed, a clever technique to see if we knew our lines without thinking about them and remembered the blocking. Then we rehearsed the play again. This time with costumes and corrected scene changes.

Everyone was on cue. We knew our lines, when to come in, when to exit. Everyone looked radiant—particularly our distinguished director, decked out in a tailored suit. Allen's hair, slicked back, made his expressive dark eyes stand out. Just thinking about going home with this man at the end of the night made me pinch myself.

Marlene was focused and deliberate. Perhaps this would be her comeback debut after all. Bill Fleishman had the comedic timing of a masterful clown, and Kevin Hawthorne, who'd replaced Bob Driscoll, played the rich owner of a manor with dignity and defiance. Frank Geraldi's sardonic sense of humor would have the audience in stitches. Charlie, the stage manager, made sure the props were in place and the curtain calls went smoothly. Other than stopping for a few snags in the scene changes, and a few minor fixes in the blocking, dress rehearsal went well. Mr. Cahill announced his appreciation.

We were given a two-hour break to eat and rest up. Everyone left the stage except Allen, who asked me to stay. He came over to me, glanced around before making his move, and then gave me a kiss on the cheek. "You're going to be great. How's everything with Emma?"

"It's all . . . okay."

"You are coming home with me, right?"

"I suppose. Unless I get a better offer."

"Let me know if you do."

"I gotta go." I gave him a kiss on the cheek. "See you later." I looked around for Charlie, the stage manager. I needed to reserve the best seats in the house—for Emma, Bert, and Sharleen.

"Charlie!" I yelled, but he didn't answer. "Charlie!" I yelled again.

"I'm over here, in the back," his voice hollered back.

I found him fiddling with the pulley. "How's it going?"

"I dunno—these new curtains," he said. "We shoulda stayed with the old ones until after the show."

"You'll make 'em work. You always do. Charlie, I have a favor to ask. Would you let me reserve some seats?" I pulled out a five, smiled, and waved it around.

He looked at the five and said, "You don't need to do that."

"Yes, I do. You deserve more."

He caved, but made me swear not to tell. I raised my three fingers, Girl Scout–style, and handed him the five.

"Fifteenth row, down center, smack in the middle of the auditorium."

"Perfect. Thank you, Charlie."

"You better go get some ribbon and mark those seats; otherwise they'll be gone."

I ran out of the theater, sprinted four blocks to the five-and-dime, purchased some yellow ribbon and a black Magic Marker.

I ran back and wrapped the ribbon carefully around the three seats in the fifteenth row, and wrote: Reserved for Emma. After all, no matter what was happening between us, it was her opening night as much as mine.

I rushed back out to the phone booth to call Emma and go over the details. Thank goodness she was home.

"Listen, Emma." Out of breath. "If Bert could pick up Sharleen at six-forty-five, and you at seven, then you'll all be at the theater by seven-fifteen, which is perfect. You need to be in your seats when the curtain opens; otherwise the seats I reserved for you will be taken."

Emma responded with a distant voice, "Yes, dear. I'll call Bert to make sure we're all there."

"It means a lot to me that you'll be here. You have no idea how much." I hung up the phone, relieved that she was coming *and* that she'd used the word *dear*.

With less than an hour left, I had to make a choice to either rest or eat. *Oh no!* I had forgotten to buy the corsage. The one I wanted to present to Emma. She had earned it, after all.

I ran over to the flower shop two blocks away and waited for the saleswoman to get off the phone. I told her I wanted to buy the most beautiful corsage in the store. She went into the cold glassed-in room and returned with a lavender Lisianthus. It was elegant. And since Emma wore lavender a lot, it would match whatever she was wearing tonight. The store owner placed the flower in a clear plastic box. I paid her with the last ten dollars to my name and ran back to the theater.

I placed Emma's flower in a small refrigerator at the back of the stage, where it would stay chilled and fresh until after the show; went to the women's room and sponge-bathed my face and neck, patting under my arms with the industrial-strength, rough paper towel; and returned to my dressing room, where I collapsed in the chair and sank deep into the wicker seat. Knowing I didn't have much time, I closed my eyes, clasped my hands on my stomach, and watched as my body began to relax . . . get centered . . . let go.

I must have fallen asleep, because I woke with a start. I got up and turned on the overhead light and noticed a burgundy rose on a small eyelet cloth. It lay there innocently on the surface of the dressing table. Attached to the rose was a small string tied to a card: "Have a ball out there! Love, Allen."

I placed the rose above my ear as I applied opening-night makeup to my face. And as I looked in the mirror and smoothed the thick pancake to my eyes and cheeks, I noticed that the canvas I was painting on was an image I no longer knew. *Who are you?* I asked the reflection. *Why do you feel so alone? There's an auditorium filled with people, and Allen, adoring you, praising you, wanting to be with you after the show.* I touched the rose. I had so much to be grateful for, but all I could think of was Emma and that I needed to call her in the morning, tell her that I was sorry . . . that I'd made a stupid, impulsive mistake and that I wanted—needed—to move back.

The bright green light on the wall started to flicker. It was the stage manager's signal meaning: ten minutes to curtain.

I finished applying the makeup, slipped on the necessary un-dergarments so nothing could show through, donned the blonde wig, and zipped up the invisible zipper at the side of the actress costume. I took one last glance at the mirror: *Okay, this is it. Make Emma proud.* I kissed my finger and touched the mirror, turned off the light, and quietly closed the door.

Tiptoeing cautiously on the black-painted cement, careful not to make any noise with my heels or trip over a prop, I moved toward the stage. I touched the black curtains with my fingers to confirm that the night was real, and eavesdropped on the audi-ence as they roared with laughter. Goose bumps were popping up on my skin; electric impulses were shooting through my body.

We were lucky; it was an intelligent audience. They laughed and were silent in all the right places. I peered around the curtains for a glimpse of the stage. The actors were pacing themselves per-fectly. Peeking out and into the audience, I could see newspaper reporters making notes on their spiral pads. I wondered if Jerry had come or if Rachel had made it. And if she got my message, did she bring Armando? Did Emma and Bert find their marked seats? Was Clifford Thorne, the playwright, here?

I heard my cue and felt a rush of energy up my spine. All thoughts of who was in the audience and who wasn't stopped; no one was allowed into my head. Sandra Billings stepped aside and made room for the character of the actress, and then the actress moved out onto the stage. All that was left to do was to listen, repeat the lines I knew so well, and respond.

Everything flowed. No matter what I did, the character was true to her essence. The audience trusted the actress completely, and they responded. They felt sad when the actress cried. They sat motionless when the actress sat quietly. My body felt wired with an electric current cranked up to the highest degree, picking up emotional frequencies within the full radius of the auditorium. I could hear people's thoughts, feel their emotions. I became the instrument for creating resistance, letting go, pulling back, letting go. The audience and I were one. And at the same time that my body, this instrument, was playing the part, I watched every move it made. I'd become the witness to my own performance and was able to stay in that awareness throughout the play: watching every move, listening to every inflection. The same response and feeling occurred when I played the intern. It was sheer perfection.

The audience loved that Allen Cahill, the director, was also playing the role of a famous playwright in the production. They loved how he meandered up and down the aisles, brushing by their seats, yelling at the actors in character. It gave the audience a chance to be voyeurs, and imagine, if only for an hour and a half, what it would be like to be in charge. The spectators were entranced, enthralled. As well they should be. Our ensemble was at their best tonight.

The curtain fell, the audience applauded, and the curtain reopened. We all took a bow and a second bow; the spectators kept applauding, and the curtain closed again. We were all ready to disperse, but the curtains reopened. Clusters of people were on their feet, shouting, "Bravo, bravo!" The rest of the audience rose in a wave. Red and white roses sailed onto the stage.

Bill Fleishman called out, "Director!" And then we all chimed in, "Director, director!" Allen Cahill came onstage and stood with the cast. The audience clapped harder. The applause rose. It was thunderous. Allen stayed with us, took a bow, and extended his arm toward the cast to show his appreciation. His gesture fueled a redoubled roar of applause. It washed over us like a current, until the curtain made its final close.

We all knew the play was a bona-fide success.

The cast members embraced each other. What a night! What an unbelievable night! I hugged everyone in sight: Charlie, Bill, Marlene, the box-office ladies Harriet and Toby. Family and friends were making their way backstage behind the curtain. Photographers and reporters were jamming their way through the crowd to get their best shots. An elderly man I'd never met came over to me in tears. He stroked my cheek and thanked me for touching his heart. Allen approached me, gave me a hug, and whispered, "You couldn't have been better. Let's go to the party together."

"Together?" I couldn't help but be sarcastic. "In the same car? Are you ready to make that leap?" I whispered back. It was one of those remarks I never should have made. "Sorry," I said. "I'd love to go with you, and thanks for the rose."

The rose. I was reminded of Emma's corsage! I excused myself and ran to the small refrigerator, pulled out the lavender Lisianthus, still elegant and graceful in its plastic container, and returned to the stage to find Emma.

Someone tapped me on the shoulder. I turned around and was ecstatic to see a familiar face. "Rachel, you came! I don't believe it. Oh my God, I'm *so* glad to see you." I pulled her into a hug that would have suffocated her *and* her unborn child, now taking up a bit more room.

"Miss you in a starring role? Are you serious? You were great, Sandra, really! Rock solid. You should be proud, Sandra Billings."

"I'm so glad you're here . . . oh my God, your stomach has really grown! How are you feeling?"

"Great! Sandra, I'd like you to meet Armando."

Armando was a knockout! He had dark wavy hair and caramel-colored skin. His black-framed glasses gave the impression of someone tough and inflexible, but as soon as his big brown eyes smiled at me, I knew he would be a kind and loving husband, a good father. He seemed perfect for Rachel.

"Hi. It's great to meet you, finally," I said as we shook hands.

"I enjoyed the show very much," Armando said in his tentative English.

"Thank you so much for coming."

"I heard your phone message," Rachel said, "but we only arrived this afternoon. Are you all right?"

"I'm better."

"We're here for a while, so we'll have lots of time to talk. Go ahead," Rachel said, gently pushing me away. "All these people are waiting to meet you. Call me tomorrow."

I gave her a final hug, turned around, and saw a line of strangers waiting to congratulate me. I smiled and shook people's hands, and then, across the stage, I saw an elderly woman with short white hair, talking to a cluster of people. Emma! I kept waiting for her to turn around, but she didn't. I excused myself from the throng and moved across the wooden stage, placed my hand on her shoulder.

"This is for you," I said and handed her the lavender flower.

The woman turned. It wasn't Emma. Turning all shades of humiliation, I stammered an apology.

Between handshaking and slaps on the back and hugs, I kept looking around for Emma. No sight of her. But I spotted Jerry and a tall woman with dark curly hair coming toward me.

"Sandra, you were fantastic. Really great! The show was terrific. I'd like you to meet Virginia Smollins. Virginia, this is Sandra."

"Nice to meet you, Virginia."

"It was a wonderful show. I'm sure you'll be very busy after this run."

"From your lips to God's ears."

"Virginia is an agent," Jerry said slyly.

She smiled at me. "Here's my card. I'd love to sit down and discuss your future."

"Seriously?"

"Seriously. Call me Monday."

"That's in three days," Jerry reminded me. "You won't forget, will you?"

"I don't think so, Jerry."

"Good. Is Emma here?"

"She should be. I haven't seen her yet."

Jerry paused, ready to wave his exit. "I'll call you," he said warmly.

"Oh . . . I moved. But I may be moving back. Let me call *you*."

"Is everything all right?"

"Yeah, yeah, everything's fine."

"Do me a favor—don't worry about your career. I believe the universe is handling everything."

Grateful for his words, I smiled.

Emma. Where was that woman? I looked out again through the curtains, backstage, around the dressing rooms, and then I saw—oh my God!—Ginger Pompidou, LaPapa's infamous witch, wrapped in her long dark cape and sporting new orange hair. I tried to duck around a group of backstage visitors to hide from her, but she saw me. *Oh well.*

"Ginger, how are you?"

"You were incredible, darling. I knew you had it in you. We have five new members at LaPapa, and we're in production with Camille's first play. You've *got* to see it, *The Iron Pot.* The play opens in two weeks at the Vanguard. This is Camille, our fabulous new playwright."

"Nice to meet you, Camille." I could sense that Camille was more to Ginger than just a playwright.

"Ginger, it's great seeing you. I'm glad you made it to the show."

Out of the corner of my eye I saw Bert Klein cutting though the crowd, moving toward me.

"Ginger, I've got to go."

"Don't forget, *The Iron Pot,* two weeks, Vanguard Theater."

"I'll try to make it."

I caught up with Bert, and we both began to speak at the same time:

"Bert, hi, where's Emma and Sharleen?"

"Sandra, you've been a challenge to find."

Bert continued, "Emma was tired. She's coming tomorrow night with her friend Jackson."

Everything stopped. Everyone went silent. *She didn't come.* Why? *Was* she tired? Was this her way of getting back at me? Had she told Bert I'd moved?

"Did you enjoy the show?" I inquired weakly.

"Best damn theater *I've* seen in quite a while. Your performance was pretty impressive."

"Thanks for coming. Bert. But why didn't you come tomorrow night with Emma?"

"I have to leave for Minneapolis tomorrow for a couple weeks. I thought I'd catch the show before I left. I, ah, might have a part for you in this film I'm producing. I'll send you a script . . . oh, for crying out loud! There's Pete Franklin, that son of a bitch. I've been trying to catch up with him. What a sleaze he is . . . Excuse me, Sandra, I'll call you at Emma's."

He didn't know.

Bert ran after the sleaze. As I headed back to my dressing room, I saw Marlene's family gathering around her, Frank Geraldi and his wife, and Bill Fleishman flirting with female reporters taking photos. From across the room, Allen motioned that he was getting the car, that I should meet him outside in five. I smiled for the final photo and rushed to my dressing room.

In less than a minute the heavy makeup was removed. The wig, unclipped from my scalp, placed on the Styrofoam head. I carefully stripped off the costume and hung it on the rack, put on my jeans, stuffed everything I needed into my bag, and switched off the light.

Emma's flower! I turned the light back on and grabbed the plastic box sitting brightly on the table, the flower still alive and luminous, though curling a bit around the edges. I hoisted my bags over my shoulders and returned the flower to the fridge, hoping that it would keep its shape for tomorrow. If not, I'd borrow some money and buy her a new one.

The balmy air brushed against my body as I came out the stage door into the night. Allen looked so proud, sitting in his white Porsche convertible, his dark hair riffling in the breeze, his arm resting casually along the seat.

"I'm glad you put the top down . . . it's such a beautiful night."

He leaned over to open my door. "How do you feel?"

"Exhilarated, exhausted, ecstatic."

"You captivated the audience."

"Get out!"

"I'm serious." He reached over and pulled me close. "You were wonderful. Didn't you see the standing ovation? Didn't you get hit by the flowers, and stampeded by reporters?" We kissed, and then he said, "Let's go."

"Wait, I have to ask you something."

He looked at me with such desire, I could hardly form the question. "I know the audience liked the show. But were *you* pleased with what I did?"

He laughed. "You went beyond my expectations, especially for opening night."

"Seriously, was there anything that I didn't bring to the characters that you wanted me to bring? Was there anything that I—"

"Sandra, you were perfect. Even when you tripped over the telephone cord and fell on the chair, you stayed in character. The audience howled. I don't have to tell you how good you were. Didn't you feel it?"

"Yeah, I guess. I never felt so connected with an audience."

"Then there's your answer. Can we go now?"

I leaned over and gave him another kiss, this time with a little more passion.

"Let's not go to the cast party," Allen declared.

"What? You're the director. You have to *at least* make an appearance."

"Do you have any idea how many cast parties I've been to?"

"That's not the point. People will expect you. And I want to go . . . we'll show our faces, have a drink, and leave." *God, I thought I was impatient.*

"If you insist."

"I insist."

CHAPTER 29

A young fox who as yet has not acquired . . .
caution goes ahead boldly . . .

It looked like Christmas. Tiny white lights framed the windows and doors of the producer's estate. Balloons and streamers hung from the ceiling, and Broadway playbills lined the walls. Detecting the scent of grilled fish and steak, Allen and I edged our way back toward the outside deck, smiling and hugging and taking in the stares from the cast and crew as we headed for the champagne.

All eyes were upon us as we walked toward the bar. Whispers and smiles, questioning stares, a few knowing glances. I smiled back, shyly, part of me apprehensive, part of me not caring what anyone thought. I was in love, I was with my man, and he was holding my hand. And as much as I wanted to know what had happened to Emma, I didn't want to think about her now. There was plenty of time for that.

Allen and I were both famished. Fortunately, a waiter walked by en route with hors d'oeuvres. There were stuffed mushrooms with crab, lobster on toast, and salmon with caviar. We decided to take one of each. The producer had opened his pocketbook for this gathering, and my stomach was grateful that he had.

We reached the bar and hugged the cast standing along the glossy wood counter. We all drank and laughed, recounted the evening, and danced and danced. Red wine, white wine, Dom Pérignon. We twisted and cha-cha'd and waltzed, until the house started to spin. And then I stopped to look, with my inebriated eyes, at all the lovely people swirling and dancing and laughing and hugging. We had done our job. The audience loved the play. We'd made a splash. Now all we had to do was see if the reviewers agreed, and keep it up night after night for the next four weeks.

Allen and I looked at each other, knowing we had more than accomplished our goal. We started to head out the door when Clifford Thorne, the playwright, stopped the music and toasted. "To the show's successful opening," he trumpeted with great pride. "And to more standing ovations." We were given more glasses of champagne to raise.

Then we left.

Like children, we snuck out and waited impatiently for the valet to bring Allen's car.

Like teenagers, we clasped hands on the stick shift as we drove to his house. The anticipation of being together was beyond . . . the beyond. Giddy, drunk on champagne and expectation, neither one of us could find a coherent word. So we sang out loud to whatever was on the radio, bellowing out tunes, whether we knew the words or not.

And then I remembered that my car was parked at the Windmill Theater. "Allen, my car is at the theater." He quickly did a U-turn without even dropping the high note from "Carry On," another one of my all-time favorite tunes.

I climbed into my Fiat and followed the Porsche back to his house. Watching him weave and ignore the yellow lines, traffic signs, and red lights would have on any other night made me a wreck. But I was just as spent myself.

chapter 30

PUSHING UPWARD has supreme success.

We staggered out of our cars and waited forever while he fumbled to unlock the door. Once inside, we kicked off our shoes and fell into each other's arms. Purse, jacket, and overnight bag were shed in a heap by the door. Allen gently pushed me against the wall and kissed me deeply, passionately. The plush carpet cradled our feet as we melted down the stairs—stair after stair, until we stopped midway to kiss again. Feeling his body pressed against mine made me weak. I could hardly stand.

Allen unbuttoned my sweater while I unbuttoned his jacket. His jacket cascaded down the steps, and we cascaded behind it, making slow headway toward his bedroom. My body was on fire. I wanted to go slowly—I wanted us to take our time, savor every second—but neither one of us was able to slow the pace.

In the bedroom, he gently peeled off my sweater, kissed my shoulders, unhooked my bra. I removed his T-shirt and unzipped his pants. We slipped off each other's underwear. Our naked bellies touched. I was lost. My mind stopped. His hands massaged my back, my breasts. As he kissed my nipples with such sweetness, my fingers caressed the length of his arms, his thighs, his erection.

We kissed, and went on kissing as we toppled onto the bed. Our bodies throbbing with so much passion, I ached for him to be inside me.

We rolled across the sheets like playful cubs, coupling like serpents twined in knots. I moaned and ran my fingers through his hair, kissed his ears, his cheeks, his throat. I grabbed his hips to pull him further inside. I'd made love before, but never like this, never with this pulsating eagerness. I was so glad we'd waited. I knew this night was a reward for our patience. It was a night I'd remember for its passionate perfection. Why must wonderful experiences like this have to end?

Limp, exhausted, we lay there in each other's arms, falling effortlessly into a deep, peaceful sleep.

The sunlight peeked in from behind the curtains, warning me that morning had come. Allen was asleep, his burly body sprawled in abandon across the tangled sheets. I gazed admiringly at his fingers, so expressive and relaxed; his shoulders and arms softly clothed with downy hair; his mouth slightly open in a light snore, lips loose, supple as a baby's. I placed my arm over his stomach and rested my cheek against his back.

Lying there behind him, eyes closed, I could feel him breathe, and found myself contentedly synchronizing my breath with his. I had never felt so relaxed with a man, so at peace. I fantasized getting up every morning for the rest of my life like this, making love again as the sun slanted through the silk curtains. Preparing breakfast, sitting out on the deck, sipping coffee.

Enough, Sandra. Be here now! I glanced at the clock sitting on his nightstand. It was seven. I wondered if the morning newspaper was here, if the editor had printed the review. Allen had said it might be out today. Carefully, quietly, so as not to disturb my sleeping bear, I slid out of bed, retrieved my scattered clothes from the carpet, and tiptoed into the bathroom to take a shower.

I was singing "Michelle, *ma belle*" as beads of hot water ran down my body and washed away the scent of Allen's cologne when the phone rang. I jumped, and spontaneously turned off the shower. I didn't know if the answering machine was off or on, or if Allen was awake. I bundled the towel around me and, without a second thought, picked up the bathroom phone.

Allen had answered. I was about to put down the receiver, but something inside me said, *Listen.*

A woman's voice spoke seductively. "Good morning," she said. "Interested in an early-morning rendezvous, along with some strawberry pancakes?"

Allen whispered back, "I'd love nothing better; only you'll have to subdue your passion until later." Then he said matter-of-factly, "Can you wait until eleven or twelve?"

"Sure," she replied, "you'll be worth the postponement. I'll just have to keep the pancakes warm until you get here."

I eased the receiver quietly back onto its cradle. Stunned, dizzy, I sat down on the toilet seat. All feeling had left my body. I wasn't sure what to do. I wanted to climb out a window, but there wasn't one. I wanted to slide under the door, sneak out so Allen wouldn't see me, so I wouldn't have to face him. *Dear God, what have I done? Tell me what to do.*

I struggled into my pants, my belt, my bra, my sweater, and thought about what I'd say to him once I opened the door. But there were too many thoughts spinning around for a coherent one to surface. I waited another moment until I was sure he'd hung up the phone. Then I gathered strength from I don't know where, took a breath, tried to compose myself, opened the door, and walked out of the bathroom.

Allen was lying there on the bed with a smile plastered on his face, motioning for me to join him. I stared at him.

"The, ah, phone?" I asked, choking out the words.

"My mother." He chuckled. "She wants me over for brunch by eleven. Come here, star. It's only"—he looked at his clock radio—"seven-fifteen. We have almost four hours."

I stood there shaking, worse than the day I'd met him at the audition, worse than the day I'd arrived in California scared to death because I didn't know a soul, worse than I'd felt remembering what Steven and Lenny had done to me all those years ago.

There was nothing I could compare this feeling to, nothing. I only knew that I was not going to break down; I was not going to lose it. I was going to stay cool and reserved and see what he had to say.

"Is Mother making strawberry pancakes or French toast for breakfast?" I asked the master impostor.

"Well, to tell you the truth, she's—"

I didn't let him finish. "Oh yes, *do* tell me the truth." So much for cool; I'd already lost it. I walked over to him ready to slap him across the face, throw him off the bed, kick him in his precious balls. But I knew I needed to save what little dignity I had left. *Reclaim what you've lost.*

"Thank you for a lovely evening, Mr. Cahill." I pulled myself together. "You gave a fine performance."

"Wait a minute, Sandra . . . come here! Please."

Screaming silent obscenities under my breath, I stormed out of the bedroom, pounded up the stairs, grabbed my purse, my overnight bag, and slammed out the door.

Thank God I brought my car. Grinding the gears, I drove down the hill. I could hardly see. Tears poured out furiously. I kept wiping my eyes, but the tears wouldn't stop. My whole body trembled. *How could I have been so stupid, so naïve, as to think he was in love with me or that I was the only one? How could I have fallen for his fake sincerity?* "Opening night is too far away," he'd said. "I can't wait that long. There isn't anyone else I'd rather be with!" *Lying, two-timing . . . !*

I kept driving. Halfway down Sunset, I found myself pulling up to the curb at La Fontaine Bakery. It was automatic, like the Fiat had driven me there. I got out of the car and headed for the door . . . and stopped at the entrance.

What the hell am I doing? But the pull to go in was *so* strong. The desire to numb these emotions was *so* intense. I paced . . . first around my car . . . then back and forth in front of the store.

I didn't *want* to go in. But the starch and the sugar would make me feel so much better. I kept pacing. *Look at you, Sandra. You're like a wild animal.* I kept walking in circles. *You're like a mouse in a maze. That's what you've become . . . a goddamned mouse in a maze.*

The realization hit me. *It's so true. Break the friggin' cycle, damn it! He's not worth it!*

I got in my car and peeled away. I drove to the Santa Monica Pier, and made a quick right into the parking lot. Only a few cars sat empty at the end of the pavement. I stopped the car, put my head against the steering wheel, and screamed.

The *I Ching* was right. Our relationship *was* Youthful Folly.

I got out of the car so I could inhale the sea air, and walked down the sandy slope toward the ocean. I looked out into the vastness and knew that as long as I was here, I was safe. I reached the water and turned, along the shore. I kept walking, more briskly now, to shake off the tension, the anger, the humiliation. The agitation was pushing my body into a run, but I pulled it back to walk. The thought of pounding my body on anything, including sand, was too abrasive.

I kicked off my shoes, needing to feel the crystals of sand on my soles, the particles filling the spaces between my toes.

What a joke! I had our whole future figured out. He'd be directing; I'd be acting. We'd be traveling. How could I have been so blind? How did my intuition fail me?

I needed to talk to someone. I was bursting at the seams. Emma, of course! *Emma—how could I have forgotten? I should have called her first thing—found out how she is.* I turned around and sprinted toward the pay phone back at the pier.

I inserted a dime, dialed Emma's number, and counted the rings before she picked up. One ring, two rings, three . . .

"Hello?"

"Oh, hi, Sharleen."

"Yes, who is this?" She sounded upset.

"It's Sandra; can I speak to Emma?"

"I'm so sorry, Sandra . . ." She hesitated. "Emma . . . Emma died this morning."

"What?" I heard the words, but they didn't sink in. "What?" I asked again. I couldn't have heard that right. *There must be a mistake.*

She repeated, "Emma died this morning." Her words made my body go limp.

"What? What happened?"

"She was sitting in her chair, reading the paper. I went to the kitchen to make some coffee . . . I came back, and her bifocals were hanging on her chest, and her eyes were closed, and the newspaper was on her lap. I . . . I thought she was asleep. But she wasn't."

Oh no. No, no. This can't be happening. Not now! Not today!

"What—what did you do?"

"I called my uncle Jackson. He called the ambulance, and Zelda. They just picked her up, a few minutes ago. I didn't know how to reach you."

They took her away without me saying good-bye, without giving her a hug, without telling her how much she meant to me.

"Are you all right, Sandra?"

"I don't know . . ."

"Do you want to come over? I'll be here for a while."

"I don't know."

I hung up the phone and sat there. I was so cold. Where was my jacket? Was it at Allen's? Did I leave it at Emma's? I thought about getting up, but I had no strength. I sat there trying to think of a reason to move. I sat there until the walls of the booth began to close in on me, and then I stood up, slowly, cautiously, like I'd just aged a hundred years. Bracing myself against the glass, I got out the door and started walking back toward the water.

The sun, the fog, everything looked filmy. My feet couldn't feel the ground. Clasping my hands around my elbows, hugging my body, I tried to stop the shivering. I really wished I had my jacket. At the waterline, I came to where my shoes were still lying, where I'd kicked them off. But they didn't look like my shoes. They looked like lifeless marine creatures that had been tossed up and abandoned by the sea. I sat down on the sand next to the foreign objects, looking out as far as I could, into the pallid sky.

As the waves slapped the posts of the pier, I knelt down, hunched forward, my forehead resting on the sand. I could feel the blood rushing to my brain. And then guilt and shame rose up with a vengeance. *I killed her.* The words pulsated inside me. *Why did I go? What made me think I had to pack up and leave?*

The *I Ching* was right: *It is not cowardice but wisdom to submit and avoid action.* It *was* cowardly of me to leave. Why hadn't I listened?

I'd been so selfish. No wonder she didn't want to go to the play.

I dug my fingers into the wet sand, digging deeper until my fingertips turned cold. Maybe if I kept digging, I could bury myself in the sand, dissolve here, and be washed away by the sea. Who would care? Who would notice?

I kept digging. Around me, the incoming waves hissed up on the sand, the seagulls wheeled above the sea.

The slapping of the waves and the sweet, salty air reminded me that life would go on whether I died here or not. I stopped digging, sat up, and placed my hands around my knees. *What do I do now?*

I listened intently, but there was nothing, nothing but the sound of the waves. As I sat there motionless, images arose, one after the other: every person I had known in my life. I watched myself walking away from each one of them, slamming doors, storming out. Like I'd done with Allen. Leaving Larry with no explanation. Never confronting my father, my mother. Steven, Lenny, Emma. I realized I'd never completed anything.

Oh, Emma. You left too soon! Dear God, show me what I need to do, where I need to go.

I sat there looking out into the ocean, into the restless movement of the waves. I closed my eyes. I waited to hear an answer. Nothing. There was only the sound of the waves. I kept listening.

And then, a wave surged within me, a wave of inner resolve. It rose up inside me like a fountain of light, coursing through every atom of my being. Energy poured through me with a lightness and freedom, as if the desire to lie down and dissolve had never been there.

I didn't fight or resist this energy, but allowed it to move on its own and propel me. I found my legs and the strength to stand up, wipe my tears, and face the ocean. Only a hint of sadness remained. There was an openness now, a vulnerability, and a new kind of humbleness. I liked it. It made me feel rooted, grounded.

The veil had lifted from inside, and outside the fog vanished. The water sparkled with the reflection of the sun. With the sun on my back, my feet firmly embracing the sand, I walked back up the beach toward the car. I wanted to go back to the place where I'd started this journey, to the place I'd never really wanted to leave.

I knocked on the door. Sharleen unbolted the lock. Her eyes were as red as mine surely were. She took hold of my shoulder, gently, and escorted me into the kitchen. The warmth there that had once embraced me had since vanished; it must have left with Emma's soul. There was no smell of chicken soup or evergreen air freshener, no crumbs on the counter, no peels of orange in the sink. Two apples sat waiting on the counter. And they'd have to go on waiting, like the rest of us.

Sharleen let me wander. I smiled, and moved on toward Emma's bedroom. Her bed was made. The bedspread was pulled up high over the feather pillow, the sides not quite even, and the crocheted blanket, the one she'd made for Josef, was placed neatly at the foot of the bed. She'd told me that there were six mistakes in the blanket; I'd never seen even one of them. I wondered when they'd take her bed away. What would happen to her dresser, her clothes? Turning back to the door, I noticed her blue dress and her white shawl laid out neatly on the chair, her matching shoes placed next to each other on the floor. *When did she know she wasn't coming to the play?*

I walked into my old room and found Sharleen's clothes scattered everywhere. Shoes were strewn across the floor, pants flung across the bed. The pictures on the walls had been rearranged. What would happen to Josef's paintings now?

I came back to the living room. Sharleen was gone, but she'd left the door cracked open. Emma's chair stood there alone, the throne now deserted. I paused, hesitant. A shaft of light appeared from the window, lighting the back of the seat. I sat down with my back against the plush green satin and placed my arms along the rich mahogany armrests, breathing in the remainder of her presence. Secretly, I hoped that Emma's wisdom and strength would seep into me. I took a deep breath, looked around, and noticed her glasses were sitting on the side table.

I put them on.

How differently Emma saw the world. The lenses, distorted for me, were clear to her. She no doubt saw *me*, like the rest of her world, quite clearly. I picked up the newspaper that lay close to her chair and saw that it was the *Los Angeles Times*, not the *New York Times*. It was open to the review.

Last night, the Los Angeles premiere of The Turning of the Century opened at the Windmill Theater to a sold-out performance. This wonderful, thought-provoking Clifford Thorne play was endearing and delightful . . . The real enchantment for the evening was watching Sandra Billings perform the dual roles of the medical intern and the actress . . . She stole our hearts. Keep a watch for this little lady . . .

She'd read it. She saw it. I hoped she was pleased.

I removed the glasses and lay them on the table, folded the newspaper, and placed it under my arm.

I moved to the dining-room table and saw that my cookbooks were set out there. A package sat next to them. On top of the package was an envelope with my name written across the top. Surprised and curious, I picked up the envelope, opened it carefully, so as not to rip the flap, and removed the paper from inside.

Dear Sandra,

Since the moment you entered my home, I knew I had received a gift. Your vigor, talent, and sense of humor uplifted me and brought purpose into my life again. There were many times I wanted to tell you this, but the words never found their way.

I want you to hear them now.

About a month ago, I had a vision of when and where I was going to die. Knowing this, I distanced myself from you so you would become detached, and learn to stand on your own. The closer the time came, the harder it was to be around you. I knew my departure would be easier with Sharleen. So I arranged for her to stay.

Sandra, everything that happens to us is a necessary part of our growth. Every encounter, every experience, teaches us something: forgiveness, compassion, strength.

Remember this and move on.

Being with you rekindled the relationship I had with my own daughter, Alexandra. She was about your age when she died in Germany from polio, a horrible disease. She too would have achieved greatness in her life, had she lived. It was her nature.

When the time is right, when you are ripe, all opportunities will reveal themselves. The same will be true with love.

It was an honor to know you.

May you walk into your destiny, with great faith.

Love always,

Emma

P.S. May this gift connect you to your spirit.

Between tears, I read the letter three more times. How could she be gone? How could this be? Why couldn't she tell me? I would have understood, and I wouldn't have left. But at least she wasn't mad. She didn't hate me.

I looked around the apartment, knowing that I would never see her, these things, this place, again. I gazed for a long time at Josef's paintings hugging the walls, the paper plates peering through the glass of the armoire, the plastic rug runners, Emma's high-back.

Should I open Emma's gift now, or wait until later? I was staring at the unopened package when the telephone rang.

"Hello?"

"Sandra? Hi, it's Jerry. I'm glad I caught you."

"Hi," I replied, trying to find my voice.

"The agent I introduced you to last night called me wanting your number. She wants you to audition for a film; she wants to sign you . . . Sandra, are you there?"

"Yes, I think I'm here. I'm not sure."

"Well, take her number. I'm late for a meeting. Call me later."

I took the number, thanked Jerry, but could not muster the words to say much else.

I returned to the dining-room table, picked up the unopened package, the cookbooks, and the newspaper with my review, and left Emma's house, leaving the door unlocked for Sharleen or whoever else wanted to enter.

Later that night, at Calvin's, I had no energy to tackle any cleaning. I was too tired to lift *anything* other than the three dimes I held cupped in my hand. A rose-colored candle burned on the table next to the bed, along with a stick of sandalwood incense. As I rolled the dimes onto the bed, the only question that came to mind was: *What next?*

The answer was hexagram 1:

1. Ch'ien / The Creative

Above: Ch'ien, Heaven, The Creative
Below: Ch'ien, Heaven, The Creative

The sage learns how best to develop himself so that his influence may endure. He must make himself strong in every way, by constantly casting out all that is inferior and degrading. Thus he attains that tirelessness which depends upon consciously limiting the fields of his activity . . .

In terms of human affairs, this symbolizes a great man who is still unrecognized. Nonetheless he remains true to himself. He does not allow himself to be influenced by outward success or failure, but confident in his strength, he bides his time . . . The time will fulfill itself.

I closed the *I Ching* and slid it over to the other side of the bed, along with the coins, the pouch, and the legal pad, and reached for Emma's package, securely tied with twine. I untied the cord and removed the paper from around the bundle.

It was my favorite painting of Josef's, the one of the beach. The one I had looked at every night in my room. It was so beautiful! How did she know? Silly question! My fingers ran around the antique frame, feeling the richness of the wood. I'd never taken the time to *really* look at it. Now, I could see every brushstroke, sense Josef's artistry in the strokes and the colors he chose, feel the love and energy emanating from the canvas.

I leaned back against the headboard of Calvin's guest bed, and propped the picture up against my knees to get a better view of the pale, expansive beach, dramatically juxtaposed against the vibrant aquamarine and teal-blue water.

As I gazed at it, I could feel all my senses merging into the beach. I was there on the sand, running, feeling the sun on my back, hearing Emma's voice: "Keep those knees high; stay on the balls of your feet."

And as I kept running and kept listening, I knew her words would stay with me, as would the words from the *I Ching*:

> *Pushing Upward has supreme success . . .*
> *The individual . . . need not be afraid, because success is assured.*

Emma had entered me.

> *Do not allow the daggers of doubt to puncture your heart. Just let them bounce off you like pellets of water.*

Emma's love would keep me rooted.

> *You are already a great actress. You only need to work on the inside.*

Her gift connected me to my spirit.
I would hold it forever in my heart.

working with
the *I Ching*

There are pivotal times in our lives when we are faced with challenging decisions, relationship questions, and work dilemmas. The *I Ching*, the ancient Chinese oracle, can help us reveal underlying issues that relate to our concerns. It can also strengthen our sense of direction, steer us onto an inspiring path—or simply confirm what we had realized all along.

Today, there are many versions of the *I Ching*. I have personally used the Wilhelm-Baynes translation, entitled *The I Ching, or Book of Changes,* published by Princeton University Press.

Most alternative editions include instructions on how to cast the oracle. For readers who may not have encountered the *I Ching* before, here is a brief description of how to "throw" the *I Ching* using the simplest method: three coins.

Formulating Your Question

When you formulate your question, it is recommended that you create a sacred space. Clear off a tabletop or other surface. You want the space to be clean, without any clutter. Focus your attention on your question, and then move gently into a state of receptivity. I usually start my question with the words: *Would _____ be for my highest good?*

Tossing the Coins

As described in *Pushing Upward,* yarrow stalks were used for centuries to cast the oracle—a very complex process. Today, most people use coins. I opt for either three dimes, three nickels, or three pennies. Ming Dynasty coins can also be used and may be found in many Asian stores. Whatever you pick, it is important that you use three of the same type of coin.

Stay focused on your subject or question when casting. Hold the three coins loosely in your hands, shake them briefly but mindfully, and then toss them six times.

The Hexagrams

The *I Ching* system consists of sixty-four six-line patterns, or *hexagrams,* each of which is composed of a stacked pair of three-line *trigrams.* The individual lines are either solid (yang) or broken (yin). The nature of the lines is traditionally determined by means of casting the coins or yarrow stalks.

The character of each line is determined by assigning a numerical value. "Heads" are counted as 3, "tails" are counted as 2. With three coins, there are four possible "throws":

Two tails and a head = 7 (yang, an unbroken line)
Three heads = 9 ("moving" yang)
Two heads and a tail = 8 (yin, a broken line)
Three tails = 6 ("moving" yin)

As you cast the coins, write down the numerical value of each throw and draw a corresponding line: a solid line for yang, a broken line for yin. Build your six-line hexagram from the bottom up. For example:

Line 6	——	= 9
Line 5	——	= 7
Line 4	——	= 7
Line 3	— —	= 8
Line 2	— —	= 8
Line 1	— —	= 6

The hexagram that you come up with is considered the "present hexagram"; it represents energies that are in play in your current situation or with regard to your query. It is a response to your question. Any version of the *I Ching* you choose will include a chart in which you can look up the hexagram you have thrown. Some oracles will include a *judgment,* an *image* corresponding to the hexagram as a whole, and *commentaries.* Plenty of food for contemplation!

Moving Lines

If you happen to throw a 6 or a 9, it is referred to as a *moving line,* or *changing line.* This means that the broken or solid line corresponding to the throw changes into its opposite, generating a second hexagram. For instance, the 6 in line 1 above, known as "6 in the first place," will become a solid line, and the 9 in line 6 above, known as "9 at the top," will become a broken line. Look up the resulting hexagram:

Line 6	— —	= 6
Line 5	——	= 7
Line 4	——	= 7

Line 3	▬ ▬	= 8
Line 2	▬ ▬	= 8
Line 1	▬▬▬	= 9

The moving lines can be very important; they provide additional perspectives, pointing to aspects of your question or the situation you may not have taken into consideration, or forces coming into play that you may not yet be aware of. When moving lines appear, they may also indicate the presence of a great deal of power or potential energy in the matter that concerns you. When you look up the description of the hexagram, you can read commentaries on the moving lines, as well as the depiction of the hexagram as a whole and of the trigrams that compose it.

To read more about the history of the *I Ching,* or learn about lectures, workshops, and other Pushing Upward offerings, please go to: **www.PushingUpward.com.**

acknowledgments

My immense gratitude and appreciation to all of the people who have supported me in birthing this story:

To Margaret Simpson, whose initial critique was the impetus for me to erase, tear up, and throw away my first draft. Without her severe critique (which took me years to digest), I would have never been able to search my soul and start the manuscript over.

To Dhruva Romanow, whose keen insight helped me to understand the significance of this story. To Heather Raymond, Joanne Ehret, Kathy Drew, Melah Skoll, Wendy Yaffee, Dina Dunaway, Roger Elkrief, Kate DeCoo, Cliff Shulman, and Ann Cafferty for their insightful critiques.

To Dale Ruff, who gave my son love and attention during the winter months skiing Vermont's mountains, allowing me the indulgence of writing.

To Ani Tuzman, who taught me to trust my heart and to write from that space.

To David Kinsley, Sheila and Sheldon Lewis, Jeff Elster, and Gene Mateson for their editorial reviews.

To Tonia Miller for reminding me to laugh when I was caught up in my drama, for disagreeing with me when I was wrong, and for hanging in there while I ranted and raved. Your spirit and honesty confirm for me why I wrote this book in the first place.

To Jim Allen and Richard Adler, who taught me about conflict. To Parvati Marcus, who was tough and critical with her edits. To Brenda Marzett, Dr. Hyla Cass, Michael Butler, and Jessica Yudelson for their feedback. To Aaron Roessler for supporting my web presence.

To Lisa Hagen, who was there when I needed her. To Jill Kramer, Shannon Littrell, and everyone at Hay House who ushered this labor of love into the world.

To Jerry DiPego, who encouraged me to be strong and tenacious, to keep going no matter what, and to stay enthusiastic during the whole, sometimes excruciating process.

To Cynthia Briggs, my editorial midwife. The one who made me go places I never would have approached without her love, compassion, and tenacity. Thank you for being my friend, my editor, my spiritual advisor, and my student. Thank you for living and breathing and birthing this book and my other books, along with me.

To Anna, who gave me her love, her time, and her space.

To my son, Brian, whose patience has been overextended since he was eight, and whose heart has been infinitely generous. I apologize for the weekends we didn't get to enjoy, the vacations we were never able to take. As you grew older, you became my toughest critic and my best cheerleader. I thank you a million, trillion times. May your intelligence and talent serve you well as you complete your own life adventure.

Finally, I would like to thank the ONE whose blessings allowed me to persevere, layer by layer, year after year, spurring me on, to go beyond my limitations and my ignorance; whose voice still moves me (when I listen) and guides me (when I see); who paved the way (when I removed my ego) for this incredible journey to come to its final destination. Thank you, from the depths of my heart.

about the author

Andrea Adler is the founder of **HolisticPR.com**, a consulting firm specializing in a holistic/spiritual approach to marketing and publicity. Recognized as the "metaphysical marketer," Andrea is an international speaker, workshop presenter, and the author of three books on Holistic Marketing: *PR for The Holistic Healer, Creating an Abundant Practice,* and *The Science of Spiritual Marketing: Initiation into Magnetism. Pushing Upward* is her breakout novel.

A recipient of the Axiom Business Book Award in 2008, and winner of the 2011–12 Los Angeles Book Festival Award for *Pushing Upward,* Andrea has been a speaker at several international conferences including Natural Awakenings Annual Conference, Mountain Biz, the American Holistic Medical Association, INATS (International New Age Trade Show), and Expo Ser in Mexico City with Deepak Chopra.

Andrea has written over 50 articles on holistic/spiritual marketing, translated in five languages, and has appeared on numerous radio and TV shows throughout the world. For 30 years she has supported small businesses, the holistic/therapeutic community, cultural creatives, and entrepreneurs in Europe, the U.S., Canada, Mexico, and Venezuela. Andrea has been a contributing writer for *Body, Mind, Spirit; Massage; Living Natural; Massage Today; Akkadian Magazine; Spirituality & Health; Tathaastu; New Connexion; Sentient Times; Kripalu; Reiki International; Marketing Holístico* (Mexico City); *UNO MISMO* (Buenos Aires); and *Vida Alternativa* (Venezuela).

Andrea has studied meditation for 30 years, living in ashrams and meditation centers in India, Paris, New York, and California. In her early twenties, Andrea was an actress both on and off Broadway. She was a member of Cafe La Mama and the improvisational group The Groundlings, and appeared in several TV shows. She also co-wrote and directed three videos at the American Film Institute.

As the founder of Professional Organizers in the early '80s, Andrea coordinated, supervised, and expedited moves for the elite in New York City and created satellite offices to support her clients. Her unique concept was so visionary that *New York* magazine, the *New York Times,* and several moving magazines wrote about her business.

In the mid-'80s while a journalist for *The Times Herald-Record,* in upstate New York, Andrea was profoundly affected by three teen suicides that occurred at a local high school. In response, she wrote a grant and received funding from Senator Charles Cook to create the Off-Off Main Street Children's Theater Company, dedicated to works by, for, and about teenagers and the challenges they face. The company ran successfully for eight years.

An actress, transformational speaker, author, savvy businesswoman, and ardent practitioner of meditation, Andrea integrates her gifts as she presents keynote lectures and her new workshop, "Pushing Upward: The Art of Living and Thriving." This workshop combines her holistic (mind-body-spirit) approach to living with the principles and concepts from *Pushing Upward.* Known for the experiential nature of her work, Andrea dives into the heart of people's passions and supports them to live their deepest desires so they thrive and push upward. Her dynamic, transformational presentation touches participants in ways that shift their lives dramatically.

Andrea lives in Santa Monica, California. Her son, Brian Adler, is a jazz composer and musician in New York City.

www.PushingUpward.com
www.HolisticPR.com

Hay House Titles of Related Interest

YOU CAN HEAL YOUR LIFE, the movie,
starring Louise Hay & Friends
(available as a 1-DVD program and an expanded 2-DVD set,
and an online streaming video)
Learn more at **www.hayhouse.com/louise-movie**

THE SHIFT, the movie,
starring Dr. Wayne W. Dyer
(available as a 1-DVD program and an expanded 2-DVD set,
and an online streaming video)
Learn more at **www.hayhouse.com/the-shift-movie**

THE FIRST RULE OF TEN: A Tenzing Norbu Mystery,
by Gay Hendricks and Tinker Lindsay

LINDEN'S LAST LIFE: The Point of No Return Is Just the Beginning,
by Alan Cohen

THE MAN WHO WANTED TO BE HAPPY, by Laurent Gounelle

SUMMER'S PATH,
WAITING FOR AUTUMN, and
WINTER MOON RISES,
by Scott Blum

THROUGH INDIGO'S EYES,
by Tara Taylor and Lorna Schultz Nicholson

All of the above are available at your local bookstore,
or may be ordered by contacting Hay House (see next page).

We hope you enjoyed this Hay House book. If you'd like to receive our online catalog featuring additional information on Hay House books and products, or if you'd like to find out more about the Hay Foundation, please contact:

Hay House, Inc., P.O. Box 5100, Carlsbad, CA 92018-5100
(760) 431-7695 or (800) 654-5126
(760) 431-6948 (fax) or (800) 650-5115 (fax)
www.hayhouse.com® • www.hayfoundation.org

———

Published in Australia by: Hay House Australia Pty. Ltd.,
18/36 Ralph St., Alexandria NSW 2015
Phone: 612-9669-4299 • *Fax:* 612-9669-4144
www.hayhouse.com.au

Published in the United Kingdom by: Hay House UK, Ltd.,
The Sixth Floor, Watson House, 54 Baker Street, London W1U 7BU
Phone: +44 (0)20 3927 7290 • *Fax:* +44 (0)20 3927 7291
www.hayhouse.co.uk

Published in India by: Hay House Publishers India,
Muskaan Complex, Plot No. 3, B-2, Vasant Kunj, New Delhi 110 070
Phone: 91-11-4176-1620 • *Fax:* 91-11-4176-1630
www.hayhouse.co.in

———

Access New Knowledge.
Anytime. Anywhere.

Learn and evolve at your own pace
with the world's leading experts.

www.hayhouseU.com

Free e-newsletters
from Hay House, the Ultimate
Resource for Inspiration

Be the first to know about Hay House's free downloads, special offers, giveaways, contests, and more!

 Get exclusive excerpts from our latest releases and videos from *Hay House Present Moments*.

 Our ***Digital Products Newsletter*** is the perfect way to stay up-to-date on our latest discounted eBooks, featured mobile apps, and Live Online and On Demand events.

 Learn with real benefits! *HayHouseU.com* is your source for the most innovative online courses from the world's leading personal growth experts. Be the first to know about new online courses and to receive exclusive discounts.

 Enjoy uplifting personal stories, how-to articles, and healing advice, along with videos and empowering quotes, within *Heal Your Life*.

Sign Up Now!

Get inspired, educate yourself, get a complimentary gift, and share the wisdom!

Visit www.hayhouse.com/newsletters to sign up today!